THE FENS

Also by Pamela Wechsler

THE GRAVES
MISSION HILL

PAMELA WECHSLER

THE
FENS

MINOTAUR BOOKS

NEW YORK

THE FENS. Copyright © 2018 by Furnace Book Productions. All rights reserved. Printed in the United States of America. For information, address St. Martin's Press, 175 Fifth Avenue, New York, N.Y. 10010.

www.minotaurbooks.com

The Library of Congress Cataloging-in-Publication Data is available upon request.

ISBN 978-1-250-07790-5 (hardcover)
ISBN 978-1-466-89023-7 (ebook)

Our books may be purchased in bulk for promotional, educational, or business use. Please contact your local bookseller or the Macmillan Corporate and Premium Sales Department at 1-800-221-7945, extension 5442, or by email at MacmillanSpecialMarkets@macmillan.com.

First Edition: May 2018

10 9 8 7 6 5 4 3 2 1

THE FENS

Chapter One

Boston hasn't had a murder in eighteen days. Most people in law enforcement kick back and enjoy a lull in crime. Not me. Whenever the homicide rate drops, my anxiety level skyrockets; my blood pressure surges and I develop a twitch in my left eye. It's not that I'm worried about job security—homicide prosecutors can always earn more in law firms, investment banks, or fast-food joints. It's that I know it won't last. At some point, there will be another murder, another crime scene, another victim.

The other assistant district attorneys make good use of the downtime. They're in their offices, drafting briefs and filing motions. My investigator has gone to the Cape for a few rounds of golf. And my victim witness advocate is at home, retiling her bathroom floor. I keep busy too—pacing around my apartment, checking and rechecking my phone.

I try to keep my neuroses under wraps, but there's no point hiding it from Ty. We've been together almost two years and he knows the drill, does his best to distract me. This week, we've been to two concerts—the Bach Society at Sanders Theatre, and the Psychedelic Furs at the House of Blues. We've seen two movies—*Gaslight* and *Spotlight*. And we've binge-watched all five seasons of *Breaking Bad*.

We also eat out a lot, spending far more than our budget allows.

1

Yesterday it was dinner, oysters at the Glenville Stops in Allston. Today it's lunch, Szechuan shrimp at the Golden Temple in Brookline. While Ty pays the bill, I check my phone for the thousandth time. Still nothing. No calls, no texts, no murders.

Ty grabs the plastic bag of leftovers and we walk a couple of blocks up Beacon Street, to the side street where his Corolla is parked. When we reach the car, Ty opens my door, rubs my back, and kisses my neck. Ty is my Ativan, so calming and protective that I almost relax.

I climb into the passenger seat, drop my bag on the floor, and adjust my seat belt.

Ty yells out. "Hey. What the—"

Outside, there's a commotion—two loud thumps. A man has appeared out of nowhere and, without a word, he tackles Ty and slams him up against the hood of the car. Ty struggles to free himself but the man has him pinned. Stunned, I bolt out of my seat, race to Ty, and jump on the man's back.

"What are you doing? Get off of him. Leave him alone!" I say.

I grab at the man's neck, but he swats me away, elbows me in the face—hard. My jaw clicks and I see a flash of light as my butt hits the ground.

"Shut up and don't move," he says.

This man is determined. I have to do something. My cell phone and pepper spray are only a few feet away, in my tote. I inch away toward the passenger door, on my hands and knees, keeping an eye on the man. He takes a swing at Ty, hitting him on the shoulder.

The man shouts at me, "I said don't move."

A glint of metal catches my eye. It's coming from the man's waistband. Fearing the worst, I strain to see what it is. It's a gun, a Glock. For a moment, everything becomes a blur. I hold my breath and freeze as the man pulls out the pistol and presses it to Ty's right temple. The man turns to me.

"When I say don't move, I mean the both of you."

I try to memorize his face. Brown hair, buzz cut, green eyes. A tattoo is on his right hand: an American eagle.

"Get up," the man says.

I stand and raise my hands in the air, in surrender.

"What do you want?" I say. "Is it the car?"

"Take my key," Ty says.

Ty fumbles with his key, dropping it on the pavement. The man doesn't bend to pick it up. He isn't interested in Ty's Toyota. This is about more than a carjacking.

The man looks around. "Where's the bag?"

"My tote is in the car," I say.

"No, not that bag—the plastic one."

Keeping my hands in the air, I use my foot to point to the sewer grate, where the bag of Chinese leftovers landed when Ty was ambushed.

"Hand it to me," the man says. "Slowly."

I pick up the bag of food and pass it to him, but his hands are occupied—one hand on the gun, the other on Ty's throat.

"Open it," the man says.

My hands are shaking, making it difficult to untie the knot. After a couple of attempts, I give up and rip the bag apart; three small white cartons spill out onto the sidewalk.

"Where are the drugs?" he says.

Ty and I look at each other, confused.

"We don't have drugs," Ty says.

The man picks up a container and inspects the contents. "What's this?"

He tosses the open box on the curb. Noodles and gooey brown sauce splash out, onto the toes of my suede pumps.

A siren blips in the distance. I hold my breath, willing it in our direction, hoping it's the police—not a fire engine or an ambulance—and that they're coming to help. Maybe someone saw the assault, heard my pleas, and called 911.

Ty and I lock eyes in solidarity. We just need to hang on a little longer. Soon, help will arrive and this maniac will be subdued and arrested. The man seems oblivious to the siren. He doesn't try to run, he doesn't even flinch.

"I want the drugs," he says.

"Look, man, there are no drugs," Ty says.

"But we have cash," I say. "I'll get my wallet."

"Stay where you are." The man waves his pistol in the air. "I don't want your money."

As the siren intensifies, the man knees Ty in the back of his legs and twists his arm. Ty grimaces in pain.

"You should get out of here," I say.

The man stops what he's doing, holsters his Glock, and turns to face me. "Why would I want to get out of here?"

"Can't you hear the siren?" I say.

"Siren?"

"Yes. The police are coming."

He shakes his head back and forth in disbelief. "Lady, I *am* the police."

Chapter Two

A marked Brookline police cruiser rounds the corner, its blue light flashing. The driver lets out two blasts of the siren and comes to a stop in front of Ty's car. I exhale. Finally, sanity will prevail. The uniform opens his door; gold chevrons, stitched on each sleeve, declare his rank.

"Sergeant," I say, "I don't know if this man is impersonating a police officer or if he really is a cop and he's completely lost his mind, but—"

"Stay back and keep those hands where I can see them."

"Me? But, I'm—" I want to tell the sergeant I'm a prosecutor and we play for the same team, but he won't give me the chance.

"If I was you, I'd stay quiet. Otherwise, I'm charging you with disorderly conduct, and both you and your cohort are going in the back of the cruiser."

"Cohort?" I say.

The man who attacked us looks Ty up and down. "Where are you folks from?"

"Where are we from?" My voice expands. "That's what this is about?"

Ty catches my eye, shakes his head. *Not now. Let me handle this.*

"We live a couple of miles away, in Brighton," Ty says.

I've been working in the DA's Office for over a decade, and I'm no stranger to allegations of racial profiling, but usually the complaints are about other jurisdictions, places far away. Ferguson, Chicago, Baltimore. Sure, Boston has a long-standing reputation for racism—in housing, schools, employment, and professional sports—pretty much everything *but* law enforcement. Other cities try to emulate our community policing model, with its close ties between law enforcement, the clergy, and neighborhood groups.

I never considered that crossing the city limits, from Boston into Brookline, would be a dangerous undertaking.

"What are you people doing around here?" the sergeant says.

"Ty, you don't have to answer." I turn to the man who started this. "What's your name, Officer?"

"Detective," he corrects me. "Detective Mike Chase."

"Detective Chase, what's the basis for your stop?"

He ignores me and the sergeant speaks up. "Mike, did you do a pat down of the suspect?"

Ty and I lock eyes. *Pat down? Suspect?*

Detective Chase kneels and frisks Ty; Chase runs his hands up one leg and down the other. Ty remains still as his pants pockets are turned inside out. It's invasive and humiliating. This has gone too far.

I plant myself in front of them, arms crossed, impossible to ignore. "I'm an assistant district attorney."

They stop what they're doing, try to look unimpressed, but I can see the sergeant's eyes dart around as he contemplates his next move. He gives me the once-over and watches as I slowly reach into my jacket pocket and take out my credentials. I flip open the top, exposing my badge.

"Abigail Endicott, chief homicide prosecutor, in the Suffolk County DA's Office," I say.

Detective Chase blanches. The sergeant reddens.

"There must've been a misunderstanding," Detective Chase says.

"No, I think we understand each other," I say.

He starts to backpedal. "I was conducting an undercover operation. There have been complaints of drug activity in the area. It was an honest mistake."

"What if I had a gun? What if Ty fought back? Someone could have been killed."

"Your boyfriend fits the description." Chase shows me a text on his phone: *Black male, approx. 5'10", wearing dark hoodie, possibly armed, accompanied by white non-hispanic female.*

"Ty is six feet two, and he's wearing a leather jacket," I say.

Detective Chase ignores the comment, turns to Ty. "I'm sorry, sir. No hard feelings, I hope."

Chase extends his hand and, to my surprise, Ty accepts.

"This has been a learning experience, a teachable moment," the sergeant says.

I want to ream them out, but Ty looks at me, then at his car, signaling he wants to get out of here. They watch as we get in the Corolla and close the doors. I'm jacked up with anger. Ty seems numb, expressionless.

I take out my phone and scroll though my contact list.

"Babe, what are you doing?"

"I'm calling the police commissioner, and then the mayor. After that I'm going to leak it to *The Globe* and the *Herald*. 'African-American Male Attacked by Rogue Brookline Police Officer While Walking with Assistant District Attorney.' It'll be tomorrow's headline."

Ty turns on the ignition. "Let's slow down. Please, don't do anything right now."

"Why not?"

"I want to figure out the best way to handle it. In the meantime, the cops can sweat it out, worrying about what we're going to do."

Ty and I are proof positive that opposites attract. I'm white, he's black. I'm from a Brahmin Beacon Hill family, his parents are aging hippies and he was raised in rural Vermont. I'm a homicide prosecutor, he's a jazz musician. I'm an adrenaline junkie, hard charging and battle ready. He's cool and measured.

"Let's take a beat; we can talk about it tonight," he says.

He pulls onto Beacon Street, toward Brighton. Before we reach the next traffic light, my phone vibrates. I look at the screen and hesitate. Taking the call will only make things worse, but I don't have a choice.

"It's Kevin."

Ty stops at the red light and turns to look at me. Boston Police detective Kevin Farnsworth is a constant source of tension between us. "Doesn't that guy ever take a day off?"

"It's probably a new murder." My heart races with a combination of excitement and dread as I slide the *accept call* button. "Afternoon, Detective, what do you got?"

"Meet me at Fenway Park?"

"Seriously? There was a murder at Fenway?" I glance at Ty, who is fiddling with the radio, pretending not to listen.

"Not exactly. No one died, but I know you're going to want in on this from the jump."

"Don't be so sure. Tell me what happened."

"It's opening day and the Sox's starting catcher, Rudy Maddox, never showed up for the game."

My heart sinks. This is not the murder case I've been waiting for. My vigil isn't over. I bite my lip and chew at a piece of loose skin, until I taste blood. "Since when do we take missing persons investigations?"

"The starting catcher for the Boston Red Sox doesn't show up on opening day, and no one has seen or heard from him—trust me, this is gonna be big."

Before I have a chance to say thanks but no thanks, my phone beeps. The screen shows that my new boss, District Attorney Stan Alvarez, is on the other line. Stan was appointed a couple of months ago, after the former DA was elected mayor. At the time the governor tapped Stan for the position, he was an FBI agent. Stan knows little about politics and even less about local prosecutions—but he's a huge sports fan.

I hang up with Kevin and grab the call.

Stan speaks first. "Did you hear about Rudy Maddox?"

This is the perfect opportunity to assert my independence and set the tone with the new boss. "I'll supervise the case, keep a close eye on it."

"I don't want you to supervise it. I want you to handle it."

I push back. "It's not a murder. It doesn't even sound like a kidnapping."

"I don't care if it's a frigging dognapping. I just got off the phone with the team owner. He's worried that his MVP has disappeared without a trace. The baseball commissioner has reached out too. And reporters are sniffing around. This could be huge and I want my top prosecutor on it."

I look at Ty, make a circle with my finger, cuing him to turn the car around.

"I'm on my way," I say. "I'll be at Fenway Park in ten minutes."

Chapter Three

I spent much of my youth behind home plate in Fenway Park. My brothers and I sat in the Endicott family box, in the front row, under the protective netting. We each had our own game-day rituals. Charlie, the oldest, would position himself near the dugout; he collected autographs, which he later sold on eBay. No surprise, now he's a venture capitalist. George, the youngest, snuck sips of beer from stray cups under the seats. No surprise, he died of a drug overdose almost ten years ago. I kept track of the scorecard, penciling in the abbreviations for each play, as though the outcome of the game depended on it. The Red Sox had an abysmal record in those years, but like most Bostonians, we were die-hard fans, always hopeful that they would turn things around.

The landmark red, white, and blue Citgo sign winks as we cross over the Turnpike, toward Kenmore Square. On Brookline Avenue, we pass a line of hot dog carts, T-shirt vendors, and ticket scalpers. When we reach Lansdowne Street, Ty pulls up behind the thirty-seven-foot-high Green Monster.

Kevin is across the street, peeling peanuts from their shells and popping them in his mouth, one by one.

Ty eyes him with suspicion. "You're not going to say anything to him about what happened, right?"

It's near impossible to make Ty jealous—I know because I've tried. There's one thing, however, that gets under his skin: Kevin. I've told him time and again that nothing has ever happened between us, and it never will. Kevin is happily married to his high school sweetheart; I'm in love with Ty, and my days of cheating are over. Still, Ty seems unconvinced. I can't blame him, given my past.

"I promise. I won't say a word." I kiss him, then once more, and get out of the car.

Kevin sees me approach, gives me a nod and a smile, and holds out the brown paper bag. "Nuts?"

"I prefer Cracker Jacks."

He tosses the bag into a trash can. "I got us a sit-down with the team manager. We might as well catch the tail end of the game while we wait."

We make our way to Gate E, where we badge the ticket taker. Inside the ballpark, I exchange nods of recognition with a plainclothes detective and a patrol officer in full tactical gear. I stopped coming to Fenway years ago, after George died; it wasn't the same without him. A lot has changed: the Sox won a couple of World Series; the park installed Wi-Fi; and bomb-sniffing dogs became fixtures at the games.

We wind our way up the ramp, past the lines at the refreshment stands: craft beer, lobster rolls, and gluten-free cookies. I prefer the old concessions: warm Bud, cold pizza, and soggy Fenway Franks.

Outside, the park is a sea of green: the field, the walls, the seats, and the drunken fan who is vomiting on his neighbor. A group of strangers are occupying our old box; my father gave up the seats years ago, opting instead to watch the game from the indoor clubhouse, where there's climate control and a full bar.

Kevin clocks me as I shade my eyes against the glare of the afternoon sun. He flags down a hawker, gives him a twenty, and grabs a dark blue Red Sox cap. He sticks the hat on my head and adjusts the visor. "Don't want you to miss any of the action."

I look over at the scoreboard. It's the bottom of the seventh and the Sox are down by five. "I'm not sure I want to see this train wreck."

Red Sox star pitcher Francis "Moe" Morrissey is on the mound. He hurls a fast one, the batter doesn't swing, and the replacement catcher, Wayne Ellis, bungles the ball. Wayne races to recover while a runner steals second base. Boston sports fans have never been shy about expressing their thoughts. The crowd of thirty-seven thousand offer a variety of chants: *We want Rudy. Rudy, Rudy. Go back to the minors, Ellis. You suck, Morrissey.*

"Moe Morrissey is the highest-paid player in the history of the sport, but he isn't worth squat without Rudy Maddox," Kevin says.

On the next pitch, the batter blasts a line drive toward Moe, who ducks, but not in time. The ball strikes him hard, on the side of his face. My head throbs in sympathy. The park goes quiet; people stand to get a better look at Moe's injury, while trainers and the team doctor race to the mound. I can't see if Moe is bleeding, but the doctor puts a towel to Moe's face. A couple of minutes later, the fans cheer in support and relief, as Moe lumbers off the field on his own.

After Moe is replaced, the game ends in a rout and the stadium empties quickly. We flag down a security guard, who walks us to the dugout, where Donnie Rourke, the team manager, is dressing down a player. Donnie, a former athlete, seems to have lost most of his muscle tone, but not his brawn. We introduce ourselves; his handshake is firm but his expression is tepid.

He signals us to follow him into the tunnel. He walks quickly and I have to struggle a little to keep pace. He barrels past the room where reporters are setting up for a postgame presser.

"I'm in no mood for the hyenas today," he says.

We round the corner, avoiding detection, until we're confronted by an ESPN sportscaster and his cameraman.

"What happened out there, Coach?"

Donnie, famous for his scowl and monosyllabic responses, doesn't disappoint: "We lost."

The reporter isn't dissuaded. "What's your strategy going forward?"

Donnie gives him the stink eye. "We're gonna win."

Someone taps me on the shoulder. I look down to see a freshly manicured fingernail.

"Abby?"

I turn to see Emma Phelps, a former Harvard classmate. She looks different: her hair is thicker, her lips bigger, and her nose smaller.

"What are you doing here?" She palms a microphone.

I'm not entirely sure why I'm here, but if I were, I wouldn't tell a reporter. I smile, try to act nonchalant, and hope she hasn't caught wind of Rudy's disappearance. "My family has season tickets."

Emma looks like a ditz, but she's not. She was managing editor of our school paper, *The Crimson*, and she doesn't miss much. "If I recall correctly, you're a prosecutor. Are you working a case?"

Before I can respond, Kevin comes to my rescue, whispers in my ear. We engage in fake conversation until Emma turns her attention, and microphone, to Donnie.

"Why wasn't Rudy Maddox behind the plate today?"

Donnie ignores the question and walks away without saying a word. Kevin and I follow him to his office, where he takes a seat behind the desk. I scan the walls, jammed with memorabilia: old blueprints of the ballpark, team pennants, and pictures of some of Boston's best—Carl Yastrzemski, Bobby Doerr, Ted Williams.

Donnie's knee bounces up and down as he arcs a baseball from one hand to the other.

"We'd like to know your thoughts. Any idea why Rudy was a no-show today?" Kevin says.

Donnie stops fidgeting and leans forward into a nonexistent microphone. "Nope."

"Is it out of character?" Kevin says.

"Yup."

I didn't expect Donnie to transform into a fountain of information, but given the significance of what's happened, I didn't think he'd treat us like the enemy.

"How are Rudy's prospects this year?" Kevin says.

"Good."

Kevin's phone vibrates; he checks the screen.

"It's the commissioner." Kevin turns to Donnie. "Not my commissioner—your commissioner—and I bet he's gonna pledge the team's full cooperation."

Donnie's face reddens as Kevin steps out into the hallway.

"Do you think this could be a power play? Maybe Rudy's trying to get attention or up his salary," I say.

Donnie clenches his jaw, as though it pains him to speak. "Rudy is one of the best catchers in the league—smart, aggressive, fast on his feet. Catchers are underrated, fans don't always give them their due, but the guys on the team and in the front office know Rudy's worth. He's appreciated and well compensated, and he knows it."

I don't believe anyone gets that kind of unconditional love, especially in the high-stakes, high-profile world of professional sports.

"We'd like to talk to the other players," I say.

Donnie looks over at Kevin, who is standing just outside the door, one ear on the phone, the other on us. "Who do you want to talk to?"

"How about the backup catcher, Wayne Ellis?"

Donnie frowns. "Wayne is new to the team and I doubt he'll have much to offer."

"He's got the most to gain from Rudy's absence."

Kevin wraps up his call, a few notches louder than necessary.

"Sure, Commissioner," Kevin says, "I'll let Donnie know you expect his full cooperation."

As soon as Kevin hangs up, Donnie says, "Follow me. Let's go find Wayne Ellis."

Chapter Four

The clubhouse is empty, except for a lanky teenager, who is gathering wet towels from the floor and stuffing them into an oversize laundry bag. Donnie points out Rudy's locker, which is unremarkable. His clean uniform, presumably the one he should have worn today, hangs on a hook.

Wayne Ellis comes out of the shower room, wrapped in a towel, drinking from a bottle of blueberry-pomegranate Gatorade. As he tilts his head back to take a swig, I try not to gawk. He's about twenty-one, which is over a decade too young for my interest; still, it's hard to resist checking him out. He's about six foot three, solid muscle, and his chiseled face is marred only by a small circle of pimples around the jawline.

He holds a phone to his ear, but ends the call as soon as he sees Donnie.

"You sucked out there today." Donnie hurls a few more insults at Wayne, then introduces us.

Wayne indicates his towel. "If you don't mind, ma'am . . ."

Ma'am—the word stings. I pivot and face the wall while Wayne drops his towel and slips into a pair of jeans. Kevin gives me the nod when it's safe to turn back around.

"Tell them whatever they want to know," Donnie says, as though he's been helpful himself.

Wayne's phone dings and he checks the screen. Donnie snatches it from Wayne's hand and lobs it into a laundry bin. The teenage maintenance worker eyes the bin, unsure if he should pluck Wayne's phone out of the pile of dirty socks.

Donnie shoos him away and turns to Wayne. "You lost your focus. If I see that phone in your hand again, I'll flush it down the john."

Donnie follows the towel kid out of the room, leaving us alone.

Wayne, eager to heed Donnie's instruction, speaks first. "What do you think happened to Rudy?"

"It's more important that we hear what *you* think," Kevin says.

Wayne's cell lets out a muffled ding from across the room. He takes a step toward it but then stops himself.

"I have to ask everyone this question, so don't take offense," Kevin lies. "Where were you last night?"

Wayne looks up in the air and racks his brain, as though he's solving a quantum physics problem. "I was at . . . I was at home."

"With anyone?"

He hesitates and looks away. "I was alone."

"How do you get along with Rudy?" I say.

"Great. He's my mentor."

Wayne's phone dings again. This time, he can't help himself; he digs through the dirty socks and underwear and retrieves it. After checking the message, he hits the mute button and looks up. "It's the first time I got to start on opening day. Folks are calling to congratulate me."

Kevin flashes a disarming smile. "Rudy being a no-show must be a big break for you."

Wayne smiles back. "It could have been, if I hadn't sucked so bad." He turns to me. "Pardon my French."

We ask Wayne a few more questions and tell him we'll be in touch. As I turn to leave, Moe Morrissey walks into the room, with an ice pack pressed up to his eye. He's as handsome in person as he is on TV, even with strips of cotton jammed up his nostrils. He could, and probably will, become a movie star when his pitching career is over—which won't be for a long time. He just re-upped with a $450 million contract.

"Donnie told me you'd be in here," Moe says.

"How are you doing?" I try not to blush. "That looked like a nasty hit."

"It's not the first time I took one to the head." He moves the ice pack long enough to show a bruise starting to form under his eye, a swollen patch of red on his otherwise perfect dark brown skin. "The doc says it's a minor nasal fracture. They're gonna do a scan, but I'll be fine. I'm more worried about Rudy."

"What do you think happened?" Kevin says.

"At first, I thought maybe his car broke down or he got in an accident, but no one has heard from him. All I know is, Rudy would never miss a game on purpose."

Wayne is on the phone, talking loudly. "Yeah, Mom, I know . . . but we lost."

Moe glares at him, until he lowers his voice.

"I'm pretty freaked out," Moe says. "He should've at least texted me."

"I know pitchers and catchers have a special relationship," Kevin says.

"It's more than that—Rudy and I are practically related. My fiancée and his wife are sisters."

I remember reading something about that in *People* last month, when I had my highlights done. The Bond sisters: Moe's fiancée, Cecilia Bond, and Rudy's wife, Rebecca Bond Maddox. Moe's arm brushes against mine; a flash of heat spreads across my face. Kevin throws me a look. *Pull it together.*

I clear my throat. "What can you tell us about his personal life? Was he into drugs, alcohol?"

Moe shakes his head, an emphatic no.

"Gambling?" I say.

"His biggest vice was chewing tobacco."

"Does his wife know anything?" Kevin says.

"I don't think she even knows he's missing yet."

"She didn't come to the game?" I say.

"No, and I doubt she watched it." Moe senses my skepticism. "She's got a new baby."

A new baby. In my experience that could be less—or more—of a reason to disappear, depending on how much Rudy wants to be a dad.

"Do you know where we can find Rebecca?" I say.

"I'll reach out to her," Moe says.

"We'd like to be the ones to tell her what's going on," I say.

It's important that we gauge Rebecca's initial reaction and determine if it's genuine. The spouse always has to be eliminated as a suspect.

As Moe walks us out of the park, I consider seeking permission to go onto the field and take a once-around-the-bases. Tagging home plate would be a thrill, and it'd give me bragging rights around the office, but someone is probably lurking in the bleachers with a cell phone. The last thing I need is a YouTube video of me frolicking around Fenway while Rudy Maddox's whereabouts are unknown.

Moe makes a call to his fiancée, hangs up, and reports his findings. "Rudy's wife, Rebecca, is at a spa called Bella Vita."

Kevin takes out his phone. "I'll check the address."

"Don't bother," I say.

It's been months since I've been to Bella Vita, but I don't need directions. I know exactly where it is—on Newbury Street, one of the chicest streets in Boston. I follow Kevin out to the car. Rebecca Maddox sounds like my kind of witness.

Chapter Five

My first meetings with victims and witnesses usually take place in places like battered women's shelters, hospital emergency rooms, or the morgue. Bella Vita is a welcome change of venue. A trip to Fenway, followed by a spa, is as good as it gets for a homicide prosecutor.

When we round the corner, from Arlington to the first block of Newbury Street, traffic is at a standstill. The area is jammed with hard hats, delivery trucks, and daredevil jaywalkers. We park in my usual spot, the loading zone in front of Brooks Brothers. When Kevin turns off the ignition, I'm so distracted by the window displays in Valentino and Armani that I open my door without looking, narrowly missing a cyclist. She gives me the finger as she whips by.

Bella Vita is between Clarendon and Dartmouth Streets, above a shop that sells hand-smocked pinafores for toddlers. At $300 a pop, the outfits are exquisite but impractical, appealing to only the most anachronistic Bostonians—like my mother, who bought most of my baby clothes here.

When we get off the elevator, I approach the receptionist. She recognizes me immediately. "Ms. Endicott, I don't see you on the appointment list."

"I'm not here for a service. I need to speak with Rebecca Maddox."

"Is she expecting you?"

I ignore the question. "It's urgent."

While she goes out back to find Rebecca, I survey the shelves, stocked with my favorite balms, cleansers, and moisturizers. I ferret out the samplers, roll up my sleeve, and squirt lavender body cream on my forearm, massaging it in all the way up to my elbow.

Kevin picks up a copy of *Men's Health* and sinks into the leather sofa. I grab the latest issue of *Vogue* and join him. I try to tune out the background music, soft jazz, so I can focus—the article on Schiaparelli's spring collection requires my undivided attention.

Kevin digs into his pocket and hands me a handkerchief.

"What's this for?"

"You're drooling."

I wave him off. "I'm trying to concentrate."

Flipping through the pages, my senses go into overdrive. Silky chiffon scarves, crisp poplin blouses, and swingy fringe skirts. Last year, when my parents chopped down the money tree and ended my monthly disbursements, I had to give up a lot—but nothing else was as painful as fashion. I was prepared to let my membership at the Athenaeum lapse and to forgo daily lattes at Starbucks, but quitting Saks and Barneys, cold turkey, has been excruciating.

My government salary barely covers the interest on the debt I've accumulated, never mind rent and food. To be fair, my parents gave me advanced warning: they told me they wouldn't support my career choice anymore. *It's too dangerous. You almost got killed. If you want to keep working there, you're on your own.* I didn't take them seriously, but they made good on the threat. I don't know how I'll ever get out of the red, but I do know it's worth it. I can't quit my job, not even for fashion.

A woman, dressed in what resembles surgeon's scrubs, comes into the reception area and reports that Rebecca Maddox is in the lounge. Kevin puts down his magazine and starts to rise, but she stops him: "It's a ladies-only zone."

Kevin looks at me and shrugs. "Have at it."

Kevin is downplaying his disappointment; he'd love to get a gander at a roomful of rich, self-indulgent, half-naked women.

As I walk past the sauna and steam, I can hear my moisture-starved cheeks cry out for help. A dozen women, wrapped in white terry-cloth robes, are scattered around the lounge. Rebecca Maddox is on a recliner, near the soaking pool, with a layer of diamond paste slathered onto her face. She has paraffin wraps on her hands, foam separators between her freshly polished toes, and a towel turban covers her hair.

A familiar-looking aesthetician finishes applying a layer of goop to Rebecca's throat and says, "I'm sorry, I didn't know you had an appointment."

I wish it were a deep pore extraction, not a missing persons investigation, that had brought me here. I smile, turn to Rebecca, and show her my credentials. Rebecca glances at my badge, then does a double take. She bolts upright and tightens the belt on her robe.

"Has something happened? Is it Chloe? Is my baby okay?"

"Your daughter is fine."

I pour her a glass of cucumber water and we relocate to the women's locker room.

"Your husband didn't show up for the game today."

She looks at me, confused, and searches my face. "What do you mean? Where is he?"

"That's what we're trying to figure out."

"Why didn't anyone call me?" She rifles through her locker until she finds her cell phone. "Holy crap, look at all these texts."

Her hands shake as she scrolls through her messages. Not

finding anything from her husband, she types out a text: *Where are you? Call me*. She hits *send* and holds the phone tightly, checking it every few seconds. "Now what?"

"It's important to stay calm." A hair dryer whirs in the background, forcing me to raise my voice a notch. "Think about the last couple of days—did he say anything, or do anything, that might give us a clue?"

"No, nothing—he was his normal self, excited about the start of the season."

"What about the baby? Is he excited to be a dad?"

"Yes. Of course. What are you implying?"

"I'm sorry, but we have to consider everything."

Rebecca lets it go, a sign that she's genuinely worried, and I feel bad I had to ask. Her eyes dart around the room; she starts to breathe quickly.

"He's never been five minutes late for anything, let alone the season opener." She grabs her chest and starts to hyperventilate.

I look around for a paper bag, but the closest I can come up with is a plastic shower cap. I scrunch the sides together and hand it to her. "Breathe into this, slowly."

It takes her a minute to regulate her breathing. If this is an act, it's an Academy Award–worthy performance.

"I have Xanax." She reaches into the side pocket of her satchel, pulls out a pill bottle, and swallows a tablet, using the cucumber water to wash it down.

"Was he in an accident? Was he carjacked? I told him not to drive that Bentley."

"So far, there's no evidence anything criminal has occurred."

"I know my husband, he didn't just blow off the game."

"We want to set up a surveillance post at your house. Is anyone there to let us in?"

She catches a glimpse of herself in the mirror and realizes that she's still wearing the face mask, which has dried and cracked. She moistens a cloth and dabs at her forehead as she continues to talk.

"Holly, the nanny, is home with my daughter. I'll let her know you're coming, and I'll meet you there."

Even under the unforgiving fluorescent lights, Rebecca's skin is flawless.

"We're monitoring Rudy's phone and credit cards. We'd like permission to do the same with yours, and to search the house, phones, and computers."

"Of course, whatever you need."

Rebecca has given verbal permission to search, but I want to get it in writing. Documenting the agreement could come in handy, especially since there's no way to predict where the investigation will take us. If we end up charging Rebecca with a crime, she could change her tune and allege that our search was illegal. The consent form will protect us against a motion to suppress. I hand her the paper and she signs it.

"One more thing. When was the last time you saw Rudy?"

She doesn't hesitate. "This morning. I was with the baby. He came into the nursery and kissed us both goodbye."

I return to the waiting room to find Kevin, lounging on the sofa, sipping green tea. He has one eye on the exotic reflexologist at the counter, and the other on a copy of *Sports Illustrated*.

"I could get used to this life," he says.

"Don't. It'll break your heart."

"Did you learn anything?"

"Not really. I don't think she knows anything. I'll fill you in when we get in the car."

On the way out, I spot a jar of my favorite regenerating serum. I pick it up, inspect the price tag, and return it to the shelf—carefully.

"Are you looking to get a shot of Botox, before we hit the road?"

"Why?" I pat the corners of my eyes. "Are my wrinkles that bad?"

"You look like a million bucks." He smiles and grabs my elbow and presses the elevator button. "C'mon, let's get out of here."

Chapter Six

Rudy and Rebecca Maddox live in a six-bedroom Victorian, in Cohasset, about a half hour south of Boston. We hit the Southeast Expressway just in time for rush-hour traffic. As Kevin weaves in and out of lanes, I call Boston Police Headquarters to organize a search team.

It takes almost an hour to reach the Braintree merge, which is the halfway point. Kevin is itching to flip on the blue light and siren and speed toward our destination, but this case is too high profile to break protocol. We have to wait with the rest of the frustrated motorists.

"It's hinky that Rebecca wasn't at the game with the other players' wives," Kevin says.

"Some women have their own lives, independent of their husbands."

"It's not like she was out curing cancer. She wasn't even carpooling kids to school. She was at a spa."

"Give her a break. She just had a baby."

"Well, if my wife was missing, my first reaction would be to get her on the horn, not send a text."

"Yeah, but you're, like, a hundred," I say. "Twentysomethings don't talk to people, they use emoticons and acronyms."

Forty minutes later, we reach our exit. Kevin cruises through the town center, passing a quaint white church and village green. We veer onto Jerusalem Road, which runs parallel to the shoreline, and continue a mile or so, until we reach the Maddoxes' home. Their backyard is like a country club, with an Olympic-size pool and tennis court. Their front yard is the Atlantic Ocean, with a dock that leads to a forty-two-foot Boston Whaler.

Kevin eyes the boat and smiles. "That's no rinky-dink canoe. It must've cost upwards of seven hundred and fifty grand. And the house, that's four million, easy. It's like the money is burning a hole in his pocket."

"Rudy can afford it.."

"Catchers don't make as much as you'd think. According to ESPN, his contract is worth three million and change."

We park in the driveway, between a Porsche and a Ferrari.

"Let's run his financials," I say.

A landscaper, hedge clippers in hand, is in the backyard trimming bushes and chatting with the housekeeper. When she sees us, she rushes inside to alert the nanny.

"For a family of three, they're well staffed," I say.

"And well equipped." Kevin points at surveillance equipment, attached to the cabana, garage, and house. "They got more cameras than a Hollywood film set."

Holly, the nanny, opens the door. She tents her hands and bows her head. *"Namaste."* She pronounces it *namas-tea,* as though she were offering a cup of Earl Grey. Her shiny blond hair, bohemian minidress, and twenty-two-year-old body are evidence of Rebecca's self-confidence. My mother's unspoken rule was that no member of the household staff could be younger or more attractive than she.

Holly was expecting us and agrees to a quick house tour. The living room is not what I'd expect from a professional athlete; it's well-appointed, with Waterford crystal decanters and New England maritime paintings. The media room, however, is exactly what I'd expect, with leather Barcaloungers and a one-hundred-inch plasma. The walls in the family room are full of vintage baseball posters and a Plexiglas-encased Red Sox jersey, with the #9 on the back.

"That's Ted Williams's uniform," Kevin says.

"No, that belongs to Rudy," Holly says.

Kevin explains that while Rudy may have purchased the jersey, someone famous wore it, and now it's a collector's item. She nods and gives him a blank stare. I hope she's good with kids, because she's not the sharpest tack in the box.

"Do you know what time Rudy got up this morning?" I say.

"Rudy is an early bird, especially on game day. I made his breakfast, always the same: three eggs, pumpernickel toast, turkey bacon, and a banana with peanut butter." She takes a breath, adjusts her posture. "It was, like, weird though, because he left without eating anything."

"Did you see him when he left the house?" Kevin says.

"No, I went upstairs to check on the baby. When I came back down, he was gone."

"Hold on a minute," I say, "did you actually lay eyes on Rudy this morning, or did you just make him breakfast and leave it for him on the kitchen table?"

She looks at the ceiling, straining to remember. "The last time I actually *saw* him was yesterday, when he and Rebecca had an argument."

"They had a tiff?" Kevin says. "About what?"

Holly crosses her arms tightly. "I don't like to spread rumors. It's bad karma."

Kevin clenches his fists, looks at her for a minute, then at me. He's great with gangsters and mopes, but millennials are more my department.

"You know what's bad karma?" I say. "Obstruction of justice."

She tucks her hair behind her ears nervously. "They were fighting about money. That's what they usually fight about."

Upstairs, we sort through Rudy's closets, which are filled with suits, everything from Armani to Zegna, as well as racks of athletic wear. In the back of the closet, buried under catcher's equipment, is a box covered with duct tape. Kevin takes out his Swiss Army knife to cut through the tape and removes the top. Inside, he finds two baseballs, carefully wrapped in tissue paper.

"Weird," Kevin says. "A couple of used regulation baseballs kept like they're worth a million bucks."

Kevin drops the balls into an evidence bag. We look in Rudy's dresser but don't find anything remarkable. As we finish looking through Rebecca's closet, the doorbell chimes and the housekeeper calls up to us to announce the arrival of the search team. Police officers and technicians go into Rudy's office, where they unpack surveillance and monitoring equipment. Three men will be stationed at the house; the rest will monitor Rudy's electronic communications. A forensic examiner seizes two iPads and three laptops. Kevin grabs a folder full of bank records.

I find a file marked *Legal Papers* and thumb through the contents. "It's Rudy's new contract with the Sox. And the signature line is blank."

Kevin leans over my shoulder and flips the page to where Rudy's salary is listed. "That's a boatload of zeros."

"If Rudy disappeared before the contract was executed, he could be in breach. That means he'd forfeit millions."

Kevin snaps some pictures and slides the contract into a plastic evidence sleeve. "If Rudy does turn up alive, and he loses all that cash, either Rebecca's gonna kill him, or he's gonna wish he was dead."

Chapter Seven

It's after midnight when we pull into the parking lot adjacent to Boston Police Headquarters. Kevin takes the key out of the ignition, stretches his arms, and lets out an exaggerated yawn. We've been on the move all day and haven't stopped for food or drink in over twelve hours. Kevin is starting to drag, but not me; I'm so amped up with nervous energy that I could sprint to the top of the John Hancock Tower.

Headquarters is closed to the public; the lobby is dark and hollow. Kevin swipes his badge over the sensor, to disarm the optical turnstiles, and once more to gain elevator access. We get off on the third floor and settle into his cubicle in the homicide unit. The duty sergeant left a stack of witness statements on Kevin's desk, and we start to slog through them.

After an hour, I start to lose focus. I need sugar. I fish around the bottom of my tote until I feel an unwrapped Life Savers. Kevin gives me his look of disapproval as I pick at the lint on the sticky candy.

"You need to join a twelve-step program. You're a sugar junkie." He grabs a couple of gluten-free, soy-free, sugar-free bars from the stash under his desk and holds them up, one in each hand. "What's your pleasure, strawberry or brownie?"

"It doesn't matter. They both taste like plywood."

He tosses me the one in the pink wrapper. I break off a piece, and when I bite into it, I feel something crack. I'm relieved when I see that it's the bar and not my tooth; I let my insurance lapse three months ago, when I had to choose between Dolce & Gabbana and Delta Dental.

Kevin goes downstairs to check on the technician who is reviewing Rudy's home-security video. As soon as the stairwell door clicks shut and the coast is clear, I grab a couple of singles from my wallet and hit up the vending machine. I select the healthiest options: Doritos, because it's cheese flavored, which almost counts as calcium; and Oreos, which, according to the package, contain one gram of fiber.

When I return to Kevin's desk, I log on to a few websites to see if word of Rudy's disappearance has spread. It's all over the internet. There are tweets of conspiracy theories. Facebook has posts about potential suspects. Instagram is flooded with photos of doppelgängers. Every major news outlet is featuring the story with the urgency usually reserved for school shootings, terrorist attacks, and Kardashian weddings.

My phone vibrates, and when I look at the screen, I notice that Stan has left a series of voice mails and texts: *What the hell is going on? Where the hell is he? Where the hell are you?* I type a response: *I kidnapped him and am holding him hostage in my basement.* Before I hit *send,* I remember Stan has the power to reassign me to prosecute narcotics or, worse, asset forfeiture. He could also fire me. I delete the message.

The next time my phone vibrates, it's Kevin: *Get your keister down to forensics, ASAP.*

Kevin has been in the computer lab for less than a half hour, and he's not an alarmist—something big must be on the video. I take the stairs, two at a time; halfway down the first flight, I lose my footing and fall forward. Grabbing on to the railing, I prevent myself from falling, but my shoe catches and my heel snaps. I try to bang it back on, hoping to rescue it—my last pair of

Pradas—but it's a lost cause. I try limping on one foot, but it's too awkward. I remove the other shoe.

"You shrank," Kevin says when I step in the room.

I hold up my broken heel. "Can I do a B and E in the evidence room? If I'm lucky, there was a shoplifting at Saks, and I'll find a pair of pumps in my size."

Kevin laughs.

"I'm not kidding."

"I know."

I look around the room. The floors are polished and the surfaces look clean, but dozens of germy defendants, and germier defense attorneys, pass though this building every day. "I can't walk around barefoot. I'll get tetanus, or typhoid, or something."

Kevin pulls two crime-scene bootees from a dispenser. "Unless you want to wear my Florsheims, you'll have to make do."

I slip the bootees on.

The cubicles are empty, except for one, where a technician is sitting in front of a monitor, fast-forwarding through footage of video from the Maddoxes' home-security cameras.

"Slow down," I say.

"It won't do any good," Kevin says.

"What's on the tape?"

"Nothing. That's the point—either the machine wasn't working or the tape was scrubbed. My money's on the latter."

Even though it's the middle of the night, I decide to call Rebecca. This is a huge development, I want to get her take on it, and chances are she's awake.

She picks up on the first ring. "Did you find him?"

I tell her about the blank video. She responds with dead air.

"Who could have tampered with it?" I say.

"Rudy is the one who knew about the cameras."

After a few more questions, it's clear that either she doesn't know what happened or she's not going to tell me.

"Try to get some sleep," I say. "I'll touch base later." She sounds

kind of hinky, but she's still a victim, and I'll treat her as such—
at least for now.

There's not much more we can do tonight. Kevin walks, and I
hobble, back to the parking lot. I'm careful not to step on anything sharp or toxic.

"I heard you sold your hoity-toity condo," he says.

"I moved to Brighton."

"That's a step down. What happened to your trust fund? Did
your folks cut you off?"

I nod. "It's their way of pressuring me to find a safer job."

"Can't blame them. Just about every job out there is safer than
ours, except maybe Navy SEAL or fighter pilot."

"Or, apparently, catcher for the Red Sox."

It's not quite sunrise when Kevin pulls up in front of my triple-
decker. The bulb on the front porch is out. I tread lightly on the
splintery front steps. Gone are the days that my doorman Manny
would greet me and usher me inside the sleek marble lobby. I
miss his cheerful greetings: *Welcome home, Abby. Hope you
caught some bad guys today.*

Ty is in bed, snoring soundly. I pour myself a glass of pinot and
turn on the shower. While I wait for the water heater to kick in,
I sip the wine and scroll through my emails; there are lots of
questions, but no answers.

I undress, step into the shower, and immediately jump out.
There's no hot water—again. I brush my teeth, wash my face,
and scrub my filthy feet. I take another glass of wine into the
bedroom with me and spill a few drops on the white sheets. Ty
rolls over and opens his eyes. So much for slipping into bed unnoticed.

"Hey, babe. Did you find Rudy?"

"Not you too," I snap at him, mindful that it's not his fault that
I've been up for almost twenty-four hours, haven't made a dent
in my investigation, and lost a pair of my favorite shoes along
the way.

"I hope you didn't try to take a shower. I meant to leave you a note—there's no hot water."

The contrasts between Ty and me usually balance each other out, making a perfect yin-yang relationship. Not tonight. I want him to be as outraged as I am, and to show it. I fluff the pillow, yanking one end of the case and shaking it, then adjust it by pounding it a couple of times.

"Let's move to a new place," I say.

"The landlord said he'd fix the water heater in the morning." Ty kisses me softly. "This place will start to feel like home. Give it time."

"It's not just that. The porch light is out. The front steps are warped."

"I'll fix the light. Every place has problems. Things in your condo were breaking all the time. The AC was always on the fritz. Remember when the elevator broke and we had to walk up seventeen flights?"

He's right. The difference is, when these things happened in the past, I could take out my black AmEx and check into the Four Seasons. I can't do that anymore. I turn out the lamp and lie back. Ty wraps his arms around me tightly. Sinking my head into the pillow, I enjoy the warmth of his body, the comfort of his breathing, and try to fall asleep.

Chapter Eight

Last year, the district attorney resigned from office and I threw my hat in the ring to replace him. A few others expressed interest in the job, but not Stan. When the governor named him, I was shocked, but I should have seen it coming. Stan was the most qualified candidate, meeting all the criteria for a political appointment: he went to a second-rate law school; he passed the bar on the third try; and he's married to the attorney general's cousin. I didn't respect him when he was a federal agent, and I don't respect him now. Still, he calls the shots—or at least he thinks he does.

When I arrive at Bulfinch Place, at the building that houses the DA's Office, I pay him a visit to feign interest in his thoughts on the investigation.

His assistant buzzes me into the bulletproof section of the executive suite. "We've been trying to reach you all morning," she says.

I check my watch. "It's only seven fifteen."

He sticks his head out the door. "You're late."

"Late? We didn't have an appointment."

He waves me into his office. Although he's occupied the space for almost six months, banker's boxes are piled floor to ceiling, the bookcases are bare, and the walls are unadorned. The only nonessentials are the two photographs on his desktop—one of his wife and kids, on Castle Island; and the other of Boston's most notorious serial killer, Whitey Bulger, in an orange prison jumpsuit. Stan was part of the FBI team that captured him; it only took sixteen years and a lucky tip from the former Miss Iceland to bring him to justice.

"Where are you on Rudy Maddox, and why haven't you called?"

I tick off the list of what we've done so far, using my fingers to distinguish each action. "We talked to Rudy's wife. We put a tap on the phones. We're monitoring his credit cards. Surveillance is sitting on the house. We interviewed his teammates. And we met with the front office."

Stan reaches into a Dunkin' Donuts bag, takes out a cruller. I didn't eat dinner last night and forgot breakfast this morning— I'm tempted to ask for half. Too late. He devours most of it in one bite.

"Who do you like so far?" he says. I don't tell him speckles of powdered sugar are stuck to his chin.

"We're looking at the replacement catcher, Wayne Ellis."

"Cast a wide net. Take a hard look at everyone on the team, and the management—don't forget the management."

I take a cleansing breath. "Good idea."

As soon as I get to my office, I disregard Stan's directive and look for Wayne Ellis's phone number.

Amber, my assistant, knocks on the door. "Ed Stone is on the phone. He wants to meet with you."

The name is familiar but I can't place him. "Who is he?"

"He sounded like he knew you." Amber does a quick Google search. "He's a family law attorney."

Of course, Ed Stone—divorce attorney to the rich and philandering. My father contacted him a few months ago, after Dad moved out of the house and into the Harvard Club.

"I don't have time to deal with my parents' drama."

Amber gets on the phone, tells him I can't talk, then puts him on hold.

"He says he represents Rebecca Maddox. He wants to know if you'll come by his office."

"Tell him I'll be there in an hour."

I don't usually cede home-court advantage, but if Rebecca Maddox is spotted here, with a divorce attorney, the rumor mill will go into overdrive.

I call Kevin and he swings by to pick me up. I expect Ed's office to be in the financial district or the Seaport, with the other high-price attorneys, but it's not. Ed's office is in a brownstone on Dartmouth Street. Everything about the place is discreet and understated: the Back Bay location; the midcentury modern furniture; and the staff, who wear muted tones and speak in soft voices.

We're escorted into a conference room. Ed stands and introduces himself. Behind him is Rebecca Maddox, barely identifiable, in a Red Sox cap and fluffy scarf, triple-wrapped around her neck.

"Rebecca wants to correct the record," Ed says.

As soon as we sit down, Kevin hits the *rec* button on his audio recorder.

Ed puts his hand out to stop Rebecca from talking. "This is off-the-record."

"It's important to be accurate," I say.

"It's a sensitive matter and we'd like the conversation to be confidential." Ed knows the rules, but it's his job to make the ask and push for more.

It's my job to push back. "Confidentiality only applies to informants."

Rebecca hesitates, clears her throat, and looks at Ed, who nods. *Go ahead, tell them.*

Rebecca keeps her head down, fixated on her $60 Bella Vita manicure. "I forgot to mention something. Rudy never came home on Sunday night."

"So, you lied to me," I say.

She doesn't respond.

"You're telling us Rudy's been missing for more than twenty-four hours," Kevin says. "The last time you saw him was Sunday?"

She nods, not looking up. "He does it all the time. Sometimes he doesn't come home for a week."

She downs a glass of water. Kevin and I wait her out, not filling in the silence.

Finally, she speaks. "I was embarrassed. The whole world doesn't need to know our business." She reaches across the table, slides the pitcher toward herself, and refills her glass. "There have been other women. A lot of them. Last week one of them called me."

"We need names," Kevin says.

"I don't know who they are." Rebecca twists her engagement ring, a flawless six-carat solitaire, and tears up. "Rudy is a good man, a good provider. I keep thinking he'll outgrow it."

"The woman who called," I say, "was she looking for money?"

"Worse. She said they were in love."

I eyeball Ed, then Rebecca. "So you filed for divorce," I say. "That's why we're here?"

"Rebecca contacted me last week. We were considering our options," Ed says.

Kevin reads between the lines. "You were waiting for Rudy to put the ink on his new contract—to make it part of the community property."

Rebecca's face sours, but she's still beautiful. "That's not fair, I loved him."

When pressed about the women, Rebecca is short on specifics and long on righteous indignation. She insists she doesn't have names, and that Rudy doesn't know she's been thinking about divorce. By the sound of it, she's still hopeful Rudy is going to return, but that could be an act. Revenge is as good a motive as any.

Kevin and I head back to the car.

"I'm not ready to cross her off the suspect list," I say, "but we should still get the names of the other women."

"Moe Morrissey is Rudy's closest friend, he might know something," Kevin says. "Let's see if we can crack the code."

Chapter Nine

Chestnut Hill is a pricey suburb, about seven miles west of Boston. The architecture—Colonial, Gothic, Georgian, and Shingle—landed it in the National Register of Historic Places. The village hosts rolling green hills, protected wetlands, and upscale shopping malls. It's also home to Moe Morrissey.

We drive through Kenmore Square and past Fenway Park, where the Sox will play tonight. There's a line outside the team store—in a show of both respect and opportunism, Donnie Rourke declared they'll be offering Rudy Maddox T-shirts at half price.

I crack my window and take in the pregame rituals.

"Get your souvenirs here!" A street vendor trundles his cart on the bumpy sidewalk.

GAME DAY PARKING $45. A sign spinner pirouettes with his placard, in the middle of the congested street.

"Hey, lady, did you drop your keys?" A pickpocket distracts his mark while slipping his hand into her purse.

It's too late to turn around, so Kevin radios a description of the perp to some plainclothes detectives. We continue down Brookline Avenue—I feel a tinge of nostalgia. To my right is Winsor, where I went to high school and studied Mesopotamian history and French literature. To my left is Brigham and Women's

Hospital, where I've conducted countless interviews with stabbing, shooting, and sexual-assault victims. I long for those days, when I could interview my victims—because they had cognitive brain function.

When we cross over the Jamaicaway, Kevin toots his horn at a Brookline police officer who is working a detail, directing cars around a construction site. The officer waves at Kevin and smiles.

"Do you know a Brookline cop named Mike Chase?" I say.

Kevin nods as he swerves to avoid a pothole. "We worked a bank robbery together, a few years back."

"What's the rap on him?"

Kevin nudges me with his elbow. "If you want, I can find out if he's single."

I swat Kevin away and let out an exaggerated sigh. "When are you going to acknowledge that I have a boyfriend?"

"Then why are you asking about Mike Chase?"

I try to conjure up a believable lie. "Someone on my team was asking about him. He's a witness in an upcoming trial."

Kevin gives me the side eye, not buying it, but plays along. "Chase did a nice job on our robbery case. He seemed like a stand-up guy."

I let it go at that. When Ty gives me the green light, I'll tell Kevin and everyone else on the force what happened. I want everyone to know who Mike Chase really is.

Kevin slows and turns down an unmarked driveway, stopping at a security gate. He looks into the monitor, presses a button, and talks into an intercom. A woman answers and the gate slides open. The Morrisseys' house is tucked away, surrounded by meticulously landscaped woods and surveillance cameras. We pass a lake, complete with swans, and a field, big enough to host the World Cup.

"I guess pitchers make more coin than catchers," I say.

"Add a couple of zeros to Rudy's paycheck; that's what Moe rakes in."

Kevin parks next to the glassed-in gym and dance studio, and we get out of the car.

"The garden has more flowers than the Arnold Arboretum," he says. "And look at the house, it's a friggin' castle."

"I hope we don't have to execute a search warrant here, it'll take forever."

Twenty yards away, a young man is hosing down a Navigator.

"You look familiar," I say. "Where have I seen you?"

He sloshes the sponge in the bucket; dirty water splashes onto my crocodile wedges. This case is killing what remains of my shoe collection.

"I work in the locker room at Fenway."

"What's your name?" I say.

"Paul Tagala, but everyone calls me Tags."

Tags tells us that after hours he works for some of the players, doing things around their houses and running errands. Kevin asks a few questions about Rudy, but Tags doesn't have much to offer.

"I helped Wayne when he moved into his apartment, but mostly I work for the pitchers."

We hand him our cards, which he inspects and stuffs in his pocket.

"Please, give us a call if you hear anything," I say.

Kevin leads the way, into the courtyard. We cross a small bridge that brings us over a koi pond and to the front door.

"You must feel right at home in a joint like this," Kevin says.

"Hardly," I say.

Kevin doesn't mean it as an insult, but that's how it lands. This place reeks of new money. In my family, an unabashed display of wealth is vulgar. My parents own three homes—a five-story town house on Beacon Hill, a six-hundred-acre farm in Vermont, and a ten-bedroom beach house on the Vineyard. They also have a flat in Chelsea—London, not New York. None of their properties, however, are accessorized by anything that remotely resembles a moat.

We're greeted at the front door by Moe's fiancée, Cecilia, a former runway model, who stands about twelve feet tall, with razor-sharp cheekbones and a swanlike neck. She brings us into the open kitchen, fully loaded, with a wood-fired pizza oven and Dacor WineStation.

"Did you know whether or not Rudy and your sister are having marital problems?" I say.

"He cheated before they got married, but Becca thought he'd outgrow it. I don't know how she puts up with it."

Moe blusters into the room; the bruise under his eye has turned purple and yellow.

"Rudy has problems keeping it in his pants," Moe says. "Always did, always will."

"You should have told us when we talked to you at the ballpark," Kevin says.

"I wasn't exactly thinking clearly." Moe points at his shiner. "I took a pretty hard blow to the head."

Cecilia takes an ice pack out of the freezer, hands it to Moe, and he presses it to the side of his face.

"How are you feeling?" I say.

"I'm fine. I'll be back on the mound in no time."

Two young boys and their nanny come in the room, asking for a snack. Cecilia gives them each a box of organic apple juice and a box of raisins and walks them to the playroom.

"We need names," Kevin says.

"I wish I could help, but I never asked for specifics."

"You've gotta know something," Kevin says.

Moe shakes his head. "Rudy has always been good at flying under the radar, staying out of the gossip columns. His endorsement deals have a morals clause and he didn't want to risk it." Moe looks around, checking to be sure Cecilia is still out of earshot. "Have you been to his apartment?"

"Apartment?" I say.

"We've only been to his house," Kevin says.

"He rents a place, in Weymouth. It's where he brought his women. I don't think Rebecca, or my fiancée, knows about it."

Cecilia comes back in the room. Moe hands her the ice pack. While she puts it back in the freezer, Moe writes down the address, folds it up, and palms it.

"Thanks for talking to us," Kevin says, extending his hand.

Moe takes the cue, and when the two men shake, Moe transfers the paper to Kevin's hand.

Chapter Ten

Kevin and I go back to headquarters, where we write up a search-warrant application. I've often declared that I could draft an affidavit in my sleep, and tonight I come close to testing my theory. I almost doze off between the paragraph about Rudy's disappearance and the section that describes the location of his apartment. When we've drafted the warrant and established probable cause to search, we drive to the courthouse and get a judge to sign it.

A couple of hours later, search warrant in hand, we travel to Rudy's hideaway. About ten miles west of Rudy's Cohasset home, Weymouth is the birthplace of Abigail Adams, wife of the president and the great-great-great-great-grandmother of my great-aunt's sister-in-law.

We get stuck at the Fore River Bridge, which has opened to let an oil tanker pass through. When we finally arrive, we find the entry team gathered outside Rudy's apartment. The orange-and-green hallway reminds me of the Ramada Inn where we stashed a reluctant witness a few years ago.

Kevin bangs on the door. "Police, open up."

There's a battering ram in the truck—we could use it to force our way inside, but we opt for a civilized entry. I go to the rental office and ask for a key. It'll attract less animus from the management, and less attention from the neighbors.

"Jeez, I had no idea Rudy Maddox was staying here." The building manager shows me the lease. "He must've used a straw."

"Who pays the rent?" I say.

"A guy leaves cash—eleven hundred dollars. Every month, he leaves it in an envelope, slips it in the mail slot."

Back upstairs, Kevin uses the key to open the door; the officers go inside to conduct a safety sweep. I glove up and slip paper bootees over my shoes. Once Kevin gives me the all clear, I join him in the living room.

Rudy's one-bedroom apartment is a far cry from his Cohasset manse. It's sparse, more man cave than the love nest I had envisioned. The walls are dimpled, the floors are carpeted, and the furniture looks like it was purchased at a fraternity yard sale.

The search is easy to conduct since the apartment has few nonessentials. The officers check the closets, cupboards, and cabinets. Technicians dust for prints. I peek in the refrigerator, which has a six-pack of Molson ale. The freezer hosts a dried-up ice-cube tray and a bottle of Stoli. An unopened box of Oreos looks tempting; I consider taking a few—it's a shame to let perfectly good cookies go to waste.

Kevin calls me into the bedroom, where I find him holding an address book. "Rudy is old-school. He keeps a little black book."

"Does it have anything inside?"

"Names—and they're all of the female persuasion."

"Smart not to store that stuff in his smartphone."

Kevin drops the address book into a plastic evidence bag. As he searches through the next drawer, I pull the blinds and check out the view of the parking lot. As I turn back around, I notice that next to the window is a picture of dogs playing baseball. It's crooked, which makes me anxious. I straighten it, but as I do, the nail comes loose.

I take the picture down and lean it against the wall. "There's a hole in the plaster."

"The landlord can send us the repair bill," Kevin says.

"No, that's not what I mean. I didn't make the hole—it looks like it was cut, intentionally."

Kevin comes over and pries off a square of plaster. He sticks his arm inside the wall—all the way up to his shoulder—and feels around.

"What's in there?" I say.

"He's keeping a secret stash."

"Of what? Guns?"

Kevin takes out his arm. He's holding something but I can't see what it is. "I'll give you a hint. It's green."

"Marijuana?"

"Nope." He turns and holds up a wad of cash, then another. The wall is full of money—thousands of $100 bills.

Chapter Eleven

We spend the next couple of days analyzing Rudy's list of women. With not a lot to go on, mostly just a name and a city, we tap into our investigative resources. Our connection at the Registry of Motor Vehicles helps track down their driver's licenses, which gives us an age, address, and photograph. Kevin taps into his database for a financial profile, which includes a list of employers. I log on to social media. A couple of clicks on Facebook and Twitter gives me what it used to take weeks to find out—information about relationship status, social activities, and recent dining experiences.

Rudy doesn't seem to have a type. The women are single, separated, divorced, and married. They are Caucasian, Asian, African-American. They're Christian, Jewish, and Buddhist. And they live everywhere—from Detroit and Denver, to Minneapolis and Miami. They represent a cross section of the country, as American as apple pie and baseball.

As much as I'd like to rack up frequent-flier miles, we don't have time to make at-home visits. We decide to do triage via Skype. That way we'll be able to lay eyes on each woman, assess her level of cooperation and credibility, and decide if she's got relevant information. Then, we'll either ask the local police departments to follow up, or we'll bring them to Boston for grand jury. Kevin will pick them up at Logan Airport or the Greyhound bus terminal, depending on how crucial they are to the case and how generous Stan is feeling.

I pick out a few promising prospects. First up is a twenty-six-year-old cancer nurse from Manhattan. I reach her at Sloan Kettering, at the tail end of her shift.

"I figured someone would be calling. I read about it in *The Times*. It's horrible." She's not the airheaded groupie that I had expected. She looks like she could use a shower and some shut-eye.

"Where did you and Rudy meet?"

"At a charity event; we were both on the board of Make-A-Wish. But I haven't seen him in a couple of years."

"Rudy's phone records show you talked to him twice last month."

"He still calls, when he knows he's going to be in the City. Sometimes we chat on the phone, but I don't fool around with married guys. At least not knowingly."

The next call is to a personal trainer in Minneapolis. She tells us she saw Rudy last month; they met up in Vegas for a two-night tryst, but she has no idea where he could be. Most of the women are equally unhelpful, but we do learn something important: a pattern is emerging.

"Nurse, physical therapist, personal trainer," I say.

"He likes people who know about anatomy. That's not unusual for athletes."

"Or most men."

"Maybe we're going at this wrong," Kevin says. "Rebecca said she got a call from one of the women last week. Let's pull Rebecca's phone records."

Kevin does a phone dump. He zeros in on last week and scans Rebecca's incoming calls. Most are easily identifiable: Rudy's cell, Cecilia's cell, the sisters' mother. He flips to the next page.

"Here's a call from the Mass General Hospital. Maybe Rudy's girlfriend is a nurse."

I dial the number and get a recording: *You have reached the office of Dr. Davidson. To make, change, or cancel an appointment, press one.* Either it's the Maddox family physician or Rudy's lover works in the doctor's office. I cut to the chase, hit zero, and get the receptionist on the phone.

"What kind of medicine does Dr. Davidson practice?"

"She's an orthopedist."

"I think I have the wrong number."

"The call fits the time frame," Kevin says, "and the caller fits the profile."

I check my watch. It's after six. We've been cooped up in my office for hours, and I'm eager to get into the field.

"Grab your coat," I say. "Let's pay Dr. Davidson a house call."

Chapter Twelve

Dr. Jane Davidson lives in 5 Longfellow Place, one of the concrete towers that make up Charles River Park. Up until about sixty years ago, the area was a jumble of tenements, occupied by a mix of immigrants: Polish, Italian, Irish, Greek, Lithuanian, Russian, Lebanese. The ethnic diversity was a rarity in a city whose neighborhoods have always been clustered according to ethnic groups. In the 1950s the tenements were bulldozed and replaced with mid- and high-rise buildings that were given names such as Whittier, Emerson, and Longfellow.

Kevin flashes his badge and asks the security guard for Jane Davidson's apartment number.

"That name doesn't ring a bell," the guard says.

"It's probably hard to keep track of everyone, coming and going," I say.

"Not really. I pretty much know everyone in here."

He scans his roster, searching his computer screen for her name, but comes up empty. "Do you have a photo? I'm pretty good with faces."

Kevin holds up a recent picture, from her Mass General ID badge.

The guard nods in recognition. "That's Dr. Shire. When she moved in, she told me she just split from her husband—Davidson must be her married name." He picks up the phone. "I'll give her a jingle, let her know you're on your way up to see her."

"No, please don't," I say. "We'd like to surprise her."

"Gotcha." He winks and hits the button to release the sliding glass door.

We take the elevator to the thirty-fifth floor.

Kevin rings the buzzer. "Boston Police. Please open the door."

There's a gap between the bottom of the door and the floor. We hear the shuffling of footsteps as a shadow comes into view and a voice calls out, "Just a sec."

A couple of minutes later, Jane Shire Davidson opens the door. She's about ten pounds heavier and six inches shorter than Rudy's wife, Rebecca. Her heavy tortoiseshell glasses are a smidgen too big for her face. Her eyes are rimmed in red, as though she's been crying.

Kevin starts to explain the reason for our visit but she stops him.

"I know Rudy is missing. I've seen it all over the news." Her voice trembles, her throat catches. "At first I thought he wasn't returning my calls because he was avoiding me."

"I take it you're more than his doctor," Kevin says.

She gestures us inside. The apartment has the generic look of a corporate rental, devoid of any personal photos or books. It doesn't look as if she plans to nest. We take seats in the living room, on the pleather sofa.

"I'd offer you coffee, but I don't have any." Her voice is deep, but not masculine.

"How long have you been living here?" I say.

She checks her watch as though she could count the minutes. "I left my husband six days ago."

She walks us over to the balcony and looks outside.

"Because of Rudy?" Kevin says.

She nods, blows her nose. "I never imagined that he'd vanish."

I walk over to windows and stand beside her. The view stretches from the waterfront to the Charles River and beyond. It reminds me of when I lived in the Back Bay, in a condo that had a view, and a terrace, and hot water.

"Did your husband know about Rudy?" I say.

She takes off her glasses, fogs them with her breath, and wipes them off with her shirtsleeve.

"My husband found out last week."

"Do you think he could have had anything to do with Rudy's disappearance?"

"I doubt it. My husband had been unfaithful more times than I can count."

"How did you and Rudy meet?" I say.

"He came in to the Mass General last year, when he injured his shoulder." She adjusts a crooked lampshade, only making it more crooked. "There were a lot of follow-up visits."

"Did he leave any of his belongings here?" Kevin says.

"I hardly have any of my own belongings in this place." She tucks her hair behind her ear. "He's only been here once."

I don't think she's lying about the nature of their relationship, but I think she's holding back. She's antsy, and fidgety. Maybe Rudy has been here more than once. Maybe she's hiding something about him or about herself. Something is making her squirm.

"Do you mind if I use your bathroom before we go?" I say.

She doesn't respond. Not exactly consent, but it's not a denial either. Kevin catches my eye. He knows I never use a witness's bathroom unless there's an emergency—like my bladder is going to burst or I want to snoop around.

On my way to the bathroom, I take a quick peek inside the bedroom. Nothing unusual. The bed is made, the comforter feels synthetic, the pillowcases look new but inexpensive. There's no sign of a male presence—nothing like a shaving kit or stray cuff links—but then again, there's no sign of a female presence either, except for the clothes in the closet.

The bathroom is barely big enough to fit a toothbrush. By law, I'm allowed to look around, but only at things that are in plain sight. Technically, I need a warrant to open cabinets or containers. Since the shower curtain is pulled back halfway, I peer behind it. Nothing is there, not even a bottle of shampoo. I flush the toilet, even though I haven't used it, and wash my hands. There's no towel in plain sight. Oops. I guess I have look in the vanity. I'm not conducting an illegal search—I need something to dry my hands.

When I open the top, I am shocked by what I see. It's not a man's razor. It's six small vials of clear liquid and a stash of syringes. Steroids.

Back in the living room, Kevin is talking to Jane, getting background information. I walk in, remain silent, and hold up a vial.

"Is that what I think it is?" Kevin says.

"Steroids. There's a drawer full of steroids in the bathroom. Tell us, what's the legitimate medical reason that allows you to keep steroids at home?"

Kevin stands and inspects the bottle.

"I'm an orthopedist," Jane says. "I dispense steroids all the time."

"I understand," I say. "That'd be a valid response if we were in your office."

"Did you give Rudy steroids?" Kevin says.

She considers her response, then murmurs, "He was my patient."

"Did you write him a prescription? A legal one?" I say. "Is there a record of the dosage?"

She walks to the window, her back to us. "I may have bent the rules."

I look to Kevin and give him a nod. "Go ahead."

He knows what to do. He unclips the handcuffs from his belt and moves to Jane. "You're under arrest for illegal possession of a Class C substance with intent to distribute." Kevin slaps opens one of the cuffs and reaches for her arm.

She trembles, starts to cry. "But I'm a doctor."

"Enjoy the title while you can," Kevin says. "When the medical board catches wind of this, you may not have an *MD* behind your name anymore."

Chapter Thirteen

Dr. Jane Davidson's arraignment is the hottest ticket in town. Reporters are lined up outside the Boston Municipal Courthouse, ready for the security check. After retrieving their keys and wallets and phones from the conveyor belt, each stands, arms extended, to be wanded. I glance at a sampling of the credentials dangling from chains around their necks: *Sports Illustrated*, *The Wall Street Journal*, *The Boston Globe*, *Entertainment Tonight*. Also in the crowd is a Boston city councillor, an investigator from the medical licensing board, and the general counsel for the Red Sox.

A cluster of prosecutors and defense attorneys are gathered by the elevator bank. I turn without acknowledging anyone and take the stairs to the fifth floor; I'm not in the mood for chitchat, and I could use the exercise.

The small courtroom is stifling. I can barely breathe, which is probably for the best. Eau de stale cigarettes and body odor are the perfumes du jour. I walk through the gallery. The three rows of pews are already jam-packed. I cross the bar to the prosecutor's table, take a seat, and pull the case file from my tote. I don't need to prepare, but studying the reports gives me something to focus on and makes me look occupied. Anything to avoid interacting with others.

A couple of minutes later, Kevin joins me at the table. Behind us, tongues are wagging. I eavesdrop on the gossip.

I heard they found Rudy last night, under the bleachers in Fenway, with a bullet in his head.

I heard Rebecca filed for divorce and that she threw his clothes out the window.

I heard Rudy's not really missing—he's just gone to rehab. This is all a publicity stunt.

A door in the front of the courtroom creaks open and a court officer busts in. He bangs on the wall to get everyone's attention. "All rise."

The courtroom quiets as Judge Victor Denton takes the stand. He doesn't need someone to announce his arrival; he's a commanding presence at six foot six and about 260 pounds. He's a former college linebacker, and he's also a former prosecutor. A few years ago, when he was in the DA's Office, we tried a difficult three-codefendant homicide together; after three guilty verdicts, and too many cocktails, we wound up at his place. It was fun, but neither of us was interested in pursuing a relationship. If this were more than a simple arraignment, he'd probably make up an excuse and withdraw from the case.

The clerk calls out, *"Commonwealth v. Jane Davidson."*

A few seconds later, Jane appears from behind a door. She's wearing pearl studs in her ears, and steel cuffs on her hands.

Her lawyer hurtles into the courtroom, wipes his forehead with a handkerchief, and files an appearance. "Preston Chisolm for the defendant. Apologies for my lateness, Your Honor. I was stuck in the line to get into the courthouse."

I've never seen this lawyer before, and he looks as if he's never laid eyes on the inside of a courtroom—at least not a municipal court arraignment session. His briefcase, big enough to double as a weekender, probably weighs more than he does. He's sporting a platinum Rolex and chunky gold cuff links with the Yale insignia: *Lux et veritas*—"light and truth."

The clerk signals Preston and hands him an appearance form, which he signs.

Kevin raises his eyebrows, wanting to tell me something. "I don't know this clown, but odds are fifty-fifty that he gets mugged in the elevator on his way out of the building."

With great ceremony, Preston unpacks a stack of legal pads, pens, and evidence books. It looks as if he were planning to be here all week.

Judge Denton reads the charges. "How do you now plead?"

Preston stands and bellows, as though he were in the grand ballroom at Buckingham Palace about to announce the arrival of the queen.

"Your Honor, may it please the court, I wish to enter a plea on behalf of my client. She is one hundred percent not guilty. And pursuant to the rules of criminal procedure, we are filing an omnibus motion—"

Judge Denton waves his hand. "No grandstanding, sir. It's only an arraignment. Save the theatrics for the jury."

"May I be heard on bail?" I say.

"You're asking for bail?" Judge Denton says. "On a simple possession charge? The defendant doesn't seem to pose a risk of flight."

In the scheme of things, a small amount of steroids doesn't call for high bail, or any bail at all, but Dr. Davidson is not your average defendant. She has money, and I need to be sure that she'll come back to court. If Rudy turns up dead, and we end up charging someone with murder, I might want to flip Jane and have her testify.

"It's not just a simple drug case. The charges are connected to a potential kidnapping, possibly a homicide investigation," I say. "The Commonwealth requests the defendant be held on one-million-dollar cash bail."

Jane starts to cry. The murmurs in the peanut gallery compete with Preston's rambling argument. He says something about the presumption of innocence, and the constitutionality of holding someone without bond. I'm not sure if the judge is listening, but if he is, he's not impressed.

"I'm allowing Ms. Endicott's request for a million dollars' cash bail, without prejudice."

"But you can't," Jane says. "I don't have that kind of cash."

"We'll be filing an appeal *sua sponte,*" Preston says.

"We're adjourned," Judge Denton says, stepping off the bench.

Aware that the world is watching, Judge Denton is playing it safe. He's leaving the heavy lifting to the judge who will inevitably hear the bail appeal.

When court recesses, Kevin goes to the police room to make some calls, and I go out into the hallway to find Preston. I find him on a bench, fumbling with papers.

"Do you want to conference the case?" I say.

"I'll check my schedule and have my paralegal contact you to make the necessary arrangements. What's your availability?"

"How about now?"

Preston should jump at the chance to hear me out. There's no downside—he doesn't have to agree to anything, and he could learn something about my case—but he doesn't seem to appreciate that. He's probably intelligent and would be the perfect choice of lawyer if we were arguing before the US Supreme Court, but this is the BMC, and I'm looking to make a bargain-basement offer. His client would be better served by a workaday ham-and-egger who knows how to play Let's Make a Deal.

After a little more back-and-forth, I suggest he confer with some of the local lawyers, and I point out a few hacks who are huddled in a corner across the hallway. Preston takes my suggestion, and a few minutes later, he returns and agrees to meet me and Kevin at the jail.

Kevin and I take the ten-minute walk to Nashua Street. I still have a headache from the stench in the courtroom, and the cool April air feels good. We cut across Charles River Park, following the cement path, and stop at Pace's for a bite. Kevin gets a tur-key sub and ice tea; I get a piece of chocolate peanut-butter cake and two cups of coffee. Next week, I'm going to give up sugar. This time I mean it.

"The doc has a nitwit for a lawyer," Kevin says.

"He's definitely out of his depth."

"There's a lot of lawyers in this town, too many if you ask me. Why not hire someone who knows the ropes?"

"Preston's firm represents the hospital. They're big and fancy, which she probably thinks is a good thing."

"That'd be like going to a brain surgeon for an ingrown toe-nail. She oughta know better."

When we reach the jail, we check in at the front desk. Kevin puts his gun in a locker and I surrender my pepper spray. We're led through a series of locked doors, each one closing before the next one opens, which always makes me claustrophobic. We wait in a conference room until Preston and Jane are brought in.

"My client demands an apology and dismissal of all charges," Preston says.

"This doesn't have to be contentious," I say. "We're here to hammer out an agreement that we can all live with. Your client can help get herself out of this mess."

Preston eyes me with suspicion, as though I might be trying to pull a fast one. Even though it's not beyond the realm, I'm not. I turn my attention to Jane.

"It's in everyone's best interest that you cooperate. It'd be to your advantage to join our efforts, rather than fight us at trial."

"What do you want me to do?" she says.

Preston puts his hand up. *I have this under control, let me handle it.* "What do you want her to do?"

For that pearl of wisdom, this guy is probably charging $750 an hour.

"Make a proffer, be truthful and tell us everything you know. In return, we'll dismiss the charges against you," I say.

"Absolutely not," Preston says. "First, you give my client immunity, then we talk."

"That's not how it works." I stand, push in my chair. "You're talking your client into a felony conviction, possible jail time, and definite loss of her medical license."

Kevin and I have an unspoken agreement to alternate between good cop and bad cop, depending on the witness. Now that I've staked my claim as the bad guy, Kevin remains seated, shakes his head, and looks at Jane.

"Let's turn it down a notch," Kevin says. "And let's not forget, Rudy Maddox is still out there somewhere, possibly still alive. Don't you want to help us find him?"

"You're not doing yourself any favors," I say.

Preston starts to argue. "My client—"

"Shut up, Preston," Jane says.

He looks at her, mouth agape, as though no one has ever shushed him before.

"You're fired," she says.

"You're making a mistake," Preston says.

She turns to me. "I'm going to represent myself."

"That's your prerogative," Preston says.

He doesn't put up a fight. He gathers his papers, his briefcase, and his fedora. When he knocks on the door, the guard comes to let him out, and he leaves without turning back.

"What do you want to know?" Jane says.

I open a file folder, take out a proffer letter, and slide it across the table. "First you have to agree with our terms."

Chapter Fourteen

A proffer is a binding contract between the prosecutor and the witness. By signing the letter, Jane agrees to answer my questions, truthfully and completely. In return, I can't use anything she says against her. She doesn't have to agree to cooperate, but if she refuses, I could still force her to testify—through a grant of immunity, which is more complicated and less pliable.

Jane flips through the pages without reading them. "Give me a pen. I can't spend another second in this place."

"Read the letter—carefully—and if you agree to the terms, sign it," I say.

She scans the document, running her index finger down the center of the page and following it with her eyes. When she's done, she looks up, and I hand her a pen.

Her hand is shaking as she signs on the dotted line. "Let's do this. I want to get it over with."

Kevin takes out his phone and flips on the audio recorder. "For the record, you've fired your attorney and decided to represent yourself."

"Yes."

"If you want to retain someone else, now's the time to tell us."

"I'll take what's coming to me. Just get me out of here."

"Why don't we start with your first interaction with Rudy Maddox," I say.

She glances down; her eyes land on her left hand, the tan line where her wedding ring used to be. "Rudy injured his shoulder last year. He came to the hospital for treatment."

"He didn't need surgery?"

"No, but he reported a significant amount of discomfort."

"So you gave him steroids," Kevin says.

"Not right away." She pauses. "And it was for legitimate treatment purposes only. It was all done in accordance with medical ethics and league rules."

I hold up the letter. "You promised to be truthful. Minimizing isn't going to help."

"That's how it started." Her eyes well with tears. "But a couple of weeks later, at a follow-up visit, he asked for growth-enhancement hormones."

"Testosterone?" I say.

She starts to speaks, stops, and nods. We all let this land, knowing that it will soon be national news. Not only has a star Red Sox player disappeared without a trace, there's a steroid scandal brewing. I take a packet of tissues from my tote, hand her a couple. She blows her nose, wipes her eyes.

"I knew he was taking advantage of me, but I didn't care. We had started seeing each other, romantically. I was falling in love."

"If it makes you feel better, Doc, I see this kind of thing all the time—from both men and women," Kevin says. "Prince or Princess Charming walks through the door and, before you know it . . ." He slams his hand on the table. "Boom, you're in—hook, line, and sinker. And as soon as they get what they want, poof, they disappear."

"I ruined my marriage, my reputation. For what?"

Kevin lets her cry for a minute. "You can recover. Everyone loves a comeback story."

"The state medical board doesn't root for a comeback, and neither will my patients."

We can't veer too far into the land of self-pity. We have to keep her on track.

"We're going to schedule you to testify in the grand jury," I say. She drops her head in her hands. "I can't."

"The good news is, as soon as you're done, we'll ask the judge to reduce the bail, and you'll be released."

Apparently, those were the magic words. She looks up and brightens. "Can we see the judge this afternoon?"

"It's too late, court has adjourned for the day," I say. "I'll get you in there tomorrow, first thing."

Jane is sent back to her cell, and the next morning she is transported to the courthouse in the prisoners' van. I meet her on the sixth floor, and a little before nine, the grand jurors start to straggle in, Dunkin' Donuts coffee cups in hand. I prefer the bitter taste of Starbucks, but I like jurors who go for Dunkie's—they tend to be more blue-collar, more grounded, and more likely to convict.

Grand jurors sit for three months at a time. This group was impaneled a month ago, which is the sweet spot; they've stopped playing junior detective, asking a million questions and spending a lot of time deliberating. On the other hand, they're not yet fully jaded—they're still attentive and prompt.

When everyone is ready, I go into the jury room and prepare the panel: "I'm initiating a grand jury investigation into the facts and circumstances surrounding the disappearance of Rudy Maddox."

The minute they hear Rudy's name, they put lids on their coffee cups and shift in their seats, sitting up a little straighter. Some exchange looks; a couple take out notebooks.

A juror in the front row, wearing a UCLA sweatshirt, raises her hand. "I have a conflict. I'm a Dodgers fan."

"I knew you looked like a foreigner," the juror in the back row says.

"Can you be fair and impartial?" I say.

"I can be open-minded about the case, but not about the Red Sox."

A woman in the middle lets out a *BOOOO*.

"Good enough," I say. "If you think you can't be fair, let me know."

I go into the waiting room to let the court officer know we're ready. He escorts Jane into the grand jury room. She walks slowly, careful not to trip on her leg irons, and takes a seat in the witness box.

I stand and face her. "Please raise your right hand."

Before I can administer the oath, a grand juror in the front row interrupts, "Hey, I know you. You're that doctor who fixed my kid's shoulder last year."

Boston is a small town and the Mass General is a big hospital. Jane registers recognition and blanches. "How is he doing?"

"Wicked good."

It's probably not a conflict of interest, but it's not worth the risk, especially since the interaction is being recorded.

"Sir, I'm going to excuse you for now. Could you please step outside until we're done with this witness?"

I administer the oath and ask Jane the same questions I asked yesterday. She doesn't hesitate to admit to her role in the affair or in providing steroids to Rudy.

"Do any members of the panel have questions?" I say.

A juror in the back row takes a bite of his Egg McMuffin and raises his hand. "No offense, but did you seriously expect Rudy to leave his wife? I mean, she's hot."

"I trusted him," Jane says. "He broke my heart."

"Let's stick to the facts of the case," I say.

I slap an evidence sticker onto the proffer letter and write, *#1*.

"Have you provided a truthful and complete proffer of all the information that you know?" I say.

Jane nods, not very convincingly.

"You have to answer out loud," I say. "The recorder doesn't pick up nods and gestures."

Jane leans forward into the mic. "I've answered all your questions truthfully. I swear."

She starts to stand, as though we're done. Not so fast.

"Have you also answered my questions *completely*?"

She looks at me, but doesn't speak. I take that as a no.

"Did you give steroids to other members of the team?"

Her thumb moves in circles on the back of her bare ring finger. Everyone, myself included, leans in. There's no doubt about what her answer will be, and as soon as the information leaks—and it will leak—the impact will be momentous. Another Boston team will become known as cheaters, and their standing in the league will be suspect for decades to come.

"Jane?"

"Rudy asked me to give steroids to one other person."

"Who?" the foreman says.

"Is this person a member of the Red Sox?" I say.

"Yes."

I take a breath and wish I didn't have to ask the next question. "What's his name?"

"It's the replacement catcher, Wayne Ellis."

Chapter Fifteen

Superman gets his strength from the sun, Spider-Man's might comes from venom. Police superpowers are rooted in probable cause. That's how detectives are able to stop speeding cars with the blast of a siren, open locked doors without using a key, and take down the bad guys with a simple command: *Stop and put your hands in the air.* Well, that plus the .45-caliber semiautomatic Glocks they keep holstered to their belts.

Kevin is itching to arrest Wayne Ellis on drug-possession charges, but we don't have probable cause. Dr. Jane Davidson's confession is solid evidence against Wayne, but not enough for an arrest warrant. That's where good lawyering comes in. Prosecutors don't carry guns, but we have subpoenas.

"We'll force him into the grand jury," I say, "and get him under oath."

Lying to police is ill-advised, but it's not necessarily a crime. Lying to a grand jury is a felony. I get on my computer, print out a subpoena, and hand it to Kevin.

"I'll serve him tonight," he says.

After he's gone, I spend time prepping for Wayne's grand jury appearance. A couple of hours later, my phone vibrates. It's a text from Ty: *Where are you? Dinner in ten minutes with your family.* I had completely forgotten, but Ty doesn't have to know.

I respond, *Of course I remember. I was just leaving. See you there.*

My family hasn't had a get-together since my father walked out on my mother, a few months ago. With no détente in sight, my sister-in-law, Missy, played the pregnancy card and suggested a family dinner. Before Charlie and I could talk her out of it, she called my parents and made a reservation at their home away from home, the Four Seasons. My mother, fresh out of a six-month stint in rehab, promised to be there, and after some prodding, my father agreed to come too. I heard he's dating someone; I hope he has the sense not to bring her. My mother is vulnerable, and now that she's sober, she's probably hopeful he'll take her back.

I drive to Boylston Street and make a halfhearted attempt to find a parking meter. After one loop around the Public Garden, I give up and stop at the hotel's valet stand. Last time I parked here, it cost me a day's pay.

"Put it on the Endicott account," I say, having no idea if there is such an account.

"Which Endicott—Charles or John?" the valet says.

"Charlie, please." My brother won't mind. He probably won't even notice.

Inside, the maître d' takes my coat and leads me into the main dining room. Ty and my brother are at a table in the center of the room. All of the neighboring tables are unoccupied, about a quarter of the dining room. The restaurant would have been filled to capacity, but my family bought out the surrounding tables—that's what they do when they want privacy. Endicotts like to be seen, but not overheard.

I kiss Ty, who looks handsome in a white oxford and blazer, and he hands me a glass of red wine. My brother Charlie, in his trademark navy-blue suit and Hermès tie, gives me a hug. His wife, Missy, marches into the room; she's carrying a vase that is brimming with an assortment of pastel roses. She snatches the restaurant's potted orchid from the table, passes it to a waiter, and replaces it with her arrangement.

Missy centers the vase on the table and admires her work: "Much better."

Missy is neurotic and compulsive, which are among the many reasons I love her. We exchange hugs; I barely feel her baby bump through her silky Akris sheath. We take seats around the table, which is filled with platters of raw seafood. Missy must have ordered them when she made the reservation.

I grab a fist-size shrimp and dip it in cocktail sauce.

"I hope Dad doesn't bring that woman he's been toting around town," Charlie says.

"He's too smart for that," I say. "It'd be a declaration of war, and he'd pay for it in the divorce settlement."

"It would devastate your mother," Missy says. "I still have a feeling they're going to get back together. Anyway, let's talk about something less depressing."

"Tell us about the baby," Ty says. "Are you going to find out if it's a boy or a girl?"

Missy beams. "We're having a girl."

Charlie takes Missy's hand and turns to me. "We'd like you to be her godmother."

I chew on my shrimp slowly, trying not to choke as I think up a valid excuse to say no. I'm thrilled for them, but I'd be a terrible godparent—it's too much responsibility. I don't even feel up to the task of dogsitting their Yorkie when they go to Positano next month.

"We're not asking you to raise her," Charlie says.

"Of course. I'd love to."

"I'd always hoped that when I had a kid, George would be the godfather," Charlie says.

We all had a lot of hopes for George. Mostly, that he would get sober, but that didn't happen. And now he's gone.

As I tilt my head and let an oyster slide down the back of my throat, my father charges in. I'm relieved he doesn't have anyone on his arm. He kisses me and Missy, gives Ty a hearty handshake, and pats Charlie on the back. Charlie sees my father every day, at the office; I'm not entirely sure what they do there—buy and sell small countries, invest in drug cartels, or trade baseball cards.

My father takes a seat across from me and says, "I've been meaning to call."

"Me too," I say. "I've been busy."

"I wasn't talking to you, Muffin. I was talking to Tyson."

Ty, as surprised as I am, puts down his glass of Sam Adams. "Did you want to talk about something specific?"

"The governor asked me to serve on an advisory committee. I'm overextended. I suggested they recruit you in my place."

"What's the subject?" I say, slightly miffed that Dad didn't ask me first.

"Something to do with community relations."

As my father flags down the waiter and orders his Glenfiddich, I lean in and whisper to Ty, "*Community relations*—that's code for police misconduct."

"Which is code for something else," Ty says.

Done with his drink order, my father turns back to Ty. "That's right, I nominated you because you're black. I also did it because you're smart, you care about your community, I think you have something to contribute, and I like you."

"This is your chance to get even with Mike Chase," I say.

"Who?" my father says. He doesn't wait for an answer. He hands Ty a business card.

Ty looks at the card and considers.

"Give him a call," my father says.

"Sure," Ty says.

We order a second round of drinks. I'm so excited about the prospect of exacting revenge on Mike Chase, I don't notice my mother's absence, until my father checks his watch.

"Where is your mother? She's forty-five minutes late."

"Odds are she's not going to show." Charlie never misses an opportunity to play backup to my father. "Let's order."

"We can give her a few more minutes," Missy says. "She's been through a lot. Facing us is probably tough."

A couple of minutes later, my mother glides into the room, looking as though she's spent the entire day getting ready to make her entrance. Her blond bob is freshly shellacked, her brows perfectly arched, her makeup professionally applied.

"Sorry to be tardy, but traffic was a bear."

I look out the window. It's true, traffic around the Public Garden is at a standstill, but her house is a four-minute walk. When she eyes my dress, a Max Mara from four seasons ago, I wish I'd chosen something that hasn't started to fade and fray from so many trips to the dry cleaner's.

My mother smiles, using only the bottom third of her face. "It's time to retire that outfit."

She gave up drinking, but not sniping. When she turns and looks behind her, we all follow her eyes. A man, definitely not a waiter, approaches. He's in a charcoal suit, like my father, and wing tips, like my father. The man puts his hand on the small of her back.

"Abigail, you remember Will Dorset," my mother says. "You went to Winsor with his daughter Meredith."

Charlie and I exchange looks. Neither of us are fans of Minnie Dorset. She was my high school rival, and Charlie dated her briefly, until she started seeing a distant cousin of the British royal family's.

"Minnie sends her regards. She always admired your pluck," Will says.

Leave it to my mother to get dumped, go to rehab, and, less than a month later, snag the only man on Beacon Hill who has more money than my father. When we're done with the awkward introductions, my father asks Charlie to get another chair.

Will, not to be out-alpha-ed, takes control of the conversation. "How's that firm of yours? Has the economy hit you hard?"

"Not at all. How's retirement?"

Coming from my father, that's the ultimate dig. He inherited enough money to stay at home and watch his investments grow, but that's not the Endicott way. Endicott men work, even though they don't have to.

My father gestures for the waiter, and we place our orders.

"Will and I are going to Palm Beach next week," my mother says.

She holds her water glass at just the right angle to flash her unadorned ring finger at my father.

"Enjoy," he says. "Bring us all a T-shirt. The place is swarming with tourist traps and souvenir shops."

When the first course finally arrives—rich, buttery langoustine—we all focus on our food with such intensity you'd think it were our last supper. In between my second and third bites, my phone vibrates. I take it out of my pocket; the screen says it's Kevin.

"I have to excuse myself."

"Muffin, not now," my father says.

"It's rude, dear," my mother says.

At least they can still agree about something—their disdain for my job. They know a call from work is about life or death, most likely the latter.

"I have to take it." I step into the hallway. "Did you serve the subpoena on Wayne Ellis?" I say to Kevin.

"Not exactly."

"What's the problem?"

Kevin takes a breath. "Where are you?"

"Back Bay." Best to be vague. If I tell him I'm at the Four Seasons, I'll never hear the end of it. "Where are you?"

"The Fens—we found a body."

I press the phone closer to my ear. "Is it Rudy Maddox? Is he dead?"

"Close, but no cigar."

My heart pounds. "Who then?"

"It's Wayne Ellis, and, yes, he's dead."

Wayne is dead.

I look back in the room. My mother is talking about Will's family castle in Scotland. Will asks my mother to hold his glass of bourbon while he searches his phone for a photo. While everyone feigns interest in the castle, my mother looks at the glass longingly. Will could have put the glass down on the table himself. He must know she's an alcoholic. I hope he's not subtly encouraging her to drink.

Ty sees me in the doorway; he excuses himself from the table, but no one seems to notice.

"They found a body in the Fens."

"Is it Rudy?" Ty says.

I shake my head. "I'll tell you about it later."

"Do you have your car?"

I hand him the valet ticket. "Can you take it home?"

"Is Kevin picking you up?" Ty says without expression.

"No, I'll take a taxi."

"Want me to grab you a coffee for the road?"

I bristle, knowing what he's hinting at. "I've only had two glasses of wine. Plus, I won't be driving."

"I'm not sure who's getting the better end of the stick, me with your family, or you with your murder."

I peer in the room. The dysfunction is palpable. Missy smiles as she struggles to make pleasant small talk. "Me," I say. "I'm definitely getting the better deal."

Chapter Sixteen

The Fens is an urban wild, near Fenway Park. In the 1800s it was fetid swampland, flooded with sewage, a threat to public health. Frederick Law Olmsted developed it as part of his Emerald Necklace. Now, it's a vibrant part of the city, a park with marshes, playing fields, and gardens. It's where kids play soccer, urban gardeners plant tomatoes, and prostitutes cruise for johns.

It's a five-minute ride from the Four Seasons, but the taxi gets stuck in a traffic snarl, in front of Symphony Hall, where a concert is letting out. I grab a pair of flats from my tote, pay the driver, and walk the last few blocks.

When I finally arrive, the crime scene is in full swing. Uniforms work crowd control, keeping the cameras away and holding back the lookie-loos. Detectives canvass the area, stopping potential witnesses on the street and knocking on doors. Technicians scour for evidence, holding flashlights and dropping orange evidence markers. Reporters have set up a staging area, on the periphery of the park.

As soon as I step into view, a swarm of cameramen and reporters shout at me. *Do you want to comment? Can you confirm the name of the victim? Does it have anything to do with Rudy Maddox's disappearance?*

I nod at the patrolman who is guarding the perimeter and duck under the yellow tape. Walking down the steep staircase, I scan the area for the brightest cluster of portable kliegs—that's where the body will be. I tread carefully, keeping to the edge of the cement path, trying to avoid the scattering of goose droppings, until I find Kevin, who is talking to an EMT.

Kevin breaks away and walks over to me. "A junkie saw Wayne laying in the grass and asked him for a light. It took him a minute to realize he was dead."

"Did the guy see anyone else in the area?"

"Sure, lots of people: George Washington, Beyoncé, the pope. He's not gonna be a great witness."

Nearby, the medical examiner, Reggie Rene, is in a cluster of dry marsh weeds, leaning over a body. I inch closer.

This is the toughest part of an investigation.

I stop in my tracks, turn to Kevin. I need more information, to lessen the shock. "What's the cause of death?"

"Gunshot wound to the head."

"How bad?"

Kevin knows what I mean. He issues a warning: "It was at close range."

My shoes sink into the muddy grass as I make my way over to Reggie. I take a couple of shallow breaths, kneel down, and lean in. I have a system, it helps me to tolerate the horror. I start low on the body and work my way up. First, I take in Wayne's feet, then slowly, my eyes travel up his legs. When I'm ready, I scan his torso, and his arms. I pause at his neck.

"He's been here a few hours." Reggie twists Wayne's arm and points at bite marks on his elbow. "Rats."

The langoustine churns in my gut as I try to settle on Wayne's face. His eyes are open; his head is resting on a pillow of blood and a smattering of brain matter. A technician snaps photographs; a forensic entomologist tweezes a couple of insects that have burrowed in Wayne's ear. When Reggie is done with his preliminary inspection, he gives his assistants the go-ahead, and they zip Wayne into a body bag. They hoist him onto a gurney and slide him into the back of the van. Yesterday, Wayne Ellis was living his dream, *the* dream.

Kevin and I walk around the reporters and get in Kevin's car. We divvy up the tasks: he tries to track down Wayne's family, and I phone Rebecca. The media is already reporting that a body was found. I want to be sure Rebecca knows it wasn't Rudy. She's grateful for the call and relieved that there's still a chance her husband is alive.

Kevin hangs up and fills me in on what he's learned about Wayne. "Twenty-three years old, and single."

"Girlfriend?"

Kevin shrugs. "He lived alone."

"Next of kin?"

"His mother, she lives in Chattanooga."

Kevin doesn't want to make the notification over the phone, so he calls the locals. A Chattanooga police officer will drive to the Ellis home and deliver the sadness in person. We'll do the follow-up.

As I wait for Kevin to finish his calls, my phone vibrates. It's Stan.

"I should always be the first to know. You should've called me the minute you found out."

"Duly noted."

"Who else knows?"

"Rudy's wife—that's all."

Emma Phelps taps on the car window. "Abby, would you like to make a comment? Off the record?"

I twist the front of my body away from her.

"Is that a reporter?" Stan says. "Don't talk to the press."

"Don't worry."

"I'll tell the front office at Fenway." Stan wants to be the big cheese.

"Roger that."

"I don't want you to call them."

"Got it, boss. I won't call anyone at Fenway."

I hang up and turn to Kevin.

He starts the car. "Where to?"

"Fenway."

"Seriously? Didn't you just tell Stan—"

"I said *I* wouldn't *call* anyone at Fenway. I didn't say anything about you. So, call them, and tell them to meet us there."

Chapter Seventeen

When we reach the Green Monster, a security guard is out-side waiting, and he lets us in the gate. We call Donnie, who sends Tags down to escort us to the front office.

"I heard on the radio they found a body," Tags says, his voice cracking.

"It wasn't Rudy," I say.

He looks relieved, but that will change when he learns the vic-tim's identity. Two catchers from the same team are gone. The prosecution is batting zero.

Fenway is dark, eerie. Donnie is in his office, along with Moe Morrissey, and Pete Taylor, whom I recognize as the team owner. The three men are on their phones, having essentially the same conversation. *I can't tell you who they found in the Fens. No comment. I'll have to get back to you.*

When Kevin taps on the door, their heads whip around. Don-nie waves us in and introduces us to Pete, who looks as if he's come from a formal event. He's dressed in black tie, minus the tie.

"You're John Endicott's daughter," Pete says.

I nod. "You know my father?"

"We went to the Business School together."

Pete doesn't identify which business school he's talking about, he just says *the* Business School, which is shorthand for Harvard.

That's how locals refer to it. I went to *the* Law School. My brother went to *the* Business School, as did my father, and apparently Pete Taylor.

We give them an update, without getting into specifics about the condition of the body.

Moe shakes his head in disbelief. "Wayne played a game this afternoon. He can't be dead."

"He was just getting started," Donnie says. "This was only his second season in the pros."

"Did you ever notice signs of drug abuse—steroids or opioids—from either Wayne or Rudy?" Kevin says.

Donnie and Pete speak at once. "Impossible."

"You think this was drug related?" Moe says. I can't tell if he's surprised or not.

"We have to ask," I say.

"None of my players were using drugs," Donnie says.

Pete starts to speak, pauses, and looks me in the eye. "The men here are like my sons. They know they can come to me for anything. I'd know if there was a problem. I know everything about them."

"Where did Wayne live?" Kevin says.

Pete looks to Donnie, who looks to Moe. Guess they don't know their players as well as they claim. I can't blame them; my parents wouldn't know my address off the top of their heads either.

"He keeps a condo in the Mandarin," Moe says.

Pete's phone rings. "It's your boss."

Stan will find out that I disobeyed him, but I don't want to be reprimanded tonight.

Kevin and I slip out and drive to police headquarters, where I make arrangements to get a search warrant for Wayne's apartment. Kevin dispatches a police detail to stand guard at the front door so no one can sneak in or out before we get there.

When we're done drafting the papers and get a judge to sign

off, we drive into the Back Bay. The sun is starting to rise; the sky is washed in an array of pinks. A well-heeled investment-banker type strides across the Public Garden, briefcase in hand. A homeless woman pushes her shopping cart toward the soup kitchen on Newbury Street. A couple of domestic workers get off the bus at Copley Square.

Word is out that Wayne's body was recovered in the park, and when we reach the Mandarin, a half dozen lookie-loos are camped out near the entrance to the building. Stanchions have been set up, to protect the residents and hotel guests from the swarm of reporters.

As Kevin and I approach, we're peppered with questions.

"Did Wayne Ellis die of an overdose?"

"Was he murdered?"

"Have you found Rudy Maddox yet?"

"Is Rudy a victim or a suspect?" This one is from Emma Phelps.

I keep my eyes trained on the door, offering no reaction.

The lobby is gleaming; the brass fixtures and the marble floor look as if they're repolished every time someone sneezes. Kevin and I approach the reception desk and I'm surprised to see who is there: Manny, the doorman from my former condo building.

He greets me with a broad smile and a hearty hug. "You're a sight for sore eyes."

"You work here now?"

"After you moved out of your condo, my tips shrunk in half. It was time to check the want ads."

There's not a lot of demand for doormen in Boston—unlike in Manhattan, most of the buildings in Beacon Hill and Back Bay are small brownstones. Kevin and Manny shake hands and exchange greetings. Kevin spent a lot of time in my old lobby, waiting for me, drinking coffee, and chatting with Manny.

"The journos out there are saying Wayne Ellis was shot."

Kevin and I look at each other. Kevin speaks first, saving me from having to dodge the question.

"You must have some inside info to share."

Manny lowers his voice. "I didn't really know him. We were both new to the building and he wasn't here very often."

"Did he get a lot of foot traffic?" I say.

Manny hands over the visitors' log. "I don't remember ever calling up to his apartment to announce a guest. Not once."

"Can you give us the security tapes for the last couple of weeks?" Kevin says.

"Whatever you need. All you gotta do is ask."

"Girlfriend?" Kevin says.

Manny shrugs. "You'd think—with a paycheck like his—but I can't say for sure. I never saw him with a woman."

"Was he a renter or an owner?" I say.

"He was a tenant. He had a one-year lease."

Wayne's pockets were deep, but not as deep as Rudy's or Moe's. Manny gives us the security video and a key to Wayne's apartment.

"This'll save us all the headache of you busting in the door," Manny says.

Kevin and I take the elevator to the tenth floor, where the search warrant team has already assembled. I pass the key to the sergeant in charge, and he opens the door and steps aside to let us in.

Chapter Eighteen

Wayne's apartment is spectacular. The view includes the Charles River, the downtown skyscrapers, and the Citgo sign. The furnishings are straight out of Design Within Reach—sleek, modern, and expensive. The bamboo floors are pristine. The floor-to-ceiling windows are smudge-free. The white marble bathroom fixtures don't have a spec of stray toothpaste or shaving cream. Either Wayne was never at home or he had daily maid service.

I wait in the living room while the search team executes the warrant. I settle into the black leather Corbusier sofa, much like one I used to own, and answer some of the emails that have been piling up. The search team checks under furniture and on top of cabinets. They open books and shake the pages. They unscrew the tops of condiment jars and empty the contents.

"They collected a couple of hairs from the drain," Kevin says. "I'll send them to the lab, but other than that, we got bubkes."

"Anything in the medicine cabinet?"

"Nothing stronger than Advil."

Kevin tells the sergeant to call us if they find anything of value. When we step off the elevator, Manny is in the lobby, waiting, eager to get an update. I can't tell him anything, which is easy since we didn't find anything. I move to give him a hug goodbye, but he stops me.

"You can't go yet."

"I've been up for twenty-four hours. I've got to go home and take a shower before I start offending people."

"But you didn't check his storage locker."

"Storage locker?"

We follow Manny onto the elevator and he presses *B3*. In the garage, past the rows of Beemers and Bentleys, are a series of locked doors. Manny stops at one, types numbers into a keypad. The lock clicks open. Manny smiles, winks, and directs us inside.

Wayne Ellis's storage room is about the size of a one-car garage. The space is filled with dozens of boxes, piled atop one another. Kevin notifies the search team, and they soon join us. After a technician photographs the area, the officers glove up and slice open the boxes.

The first ten boxes contain clothes, linens, dishes—things that probably came from Wayne's old apartment. The next group is filled with papers: tax returns, contracts, and receipts. These are hauled off and transported into a police van.

"Go home and catch some shut-eye," Kevin says. "I'll give you a jingle if we find anything in here."

The air is stale, my eyelids are heavy, and the fluorescent over-head is giving me a headache. "I'm fine."

After another hour of sorting through Wayne's possessions, an officer rips open one of the last boxes.

"Yowza." He holds up a wad of cash—just like we found in Rudy's Weymouth hideaway—a box of $100 bills.

"I wonder if all players hate banks, or if it's just the catchers," Kevin says.

"They probably didn't want to declare the money because it's dirty," I say.

"They could be trafficking in steroids."

I shake my head. "It wouldn't be worth the risk."

"Maybe they were betting on games."

Kevin offers to give me a ride home. When we get outside, I shield my eyes against the glare of the noonday sun. Boylston Street is bustling with pedestrians, cyclists, and motorists, many of whom are triple-parked outside the shops and restaurants.

Somewhere between Kenmore Square and BU's towering law center, I doze off. Kevin gives me a nudge when we're at my front door. I drag myself inside, kick off my shoes, and fall asleep on the couch. A couple of hours later, feeling almost refreshed, I wake up to the sound of my phone. It's the medical examiner.

"I heard you had a long night. I went ahead and autopsied Wayne Ellis without you."

"Sorry I missed it," I lie.

"I found something."

Reggie is competent, but he tends to be theatrical; he takes a dramatic pause. I give him his moment.

"There were traces of steroids in Wayne's system."

"I'm way ahead of you on that one."

"I recovered a bullet fragment from the occipital bone."

This would be good news if we had a gun to compare it to, but until then, it's just a piece of shrapnel that doesn't lead anywhere. I thank Reggie and check my phone. Sixty-three emails, twelve texts, and nine voice mails. I listen to the first phone recording. It's Stan.

"Steroids?" Stan's voice is loud and angry. "The press office is being bombarded with questions about a steroids scandal. It's all anyone in the city is talking about. You should have given me a heads-up."

My apartment is dark. I sit up and reach for the lamp. Fumbling with the cord, I elbow a glass vase full of yellow tulips. It falls to the floor, water spills, the flower petals detach from their stems, and the glass shatters into a series of sharp, jagged pieces. The vase was expensive, handblown Venetian glass, but today it doesn't seem like a big loss.

Chapter Nineteen

It takes an entire roll of paper towels to soak up the puddle of water and remove the shards of glass. When I'm done, I toss the flowers in the trash and call Stan to apologize and explain. He's upset I didn't tell him about the steroids, but he's more upset that my photo is plastered all over the news, instead of his. He's becoming a politician faster than I'd anticipated.

Ty is at the gym. Recently, he took up boxing and he's trying to get me to do it with him. He thinks it'll be good for me to exercise and get out my aggressions, and I know he's right. I told him I'm too uncoordinated to box, but the real reason I've resisted is I'm afraid that once I start hitting people, I'll never stop.

I surprise Ty with an impromptu dinner invitation. He has to play a gig at Wally's in a few hours, so we don't have a lot of time. We agree on Anchovies, in the South End. It's cheap and has good food, plus there are back booths where I can dine unnoticed. Ty and I went to Anchovies on our first date, which always makes it a good choice—especially when we've hit a rough patch.

Anchovies is always packed and tonight is no different. I elbow my way past the crowded bar.

A woman calls out, "Hey, you're the lady on TV."

I keep my head down. A man, wielding an Amstel Light as though it were a lightsaber, blocks my path. "Hey, I know you."

"You have me confused with someone else."

He stands in place and it's impossible to go around him. "You don't even remember me?"

I shake my head.

He's not giving up. "You sent me away for a deuce."

A deuce—if this guy only served two years in prison, it means he didn't kill anyone, and he's only moderately dangerous. He probably sold heroin or held up a gas station. He doesn't look familiar, but that doesn't mean anything—I have all I can do to recognize my murderers. I can't keep track of my nonhomicidal felons.

Ty sees me and comes to my rescue. "Everything okay here?"

The man returns to his barstool, and Ty leads me to our table in the back of the restaurant. When he smiles and kisses me, it confirms what I already know: Ty is handsome and charming, and I'm lucky to have him in my life. And not just because he has a glass of red wine waiting for me on the table.

"I read about the steroids. You making progress on your case?"

"As Kevin would say, we got bubkes." I regret mentioning Kevin as soon as I see Ty's expression harden.

The waiter takes our orders: stuffed peppers for me, linguine with mussels for Ty, and two more glasses of Chianti. When the food arrives, we both dig in. I haven't eaten since yesterday and I'm a little woozy from the alcohol.

"Did you report the Brookline thing yet?"

I expect him to snap at me or at least roll his eyes, but he doesn't. "I will. I'm on it."

"When?" I hate myself but can't seem to stop.

"Babe, chill. We're not in court, don't cross-examine me."

Ty twirls pasta around on his fork and I down the second glass of wine and order a third. He raises his eyebrows in disapproval.

"You're one to talk," I say.

"I'm not a public figure, out in public. No judgments—but you've been drinking a lot lately. I know you're under a lot of stress, but still, maybe you should take it easy."

He signals the waiter for two cups of cappuccino. It looks delicious, but I let mine remain untouched, in protest of Ty's new-found paternalistic oversight. My phone vibrates. I look at the screen, then at Ty. I don't have to tell him who it is.

"Hey, Kevin, whassup?"

"You okay there?. You sound a little under the weather."

Under the weather is Kevin-speak for "you've had one too many." I don't like this new thing where everyone feels at liberty to micromanage my alcohol consumption.

"I'm in the middle of dinner."

"I got Wayne Ellis's phone records."

Ty is watching, fiddling with his phone, but I know he's got both ears on the content and tone of my conversation. I keep my words to the bare minimum. "Anything interesting?"

"He called his mother every day."

"And?"

"He's got a significant other. Kind of a secret lover."

This is news. It could be a break in the case.

"What's her name?"

"*His* name is Graham Davenport."

It didn't occur to me that Wayne might be gay, but I'm not surprised.

Ty clears his throat, reminding me we're on a date. I look at him, but keep talking to Kevin.

"Is the boyfriend local?"

"He lives in Charlestown."

"You want to take a ride out there?"

"Tomorrow," Kevin says. "When you're feeling better."

I hang up.

Ty signals for the check. "Did you drive here?" He holds out his hand, palm up, and I give him my car key. "I'll drop you off at home and Uber to my gig."

Ty leads me through the crowd at the bar.

The felon with the lightsaber calls out, "You're the reason I spent two years away from my kids."

"No, *you're* the reason you went to prison. I didn't commit a felony."

"Babe, don't argue with him," Ty says.

"I don't know how you sleep at night," the man says.

I almost tell him I don't sleep at night, but not because I sent him to prison. I don't sleep because I'm busy working. Or worrying about my victims.

Ty takes my elbow. "C'mon babe."

I jerk my arm away, lose control of my tote, and it goes flying. As I take a step forward, my ankle gets tangled in the strap. I fall forward, Ty reaches for me, but I go down hard and land on the sticky floor.

I look up to see the man, holding his cell phone. "Smile."

The camera clicks twice, then a third time. This is not what I need right now. Soon, a picture of me—on my hands and knees, hair in my eyes, dazed expression on my face—will be splashed all over the internet.

Chapter Twenty

The next day, Kevin and I interview Wayne's boyfriend, Graham Davenport. He lives in Charlestown, one of Boston's smaller neighborhoods. Charlestown only occupies about one square mile, but it holds a lot of history. The USS *Constitution* is docked in the harbor. The Bunker Hill Monument is perched high atop the steep hill. The area also hosts the highest population, nationwide, of bank robbers.

Graham's apartment is in the Navy Yard, in a building designed to look like an ocean liner. He buzzes us in and meets us outside his apartment, on the third-floor landing. His face is wan, his eyes unfocused, and a silver-dollar-size stain is on the front of his polo shirt. He reminds me of what I must have looked like last night in Anchovies.

"Can we talk out here in the hall? My place isn't really presentable."

"Don't worry. We've seen it all," Kevin says, peering over Graham's head, into the apartment.

Graham hesitates, then stands aside. Unpresentable isn't an apt description; it's a massive understatement. The place looks, and smells, like a crime scene. The loft is modern and spacious, with a killer view of the harbor, but something's very wrong. Every surface is covered—the floors, tables, countertops, bookcases—with an assortment of clothes, papers, exercise equipment, and trash.

"Was there a break-in recently?" Kevin says.

"No."

The only other explanation for the state of the apartment is that Graham is a hoarder. He picks up a stack of yellowing newspapers and piles them on another stack of newspapers, about three feet away. We all remain standing; even though there are chairs and a sofa, there's not enough empty space on them to sit. I try to ignore my surroundings, keeping my hands clasped in front of me, careful not to touch anything.

"I'm sorry for your loss." I don't say, *I know what you're going through,* even though I do know exactly what he's going through. The love of my life was murdered two years ago. This meeting, however, isn't about my loss, it's about his.

"It's complicated." Graham tears up. "I'm trying to respect Wayne's privacy, but it's hard to act like we were just really good friends."

"How long had you been together?"

"A few years—we met in Kentucky, when he was playing in the minors."

Graham blows his nose, bunches up the dirty tissue, and slips it into a drawer in the open kitchen.

"It's not going to be secret for much longer," Kevin says. "We won't release the information, but it's bound to leak out."

Leaks are an inevitable part of any homicide investigation, especially the high-profile ones. There's little we can do to control the information flow. I've even leaked things to the press myself—if it helps further the investigation—but in this case that'd be counterproductive.

"I guess it doesn't really matter anymore. Wayne was the one who wanted to keep it secret." Graham walks around a cluster of empty shopping bags and opens the refrigerator. I turn my head away, I can't bear to see what's inside. "Would you like something to drink?"

I'd love a glass of water. I'm dehydrated from last night, and I've already consumed the Poland Spring bottles I carry around in my tote.

"No thanks," I say.

Graham pours himself a paper cup full of lemonade and takes a series of small sips.

"It's embarrassing to live like this. Wayne hated coming here, but he didn't want to be seen with me at his place." Graham looks around the apartment, stopping at a mound of trash bags. "It's gotten worse, I've gotten worse, in the past few weeks. Anxiety."

"Was something particular going on, before the murder, that caused you to be on edge?" I say.

"Sure, lots of things. The relationship, the secrecy, the move to Boston." He puts down his cup, crosses his arms tightly. "And the threats."

"You were being threatened?" Kevin says.

"Not me—Wayne. He was pretty freaked about it."

"Extortion?" I say.

Graham nods. "I think so."

"Pro athletes are starting to come out," Kevin says. "Is it really that big a deal? Still?"

Graham nods. "Wayne didn't want to be known as the gay baseball player. He wanted to come out on his own terms, when he was more established."

"Wayne was using steroids." Kevin tries to gauge Graham's reaction. "Did you know that?"

Graham looks away, starts to talk, then stops himself.

"We're not trying to disparage him," I say. "We're trying to find out who killed him. It could be relevant."

"When did he start using?" Kevin says.

"My best guess is about six months ago. His skin started breaking out, his mood was up and down. I confronted him about it."

"What did he say?" Kevin says.

"He denied it. I think he didn't want me to worry."

"Do you know what he did last night, after the game?" I say.

"He said he had to finish some things at work. I think he had a meeting with the coach or something."

Graham rubs his hand over his chin and I notice his watch. A platinum Patek Philippe; my father has one. I gave it to him for his fiftieth birthday and it's easily worth $50,000.

"What do you do for work?" I say.

"I'm taking classes at Bunker Hill." He catches me eyeing the Porsche key on top of an end table, partially hidden under an empty Heath bar wrapper. "Wayne was generous."

Kevin and I exchange looks. Maybe Wayne was generous. Or maybe Graham was the one who was extorting money from him.

"Would you be willing to give a DNA sample?" I say.

He doesn't hesitate and agrees to come by the police station tomorrow to take the test. Odds are seventy–thirty he doesn't show up.

I'm almost out the door when I remember something and turn back around. "Did Wayne keep any of his things here?"

"Some clothes, a razor. That's about it."

"What about drugs or money?"

"Definitely not, but he did leave something I thought was weird." Graham walks over to a teak side table, covered with papers.

I start to sort through some of the pages, but Graham stops me. "Not the papers, the table. It didn't make sense, the last thing I needed was more stuff, but he really wanted me to have it."

The table has a thick pedestal base, and the style doesn't match the rest of the room. Kevin puts one hand on either side of the table, tilts it on its side, and rolls it around a little. Something rattles inside.

"I need a screwdriver," Kevin says.

Graham opens a tattered cardboard box and displays a dozen screwdrivers of all shapes and sizes. Kevin grabs one, removes some screws, then pries off the tabletop. He reaches inside and pulls out a wad of bubble wrap.

"What's in it?" Graham says.

Kevin unwraps the package and discovers the contents: a scuffed-up baseball.

"Any idea why he would have kept this?" Kevin says.

"None."

"It's gotta mean something," I say.

Chapter Twenty-One

Unlike the majority of my witnesses, Graham makes good on his promise. The next day, he shows up at Boston Police Headquarters and allows a technician to swab the inside of his cheek. The DNA results are not surprising: Graham's profile doesn't match anything relating to the case, but it was worth a try. We can eliminate him as a suspect, at least for now.

I stop by the executive suite in Bulfinch to let Stan know. It's an easy way to appease him. He's been threatening to take me off the case, and I want to make him feel that he's in the loop.

I find him in a conference room, at the tail end of a press conference. It sounds as if he's just announced the arrest of a sicko who's been preying on children. The reporters hurl a bunch of questions at him—none of them pertain to the case he's been describing. The only thing reporters seem to care about these days is the Red Sox.

I slip past the door, unnoticed, and wait for him in his office.

"You'd better have something for me," he says.

Unfortunately, I don't, and I'm running out of options. "Don't worry, we have plenty of options."

"Baloney."

"We could do a DNA dragnet, swab everyone."

He shakes his head in frustration. "We can't get warrants for an entire ball club."

"We don't need warrants—we have Donnie. He can get the players to cooperate, without a court order."

"You're assuming management is going to help. My money's on them not wanting to risk the exposure."

"Donnie is savvy. He'll comply. Otherwise, it'd be a public relations disaster."

Stan thinks about it for a minute. He may not know a lot about local investigations, but he's an expert on communication shortfalls. He allows the hint of a smile. It's been so long since I've seen anything other than a grimace on his face that he's almost unrecognizable.

"I'll call Donnie. He can make it happen." Stan dials Donnie's cell and puts him on speakerphone. He makes the ask and Donnie agrees to cooperate—at least in theory. Stan has a tough time pinning him down.

"Give me a couple of weeks, and I'll call you when we get back from our road trip," Donnie says.

Stan looks at me; I shake my head.

"We need samples before you leave town. It'll only take about an hour, total," Stan says. "We'll send the technicians to you."

Donnie hedges, Stan pushes back. I tune them out, trying to figure out Donnie's real concern. He's not trying to protect a killer; Donnie wants the case solved as much as anyone else. I realize why he's hedging: steroids. Donnie is afraid the test will reveal that some of the players were using performance-enhancing drugs, and he wants to buy time to get it out of their systems.

"We don't need to draw blood," I say, "just a quick cheek swab for DNA."

That seems to allay Donnie's concerns. "Okay, sure, come on by the clubhouse."

After we hang up, Stan says, "Be sure to get Donnie's DNA too."

Kevin arranges for a couple of lab technicians to meet us at Fenway. When we arrive, Tags comes to Gate E and escorts us inside. The procedure takes about an hour and a half. The players and coaches line up, and the technicians swab the inside of their cheeks. Tags stands off to the side, watching, looking anxious. His toe taps up and down, up and down. He may as well be wearing a sign that says *Hey! Test me too.*

"Tags," I say, "we'd like to get your DNA sample too."

Tags pretends not to hear me, but Moe is standing nearby and says, "Tags, I hope you're going to cooperate with the police."

He stops tapping his foot, rubs his forehead. "Sure, whatever I can do to help."

Tags closes his eyes, tilts his head back, and opens his mouth wide, as though he's about to get a root canal.

"Relax," the technician says. "It's not going to hurt."

When everyone has given a sample, Kevin and I head back to our cars.

"I'll catch up with you later," I say.

"You got a hot date?"

"My friend's baby shower." Technically, it's not my friend's event, it's my sister-in-law's, but I want Kevin to think my social circle extends beyond immediate family. Even if it doesn't.

Kevin laughs. "You don't have friends. When I first met you, like a decade ago, you had a social life. As far as I can tell, you haven't gone to a party since your brother's wedding, and only because you couldn't find an excuse to get out of it."

"That's not true," I say, even though it is.

I used to have friends, lots of them, in college and law school. After I took this job, I always had a stack of invitations on my desk—birthdays, weddings, fund-raisers—but something always got in the way. People grew tired of my no-shows, and eventually the invites dried up; the last time I was asked to anything was my college roommate's anniversary party. I was all dressed up, ready to head out the door, when I was called to a quadruple slaying in Dorchester. I stood over four dead bodies, in a floor-length Dior.

At first I felt a little lonely, but I don't miss the cocktail party circuit anymore. After my tenth visit to a murder scene, I lost interest in making small talk over canapés and cosmopolitans.

Today's baby shower is obligatory, since I'm the godmother. My mother is hosting the event, which in this case is a good thing. It means that the only baby shower games will be mind games, like how to tell if you're being praised or insulted when someone says, *You're so thin*. Or: *When was your last vacation?* Or: *Your work sounds so . . . interesting*. On the upside, there won't be any inane baby shower activities, no rounds of pregnant Twister, baby bottle bowling, or guess the baby food.

The lunch—or as my mother calls it, the "luncheon"—is at the Alden Club, on Fairfield Street in the Back Bay. My great-grandmother was one of the club founders, and my grandmother gave me a membership for my sixteenth birthday. It's a place where Bostonians wear black tie and ancestral diamonds. Members chat about where their children prep and where they summer, and they complain about how hard it is to find decent help. It's all a desperate effort to convince themselves, and one another, that they are still relevant.

When I walk into the dining room, the women are pecking at their plates of baked sole and overcooked vegetables, pretending to eat. My mother gives me an air kiss, and I can smell the booze on her breath. My stomach drops. Her wineglass is empty. She must be doing her drinking in private, in the powder room or the back of her Town Car.

"I'm so glad you could make it," Missy says. "I know how busy you are."

Coming from anyone else, that would be a dig, but not from

Missy. She is her usual gracious self. She looks radiant; her brown hair is shiny, and her cheeks are rosy. Missy's mother sits beside her, looking out of place in this room full of snobs. Missy learned how to pass for a blue blood—the understated but expensive outfits, the barely there makeup that took an hour to apply, the simple but flawless diamond studs. Missy's mother, Pat, however, will never assimilate—with her synthetic dress and garish pin—and I adore her. She's my favorite relative.

"Missy tells me you're still with the DA's Office," Pat says. "That was quite a scare you had last year."

Before I can respond, my mother interrupts, "We've tried every which way to Sunday, but we can't get her to move on with her career. At first, it appeared admirable—her decision to go into public service. But now, it's beyond the pale."

"Mother—"

She cuts me off. "Don't shush me, it's impolite."

Missy signals the waiter. "Let's all have some coffee and cake."

My mother grabs her clutch and goes to the ladies' room—probably for a shot of whiskey, or whatever she's got stashed in that bag.

"I'd love to come by and see your new apartment," Missy says.

I picture Missy and my brother taking a tour of my seven-hundred-square-foot walk-up. We'd all have to try to be upbeat and overcompensate for the awkwardness.

"There's not a lot to see," I say.

"There's you, and there's Ty," she says. "That's all I need."

When Missy crossed the three-month threshold, she took a leave of absence from her job as a fund manager. She has a Harvard MBA, and she's pretty high up the food chain at Fidelity. I can't imagine what she's doing with her time now. She has a full-time housekeeper, and a part-time everything else she needs. She sounds a little stir-crazy.

When my mother comes sashaying back to the table, looking re-lipsticked and refueled, I bid my goodbyes.

"But you just got here," Missy says.

"Where are you going?" my mother says. "To meet another one of your murderers?"

"No. I'm going to meet another one of my victims."

Chapter Twenty-Two

Kevin meets me in Boston Police Headquarters, outside the third-floor conference room. I peek in the window and catch a glimpse of the two heartbroken women, seated across from each other. The mothers of Wayne and Rudy have much in common: they're each in their midforties; they live in the South; and they're grieving deeply. They also have a lot of differences: Wayne's mother, Lenora, is single and modest—in both attitude and attire; Rudy's mother, June, is married and flashy—with a chunky gold chain, and Gucci purse. Rudy's father, Clyde, is sporting reptile boots and a turquoise belt buckle. The biggest difference, however, is that the Maddoxes can still hold out a glimmer of hope their son is alive.

I turn back to Kevin and speak quietly. "Did you run their financials?"

"Last year, Rudy's parents went from an eight-hundred-foot, one-bedroom apartment to a million-dollar split-level ranch, paid for in cash."

"What about Wayne?"

"His mother had a small influx of cash, not as much as the Maddoxes, but still suspicious. The numbers don't add up."

I take a breath before opening the door. When we walk in,

Wayne's mother is in the middle of describing the day her son made it to the majors: "Proudest day of my life."

Kevin introduces me to the families.

"I'm sorry we have to meet under these circumstances," I say.

I say this to all my victims' families when we first meet. It's not original but it's heartfelt and true, and I've never been able to come up with anything more appropriate.

Kevin gives them an update on the investigation. They ask a few follow-up questions. There's not much we can tell them, but this is a good opportunity to learn about their sons.

"Rudy is a devoted husband, a good father," Mrs. Maddox says.

"When he's not chasing skirts." Mrs. Maddox elbows her husband but he rolls his eyes and keeps talking. "We have to say the truth, June. Otherwise, how are they going to figure out what happened?"

"What about you, Ms. Ellis?" I say. "Do you know anything about Wayne's personal life?"

"I knew he was gay," she says without missing a beat. "I'm pretty sure I knew before he did."

I wonder how much my parents know about me. I had been dating Ty, practically living with him, for a year before I mentioned his existence. They don't know that before Ty I was in love with a fellow prosecutor, who was married, and that he was the one who was murdered last year. And they don't understand that I spend my days in a world of loss, and pain.

"We have reason to believe that both Rudy and Wayne had additional sources of income," Kevin says.

"You mean from the sneakers?" Mr. Maddox says.

"We didn't find any endorsement deals," I say.

"He told us he had a big contract with Nike."

So that's how he explained the infusion of cash.

"Do you know if Rudy or Wayne had any involvement in drugs or gambling?" Kevin says.

They all shake their heads in disbelief. It seems that none of the parents have information, at least none that they're willing to offer.

Mrs. Maddox tears up. "Are you any closer to finding our son? Do you think he's still alive?"

I put my hand on her arm and she drops her head, closes her eyes.

"We don't know," I say.

"When was the last time you saw Rudy?" Kevin says.

"He was home in March, for his cousin's wedding," Mr. Maddox says.

"Tell them about the box," Mrs. Maddox says to her husband.

"One day I went out to clean the garage. I found a small box. It was a baseball, all wrapped in bubble wrap. I thought it was kind of weird that he never mentioned it."

Kevin and I exchange looks.

"Did you ask him about it?" Kevin says.

Mr. Maddox nods. "He said it was a souvenir."

Rudy and Wayne both stashed souvenir baseballs in strange places. Maybe it's a thing that catchers do. Or maybe they're hiding something inside the balls.

"We need that baseball," Kevin says.

My cell phone vibrates. I check the screen and read the text. *Got a hit on the tissue we found in the Fens.* I excuse myself, and Kevin and I step into the hallway.

"Any bets on whose DNA is on that tissue?" I say.

He shrugs. "Donnie?"

When I call the crime lab, the DNA examiner picks up on the first ring.

"What do you got?" I say.

"The tissue we collected at Wayne's murder scene, in the Fens, came back as a match."

"Cut to the chase."

"Paul Tagala."

Kevin pulls at my arm. "Who is it?"

I end the call. "It was Tags."

"The towel boy?"

"Yup."

Chapter Twenty-Three

Unlike 99 percent of the people I interact with every day—lawyers, defendants, witnesses, even cops—DNA doesn't lie. There's no doubt Tags was involved in Wayne's murder. We can prove he was at or near the crime scene, which gives us means and opportunity, but we still don't have intent. The law doesn't require us to prove motive; it's not an element of the crime, but I want to know why Tags would want to kill Wayne—and the jury will want to know too.

Still, Kevin is itching to make an arrest. I think that'd be jumping the gun. The Fens is practically within spitting distance of Fenway. A good defense attorney could raise reasonable doubt: he could argue Tags was in the area for another reason, or that he may have tossed the tissue out the window as he drove by, on his way home from work.

"We need more: a witness, forensics, or a confession," I say.

"I know you think you're playing it safe, but you're not."

"I'd lose at trial."

"This guy is a dangerous son of a gun. While we're wasting time, spinning our wheels, he could off someone else. You'd never forgive yourself."

There's no right answer. We could arrest Tags and keep him off the street while we look for more evidence. But his lawyer will file a motion to dismiss, and as soon as we get to court, the charges won't stick and we'll be back to square one.

"Let's go talk to him," Kevin says, "shake his tree."

When we get to Fenway, the Sox are playing the Yankees. Judging by the length of the beer line, the game is in the seventh-inning stretch. Not wanting to set off alarm bells, we go directly to the locker room.

We slip into the room, unnoticed. Tags's back is to us; he's folding laundry, keeping one eye on the TV monitor that is showing the game.

"Who's winning?" Kevin says.

Tags, startled, turns. He looks at us and winces slightly. "The Yankees are up by three."

I pretend to care. "That's too bad."

"The good news is that Moe is back on the mound."

"The bad news is we need to take you in for questioning," Kevin says.

Tags looks at Kevin, then at me. We both stand in place, silent. "What? Why?"

"We'll tell you when we get to the station." Kevin is not in the mood to give an explanation.

Tags picks up an armful of towels, hurls them in our direction, as if that's going to save him, and bolts toward the door. Perfect—he's helping my case. I can argue to the judge that Tags's running from the police shows consciousness of guilt. That's the missing piece that gets me to probable cause. But first we have to catch him.

As Tags races by me, I try to grab him by the shirt, but he whacks me in the eye with his forearm. I fall back on my butt and, for a brief moment, see a flash of stars. I get right back up. This is nothing—I've been hit harder, by more menacing felons.

Kevin chases Tags out the door. I look down at my two-inch heels and wish I'd chosen different footwear. I tail behind, following them into the concessions area. Tags zigzags around the refreshment stands, with Kevin in hot pursuit. People jump out of their way, leaving them a path to navigate. No one is sure whom to root for; the men look like a couple of rowdy fans—until Kevin holds up his badge and shouts, "Boston Police."

A vigilant fan, with a cup full of sudsy Bud, chucks the beer at Tags—and misses. Unfortunately, most of it splashes on my suit jacket. Another fan sticks out her foot, catching Tags midstep, and he goes flying forward and falls on the cement.

Kevin races over, puts his knee on Tags's back, and holds him down. "Don't even think about moving."

A couple of security guards and a police officer rush over. The fans are confused, shouting. *He wasn't doing nothing. Police brutality. Leave him alone. That was a waste of a perfectly good cup of beer.*

"Wait a minute," someone says. "Is he the guy who killed Wayne and Rudy?"

Hearing that, a dozen people, including a couple of cops, take out their phones and snap selfies.

Kevin slaps the cuffs on Tags and yanks him to his feet. "Paul Tagala, you're under arrest."

The cameramen who were covering the game follow as Kevin walks Tags out to the car—an unintended perp walk. Kevin protects the top of Tags's head, puts him in the back of the car, and slams the door. As soon as I settle into the passenger seat, both of our phones light up. The Red Sox front office is calling Kevin. The DA's press office is trying to reach me. We both send the calls to voice mail.

Our first stop is the local police station, Area B-2 in Dudley Square, for booking and processing. At the counter, Tags surrenders his wallet and his watch.

"Where do you live?" the booking officer says.

"With my grandmother and two sisters, at Eight Thomas Street in Dorchester."

"Age?"

"Eighteen." His voice catches.

"Too bad for you—you missed the cut off for juvie," the officer says.

Tags is breaking out in a rash: red blotches, the size of dimes, spread across his neck. He scratches at his wrists, where similar spots are starting to form. When we're done with booking, we head over to Boston Police Headquarters for major-case prints and photographs. Then, Kevin takes him to the interrogation room.

I go into the sergeant's office to watch them on the TV monitor.

"You smell like a brewery," the sergeant says.

In the interrogation room, Kevin gives Tags his Miranda rights. "You have the right to speak to an attorney."

"Uh-huh."

"Do you waive that right?"

"Nope."

Kevin keeps an even tone as he masks his disappointment. "You want a lawyer?"

"Yup." Tags's behavior is more confident, resolved, than I had anticipated. If it weren't for the ever-increasing splotches on his neck, I might have bought his act.

"Can you afford to hire one?"

"Nope."

That's my cue—the interview is over. I call the Committee for Public Counsel Services, or the Committee as we mockingly refer to them. A woman tells me she already heard about the arrest and was expecting the call. In less than an hour, I go down to the lobby to greet public defender Tracey Miller.

Tracey is a true believer, an aging hippie, with frizzy gray hair, unadorned lips, and comfortable shoes. "My client does not wish to make a statement."

"How can you say that? You haven't even talked to him yet."

I'm annoyed, but not surprised. I've known Tracey for years, and she's never let a client talk to us without immunity, and even then, it's a struggle. Kevin lets her into the interrogation room, and as much as it hurts, we turn off the camera, allowing them their attorney-client privacy.

A few minutes later, Tracey emerges, to tell us what we already know. "He's exercising his right to remain silent."

"Can you do us a solid and ask him where he buried Rudy?" I say.

"He says he doesn't know because he didn't kill him."

If it were up to me, I'd ask Kevin to arrest Tracey for obstruction of justice, but I know she's just doing her job.

"If Tags changes his mind and helps us locate the body," I say, "we'll cut him a break at sentencing."

Tracey smirks. "There's not going to be a sentencing because you'll never be able to prove your case."

This discussion isn't going to be fruitful. I call the sheriff's deputies, who come to transport Tags to the jail. When Tags stands and puts his arms behind his back, the rash is redder than ever, particularly in contrast to the white strip where his watch made a tan line.

After Tags is gone, Kevin and I huddle in his cubicle.

"Did you notice what kind of watch he was wearing?" I say.

"Now's not the time to talk fashion."

"Just check the booking sheet."

Kevin scans the property list. "The watch was a Pacer." He looks at me. "Why are you smiling?"

"I gave one of those to Ty, for Valentine's Day."

"You're an ace in the courtroom, but you could use some help in the romance department. Who gives their true love a gadget that counts your steps?"

"It also tracks your movement. It's got a built-in GPS."

"Is that why you gave it to your boyfriend—to facilitate stalking?"

"No, but if Tags was wearing the watch when he did the murder, we'll be able to see where he was that night."

Chapter Twenty-Four

The next morning, I drive over to the Roxbury District Court, where Tags is scheduled to be arraigned. Parking is tight, and after circling the block twice, I pull into the police lot, where I squeeze into an illegal space and hope I don't get towed. There's a line outside the courthouse door; it reaches out to the sidewalk and snakes around the bend in the road.

I walk in the street, adjacent to the line, and survey the crowd. There are lots of familiar faces: prosecutors and detectives who are here on other cases; reporters, including Emma Phelps; defense attorneys, including Tags's lawyer, Tracey Miller; a woman with a black eye and an Ace bandage wrapped around her wrist; and a smattering of gang members, many of whom I've dealt with as defendants or victims, or sometimes both.

I badge my way through security and take the stairs to the second floor. I elbow my way into the courtroom, take a seat at the prosecutor's table, and text Kevin: *Any luck with the Pacer records?* He texts back immediately, *I got bubkes. Time to work your hocus pocus.*

The court officer calls order, and Judge Ramona Harper takes the bench. She's a judge who hates to judge, a hack, in it for the job stability, the pension, and the dental plan. I've appeared in front of her a dozen times, and I've never heard her voice—not once, not even to say good morning. The clerk does Judge Harper's bidding; the judge scribbles on a legal pad, hands her notes to the clerk, who then announces the decision. That's fine when the charges are shoplifting or breaking into a car, but it doesn't work with a murder case.

"Mr. Tagala, how do you now plead?" the clerk says.

Tags takes a breath; his hands are clasped in front of him as though he were in church about to take Communion. "Not guilty."

"Is there a request for bail?" the clerk says.

I stand and argue why Tags should be held without bail: the serious nature of the charges, risk of flight, the danger to the community. Tracey makes her case why Tags should be released pending trial: he has no prior criminal record, strong roots in the community, no reason to flee.

The judge checks some boxes on the bail form, jots down a few words, and hands the paper to her clerk. "Mr. Tagala, you are hereby ordered to be held without bail."

It's expected that a defendant will be held without bail in a murder case, but Tracey puts up a good front by acting surprised. She shakes her head in disappointment, whispers to Tags, and consults with a colleague who is seated behind her.

"Does either party have anything else on the docket?" the clerk says.

"Ms. Endicott has sent a subpoena to Pacer, requesting my client's GPS records. We're filing a motion to quash the subpoena," Tracey says.

I wasn't expecting Tracey to make a preemptive strike. The judge looks to me for a response.

"Objection," I say. "The defendant has no standing. The subpoena was sent to the corporation; we're not asking for Mr. Tagala's attorney's opinion."

"We're offering it," Tracey says. "Mr. Tagala's privacy rights will be infringed if the court allows the government to obtain a list of his whereabouts. It's akin to Big Brother, an ex post facto search warrant."

Tracey is the kind of lawyer who thinks that if she throws around a Latin phrase every now and then, she'll confuse the judge and win her argument.

I can see her *ex post facto* and raise her one. "This is a matter of stare decisis, it is not a case of first impression. The law is clear. We subpoena GPS records from cars after a crash, we should be permitted to do the same with a wristwatch after a murder. The intrusion is no more, or no less."

The Pacer records are our only hope of finding Rudy. The data is key to both helping me win the case and giving Rudy's family peace of mind.

Judge Harper waves us up to sidebar. She clears her throat, preparing to speak, and we lean in, eager to hear her voice.

"I tend to agree with Ms. Endicott." She has a thick Boston accent, and a lisp, not a harmonious combination, but her words couldn't be sweeter. "The defendant's motion to quash is hereby denied."

She bangs her gavel, stands, and retires to her chambers. She's put in a good twenty minutes of work—time for a coffee break.

A few hours later, when I'm back at Bulfinch, Pacer emails the information to me. Kevin joins me in my office as I'm trying to make sense of the data.

"What do you got?" Kevin says.

"It uses military time, which has always been a challenge for me, and geographic subsections, which are categorized by a series of numbers and letters."

"Let's cut through the malarkey. We already know that he spent the day at Fenway because we got him on video."

"According to this printout, he left the ballpark late, after midnight."

"Where did he go?" Kevin says.

"His grandmother's apartment on Thomas Street, and it looks like he went straight there."

I hand Kevin a few pages and he gives them the once-over.

"So, chances are, he hid the body in, or near, the house," Kevin says.

Kevin makes some calls, requests that a warrant and a search team meet us at the Thomas Street apartment. We drive out of the city, onto the Southeast Expressway, past the enormous rainbow-swashed storage tanks, and onto Morrissey Boulevard. When we get near Lambert's—their bologna sandwiches are not to be missed—I remember to call Stan. I vowed to keep him in the know, and I've broken that promise—again.

He picks up on the first ring.

"We're thinking about heading out to Dorchester," I say with all the deference I can muster. "I wanted to check with you first."

"You're a lousy liar. Look up."

"What?"

"In the sky. Can't you see them in the air?"

A helicopter is hovering above.

"Are we being followed?"

"Your road trip is being broadcast live on the three major networks." He slams down the receiver.

Thomas Street is in Dorchester, or Dot as it's known to residents; it's Boston's largest neighborhood. On a map, Dorchester is divided into sections, such as Savin Hill, Upham's Corner, and Codman Square. But locals self-identify according to parish, such as St. Gregory's or St. Brendan's. When people say that they grew up in Dot, no one asks which neighborhood, or which street; people ask which parish.

Tags's grandmother's apartment is near Carney Hospital, where she works part-time as a nurse's aide. Reporters have assembled both on the sidewalk outside the Carney and outside the triple-decker. Police officers are directing traffic and working crowd control.

We stop on Thomas Street, park in front of Ms. Tagala's drive-way. She peers out of the first-floor window, from behind the yellowing lace curtains; our eyes meet. I hold up my badge and wave, and she comes to the door. Cameras snap and reporters shout; Ms. Tagala hesitates before letting us into her apartment.

The apartment is small, about the same size as mine. She tells us she lives here with her two granddaughters, ages seven and two, and her grandson, Tags. There's one bedroom, where she and the girls sleep, and a small alcove for Tags—not that he'll need it anymore. His new home is the Nashua Street Jail.

Ms. Tagala sits on a folding chair, near the two-year-old, who is on the floor, banging a saucepan with a wooden spoon. Kevin and I squeeze into the small couch, sitting knee to knee, elbow to elbow.

Ms. Tagala is about fifty, a few years older than Kevin. Her hair is pulled back into a tight, unflattering ponytail. She doesn't smell like cigarettes, but the wrinkles around her mouth tell me that at some point she was a hard-core smoker.

"Where are Tags's parents?" I say.

"His father is dead and his mother is in jail."

"What happened?"

"Heroin is what happened. Addiction got the better of them both."

"That must be tough on everyone," I say.

"I don't expect you to understand."

I don't argue the point, but I could. I may not know what it's like to live in a cramped apartment with three grandchildren, but I do know a lot about losing a loved one to addiction.

"Detective Farnsworth and I are here to collect evidence."

"I'm not going to help you send my grandson to prison."

"We have a search warrant," I say, "but it'd be less intrusive if you cooperate."

We could play hardball—handcuff her while we slice open the pillows and go through her drawers—but children are involved.

"How about you take the baby to a neighbor's house while the officers conduct the search?"

"I know the routine. The police have been in here before, looking for my daughter and her drugs."

Ms. Tagala goes next door; seven police officers come in and look through Tags's belongings. They bag clothes, shoes, and personal papers as evidence. They walk the search dog through the apartment, down the back stairs, and into the basement. After all that, they come up empty.

I peek out the window, at the postage stamp–size plot of land behind the house. "Have them take the dog out to the backyard."

Kevin rolls his eyes.

"We have to cross the t's and dot the i's," I say.

Kevin directs the team out back. We both know they won't find anything, and they don't.

"According to Pacer, he was only in two places," Kevin says. "He was here and at Fenway."

"Maybe Rudy wasn't with him. Maybe someone else killed him. Or maybe he's still alive."

"Unlikely."

"Then maybe Rudy was murdered inside Fenway Park," I say. "Which means his body could still be there."

Chapter Twenty-Five

Getting a warrant to search Fenway Park is not a simple endeavor. First, I have to talk to Stan about it and get his assent. I can hide a lot of things from Stan and I can try to skirt the rules, but I'd never get away with this. Then, we have to draw up a warrant, citing sufficient probable cause to prove Rudy's body might be inside the park. Then, we have to get a judge to sign off. Given the number of Sox fans among the judiciary, this turns out to be the easiest part. Judges want to know what happened to Rudy as much as the rest of us.

Several hours later, Fenway Park is designated a crime scene—and it looks every bit the part. Uniforms are stationed outside the gates, barring entry. Yellow tape and barricades have been set up to block off the surrounding streets. Clusters of fans, dozens deep, are gathered on Brookline Avenue, hoping to catch a glimpse of the action. News trucks are lined up behind the Van Ness Street barrier, their satellite dishes extended, some broadcasting live.

Searching a place of this scale is a massive undertaking. The park holds over thirty-seven thousand seats. There are dozens of tunnels, closets, overhangs, and hideaways. Officers fan out; scent dogs and forensic experts are rushed in. This operation could take weeks.

Kevin and I move past the shuttered concession stands and outside to the field. The head groundskeeper flips on the light towers. It feels as if someone should belt out the national anthem, but tonight there will be no first pitch, no one will call out for popcorn or Cracker Jacks. We're not root-root-rooting for the home team, we're rooting for the discovery of a dead body.

The visitors' dugout serves as the command post, where a sergeant distributes assignments, along with flashlights and maps. I set up shop here too, fielding phone calls, mostly from Stan and his press secretary, who are back at Bulfinch. Prosecutors aren't part of search teams; our role is to supervise, authorize, and advise—at least in theory. In reality, police officers ignore us until someone screws up or needs an official signature.

An hour into the search my phone shows that the team owner is calling. I can barely hear him, which is not a bad thing. The static and echoes of police radios are drowning out his fury.

"I'm out here, at the gate, and they're telling me I can't come in."

"I'm sorry, but entry is restricted to essential police personnel."

"It's my ballpark."

"You'll have full access, as soon as we release the property."

I don't tell him everyone is still a potential suspect, including him, the members of his management staff and team—but he seems to get the point. He hangs up without salutation. Two minutes later, Stan calls and I let it go to voice mail.

The cold night air sets in, and when the temperature drops into the forties, I abandon my post and go inside to warm up. I pass the concession stands, where the smell of popcorn makes my stomach grumble. I scavenge around for a stray candy bar, anything to quell my hunger. A stack of paper cups is near the soft serve machine. I take one, hold it under the spout, and lift the lever, hoping for a swirl of chocolate ice cream. Nothing comes out.

"You should take off and get some chow." Kevin surprises me. "I'll give you a jingle if anything comes up."

Sweet Cheeks is within walking distance and Ty probably

hasn't left for his gig yet. We could meet there for ribs and butterscotch pudding, not necessarily in that order. The thought of the creamy caramelly confection makes me want to bolt out the door.

"I'm not hungry."

"Go ahead, I'll cover for you."

No one will miss me. It's not as if I were going to climb up to the rafters and look for evidence or dig up the dirt behind home plate. But Kevin would never leave me in the middle of one of my trials, especially not to go to a restaurant. I'm not going to abandon him during a police search.

He holds up a Snickers bar and smiles. I snatch the bar from his hand, inhale almost half of it in one mouthful. As I'm midway into my second bite, my pocket vibrates. It's a message from a blocked number: *Meet me outside Gate D.* I text back, *Who is this?* The response is nonresponsive: *Come alone. And don't tell anyone.*

"Anything good?" Kevin says.

"No," I lie. I certainly don't owe the mystery texter any allegiance of secrecy, but I don't want to scare him off by bringing someone with me.

Kevin knows when I'm holding back and he isn't buying it. "Fine, have your secrets."

I scarf down the rest of the candy. "I'm going for a walk."

Kevin brushes his finger across his front teeth. "You've got chocolate on your choppers."

Venturing out alone is not the smartest move, but as usual, my curiosity trumps my survival instinct. I look over my shoulder, make sure no one is following me, and head over to the home plate concourse and out Gate D.

Chapter Twenty-Six

The perimeter of the park is dark and quiet. The crowds must have lost interest and gone home for the night. Yawkey Way is still blocked off, the souvenir shops are shuttered, Red Sox championship banners flap in the wind. A voice calls out.

"Abby—over here."

Startled, I turn to see who it is. Twenty feet away, there's a shadowy figure, partially obstructed by a green steel pillar. Stepping into the darkness, I regret my decision to come here alone. At the very least I should have told Kevin where I was going.

It's too creepy, even for me. I turn to head back inside the gate, but when I pull on the door handle, I learn that it's locked. Clutching my purse, I feel around for my canister of pepper spray; my trigger finger is on the nozzle, ready to aim and fire.

"Where are you going?" It's a woman and she doesn't sound like a killer, but neither did my last defendant, Chip Aldridge.

I keep my guard up. Fool me once. "Who is that?"

"It's me."

The woman waves at me; her hands are empty. If she has a weapon, it's concealed, and it will take her a minute to pull it out. I palm the pepper spray, but my hand is sweaty and I drop it on the pavement. It pings and bounces a few feet away. I bend to pick it up, keeping my eyes trained on her, trying to make out her features.

When she steps forward, into the light, I'm both relieved and furious that it's not the homicidal maniac I was expecting. Instead, it's Emma Phelps.

"Christ, Emma. I'm busy. You can't drag me out here in the middle of an investigation."

"This is about the investigation."

"I'm not going to make a statement."

She grabs my arm and whispers, "Come with me."

I shake her off. "I've got to go."

She blocks my path. "I promise, you won't be disappointed."

I follow Emma up Yawkey Way, until we reach an unlit alley. She stops and extends her hand, gesturing me forward.

"You first," I say.

She picks up the pace and I try to keep up, but the pavement is uneven, which makes it difficult. I stumble on a rock, regain my footing.

"Where are we going?" I'm two parts annoyed, one part fearful.

She points at a fire escape, grabs on to the steel ladder, and hoists herself up.

As she navigates the first two rungs, I stand firm. "There are NO TRESPASSING signs all over this building."

"I'm fairly positive no one is going to arrest you." She moves to the third rung.

I struggle to pull myself up the ladder, promising myself to start a regimen of biceps curls and cardio tomorrow. It's a four-story building; when we reach the roof, I realize my hands are sweaty and slippery. I pause, worried that I'll lose my grip. Emma offers her hand to help, but I refuse. I'd rather plunge to my death than act the damsel in distress to Emma Phelps.

I manage to step onto the roof, which is flat and gravelly. As my adrenaline surge starts to subside, I take in the expansive view of the area around Fenway.

"This is where I was on the night Rudy went missing," Emma says. "I was reporting on the game."

She takes out her iPad and holds it up.

"Cut to the chase. What's on the tape?"

"First, we have to reach an understanding."

"Show me what you have."

"You have to promise me an exclusive."

"I don't make blind agreements."

Emma and I both competed on the debate team, or debate *union* as it's called at Harvard. She never backed down from her position, and neither did I.

"There has to be a compromise," she says.

"Give me an offer of proof."

"Paul Tagala is on the tape. I didn't know it until I was in the editing booth today."

I look out at the Citgo sign, masking my excitement. This could be the break we've been looking for.

"Deal. Show me Tags on that tape and you get the exclusive."

She hits play. It's *Emma*, reporting, talking into a mic. She pauses the video and zooms in on the background, hits play again. A man comes out of the ballpark, wheeling a large laundry bin. His face is obscured by a Red Sox baseball cap. When he looks over, into the light, he freezes.

"He's looking at me. He can see that someone is on the roof."

It could be Tags, but it could be a lot of other people.

As I'm about to dismiss her, she stops me. "Keep watching."

She restarts the tape and we watch as the man hunches over and pushes the laundry bin until he's out of sight. About four minutes later, an SUV pulls onto the street; its headlights are off, and the driver isn't visible. The car takes a quick turn, away from the news crew, and speeds off. Emma stops the footage, capturing the rear of the car, and zeros in on the license plate.

"A source at the registry ran the numbers."

"The plate came back to Paul Tagala?"

She nods.

"And you think Rudy's body was in the laundry bin he was pushing?"

"Don't you?"

As much as I'd like to, I can't argue with her. She's probably right.

"I've lived up to my end of the bargain," she says.

I resist the urge to grab the tablet from her hand, stuff it in my tote, and run. Too bad I have to obtain the evidence lawfully. The rules require either Emma's consent, or a grand jury subpoena—and right now, I don't have either.

"Tell me what you're looking for," I say, hoping she doesn't ask to be there when we find the body.

"I want to be there when you find the body."

I feign surprise and take a moment to consider. "I'll have to talk to my detective."

I want to welsh on the agreement and force her hand with a subpoena, but that would be career suicide. Prosecutors are only as good as their promises.

As she makes her way down the ladder, I stay behind and text Kevin: *Meet me outside Gate D*. I'd like to send out an SOS text to the fire department, requesting someone to come carry me down the ladder. Instead I work my way, slowly, back to the ground.

Chapter Twenty-Seven

Emma and I round the corner, from the alley, onto Yawkey Way. Kevin is already there, standing in front of Gate D. He sees us before we see him. I can't make out his features, but I know he's not smiling.

"He's cute," Emma says as he approaches. "Married?"

I throw her a look. *As if.*

"What's going on?" Kevin plays it neutral, masking his surprise and disapproval of what he's seeing. I take his arm and usher him a few feet away from Emma.

"I know what it looks like, but before you rip me a new one, hear me out."

Kevin keeps his voice at a whisper. "Have you gone over to the dark side?" He's never been shy about expressing his disdain for members of the fourth estate. "No wonder you went on a secret spy mission—you knew I'd talk you out of it."

"You're going to change your tune when you see what I discovered."

"You're the last person I'd suspect would leak information that could hurt our case. That's what you're doing, right?"

"Not exactly."

I signal Emma, who hands me the tablet, and I play the video for him. "According to Emma, the plate comes back to Tags."

He keeps his back to Emma but speaks loud enough for her to hear. "I'm going to run it again. I don't trust reporters."

He uses his iPad to connect with the database at the Registry of Motor Vehicles. It checks out—it's Paul Tagala's car. That means Tags transported Rudy's body somewhere, and we have to find out where that is.

"What's the catch?" Kevin says.

I hesitate and close my eyes, preparing to get an earful. "I agreed to let Emma be present when we search for the body."

Kevin is quiet. Silence is the worst kind of reprimand he can give. He walks away; I follow, pleading my case.

"You make deals with the devil every time you use an informant."

"This is different. If word gets out prematurely, it could compromise the investigation."

"We need that tape. It's the link that will prove Tags's involvement in Rudy's murder." I take a breath. "She uses us, we use her."

Kevin takes a minute before speaking. "Fine. Tell her where I'm parked. She can follow us, but not too close."

While I work out the logistics and ground rules with Emma, Kevin calls off the search in Fenway. Everyone is curious about why it's over, but Kevin just tells them it's being suspended for now. As soon as Kevin is able to review the Pacer data, he charts out Tags's trip from the ballpark to his home in Dorchester.

"Rudy's body has to be somewhere between the two locations," Kevin says.

The search teams are redeployed to cover the seven- mile route, and they're instructed to look inside any container big enough to stash a body, or body parts.

As we drive past Boston Medical Center, I consult the map. I've been in this area five times in the last month—twice to the hospital to visit victims and interview their doctors, and once to the Office of the Chief Medical Examiner. Last Sunday, I was a couple of blocks over, at the Goodwill donation trailer, dropping off clothes and linens that I don't have space for in my closets anymore.

"Let's take a detour to the Goodwill," I say.

Kevin assembles a crew, who sort through the donation bins and drop-off trailer. There are dozens of shopping bags, full of shoes, coats, and T-shirts—but no Rudy. When we're done, we walk past a homeless man, who is digging through a trash can. I hand him a five and we get in the car.

"Isn't there a dump around here?" I say.

"There's a transfer station in Roxbury."

Kevin flips on the light and siren and speeds up Albany Street. Cruisers and unmarked police cars stay close behind. I'm glad I can't see Emma, but I'm sure she's not far away.

Within a half hour, a couple of dozen uniforms and plainclothes detectives are scouring the trash containers and scrap heaps. I wait near the entrance gate and use the time to call Stan.

He's not surprised when I give him the update. "Yeah, I know. Emma Phelps is reporting live from the transfer station."

My jaw clenches. I have no doubt that Rudy's body is here. Emma could have at least waited until we make the notifications to next of kin. This is not how Rebecca should learn about her husband's death.

"Where is she?" I say.

"Near the back gate. How the hell did she find out?"

Before I can make up an answer, Kevin calls me over.

"Gotta go," I say.

I rush toward a group of officers who are huddled near a heap of scrap metal. When I reach them, they make space for me. Kevin nods and I look down.

Half of his head is missing and his body is decomposing, but there's no mistaking who he is. Rudy Maddox.

Chapter Twenty-Eight

Death notifications land like lightning bolts. They shoot from the sky, often without warning, bringing fear, chaos, and destruction. I've experienced it from both sides. I've delivered the news: *I'm sorry to tell you that your husband has been the victim of a violent crime.* And I've received it: *Abby, your brother has passed away. We need you to go to the morgue to identify his body.*

When a victim has been missing for a period of time, it's still shocking when you learn the body has been discovered—but it's not unexpected, and sometimes, it's a relief. There is nothing more to hope for, but finally, there is something tangible to grieve. And maybe there are answers.

Now that we've found Rudy's body, we want to make the notification as quickly as possible. Kevin and I set out to Cohasset to talk to Rebecca. It'll be tough to hear the news, but it will be worse if she learns about it by watching Emma Phelps's report.

"Let's call Moe and see if he can meet us at Rebecca's," Kevin says. "She's gonna need all the support she can get."

I reach for my phone and see a dozen texts, most from Stan. The news has hit the stratosphere. "Word is out."

Kevin steps on the gas, as though he can outpace the internet.

When I call Moe, he picks up on the first ring.

"I heard," he says, his voice cracking.

The sound of a woman crying echoes in the background. "Is that Rebecca?"

"No, it's my fiancée, Cecilia. We're in the car, on our way to Rebecca's."

"We'll meet you there."

When we arrive, the light above the front door is on, casting a blurry glow in the marine layer. Moe opens the door. The last remnant of the bruise under his eye is still visible, and he gestures us inside.

Rebecca is in the living room, head in hands. She's being comforted by her sister, Cecilia, and the nanny, Holly. The women are in their nightclothes: Holly in boxers and a tank; Cecilia in pajama pants and a T; Rebecca in an oversize Red Sox shirt.

Rebecca looks up at us, her eyes full of tears. "Tell me it's not true."

"I'm sorry," I say.

I tell her about finding Rudy in the transfer station, leaving out the parts about the condition of his body.

"That's it," she says, "there's nothing more to hope for."

"You can hope that they catch the bastard," Moe says.

Phones ring constantly. Holly leaves the room to answer the house phone.

Moe looks at his cell, pockets it, and says to us softly, "They're saying on the news that Tags did it."

"Did he?" Cecilia says.

"He's our prime suspect," Kevin says.

Moe shakes his head. "There's no way."

"We're building a strong case against him," I say.

"He's been in and out of our house," Moe says.

"Maybe he was going to kill you too," Cecilia says.

"Why? Why would he do that?"

"We're not certain of the motive," I say.

"We need to know if there's anything strange about Tags's relationship with either Rudy or Wayne," Kevin says.

Moe shakes his head. "As far as I knew, Tags was a good kid, a hard worker. He said he was using the extra money we paid him to take care of his family."

"We let him near our kids," Cecilia says.

The baby starts to cry; her voice shrieks through the monitor. Rebecca goes upstairs and we can hear her sob as she tries to comfort her child. Moe puts his arm around Cecilia, who lets out a gasp and then a torrent of tears.

"Rudy was living beyond his means," Kevin says. "Was he gambling?"

"You mean betting on games?" Moe says. "No way."

"He had a lot of cash that was unaccounted for," I say. "It could have something to do with his murder."

This is a good place to end the conversation. It will give Moe something to think about, in case he's holding back. I tell them I'm going to continue with the grand jury. "I'll let you know when we've secured an indictment."

Outside, the sun is coming up over the ocean; there are no clouds, no ranges of hues, just a ball of fiery orange. We drive along the rocky shoreline and I doze off somewhere between Hingham and Weymouth. I wake myself up when my head snaps forward. Wiping the sleep from my eyes, I see that we're a couple of blocks from my apartment.

"I need to lock in Emma Phelps's testimony and get that video into the grand jury," I say.

"I'll serve her, pronto. If we're lucky, I'll catch her right when her head hits the pillow. Once she sees the subpoena, she'll never get to sleep."

Upstairs, Ty is in bed, snoring lightly, and shows no signs of stirring. I have to be in court in a few hours, and I decide to stay awake until then. If I go to bed now, I'll never be able to rally for the grand jury. I put a cup of Starbucks in the Keurig and turn on the news. It's no surprise that Rudy is the lead story on every station.

I flip to Emma's report; there's an establishing shot of the transfer station. I pour cream into my coffee, dump in a heaping spoonful of sugar, and gulp it down. As soon as the acid starts to burn in my gut, I decide that from now on I'm going to switch to herbal tea. Then, I make a second cup of coffee and watch a long shot of Rudy's lifeless body being zipped into the body bag and hoisted onto the stretcher. The assistants slide the gurney into the back of the van and slam closed the double doors. My stomach churns when I think about Rebecca, and I hope she doesn't watch the video.

Overly amped up after my third cup of coffee, I notice Ty's laptop is open. Staring at the screen for a minute, I will it to come out of sleep mode. When it remains dark, I know I shouldn't, but I brush my fingers against the mouse pad and take a peek. He's usually working on something music related, but not today.

Ty has been doing research: police-community relations; racial profiling; illegal stop and search. He's composing an agenda for a meeting of the governor's commission. At last, he's making good on his promise; he's going to report what happened in Brookline.

Hearing footsteps behind me, I whip around to see Ty.

"Babe, you shouldn't be looking in other people's stuff."

Busted. "Sorry, occupational hazard."

I smile. He doesn't smile back. He turns on the kettle.

"I'd say I'll never do it again, but I promised not to lie anymore."

"It's not funny." His body stiffens, his face is serious. "Look, I don't have anything to hide, but that doesn't mean you can snoop through my stuff." Ty rarely expresses anger, so for him, this is a warning shot. I've crossed a line.

"I know, you're right." My cell phone sounds. I check the screen. "I have to take this."

"Of course you do. Say hi to Kevin." He turns his back and walks away.

"For your information, it's Stan," I lie.

I walk into the bedroom and close the door. "Hi, Kevin. What's up?"

"Emma Phelps has been served. And she's not a happy camper."

"Good, mission accomplished."

Chapter Twenty-Nine

It's a lot easier to secure an indictment in the grand jury than it is to get a guilty verdict at trial. In the grand jury, only a majority of the twenty-three-member panel is required to reach a decision; in felony trials, twelve jurors must reach a unanimous verdict. In the grand jury I only need probable cause to get an indictment; at trial, the standard is proof of guilt beyond a reasonable doubt. And grand jurors can consider hearsay evidence, but trial jurors can't. An indictment doesn't do me any good if I can't prove the case at trial.

When I walk in the grand jury room, most of the panel are scanning news reports on their tablets, or thumbing through *The Globe* or the *Herald*. As soon as they see me, they put their papers down, close their tablets. The grand jurors have been eagerly awaiting my appearance, and almost everyone is excited. The exception is the physician's assistant, seated in the front row. She's angry the Sox have lost their last three games, and she seems to think it's my fault.

"Moe lost his best friend. His game is off, he may never recover," she says. "Now we have no shot at the championship."

I ignore the comment, try to keep them on course. "This morning, you're going to hear testimony from one witness."

"Is it one of the players?" someone says.

"No."

The group lets out a communal sigh of disappointment, but they perk up when I announce the name of the witness.

"Emma Phelps, the TV lady?" the physician's assistant says.

I nod and set up the TV screen. Emma has been subpoenaed and so has her video. I want to play the footage while she's on the stand. She can describe what she saw: Tags leaving the stadium, pushing the laundry bin. Her testimony will support my theory that Rudy was in that bin, dead. And that Tags is responsible for the murders of Rudy and Wayne.

When I go out to the waiting room, I almost don't recognize Emma. She's scaled down her act by about five octaves; her hair is pulled into a tight ponytail, and her makeup is minimal. She looks as if she needs sleep as badly as I do, which makes me smile.

"Emma, you're up."

As she follows me into the grand jury room, she suppresses a yawn. I administer the oath and she answers the preliminary questions begrudgingly—name, occupation, employer. It takes her a while to recall how long she's been with the station. She's sluggish, expressionless, a far cry from her chipper TV personality.

Since Emma is being difficult, I needle her by asking her age.

"Thirty-seven." She glares at me. "Same as you."

I'm thirty-six, but this isn't the time to quibble.

"I'm going to play the video from the night Rudy disappeared."

I cue up the machine and extend my hand, waiting for her to hand me the footage.

"I didn't bring it."

I try not to react. "It was subpoenaed."

She looks me directly in the eye. "I'm asserting my rights under the First Amendment to the United States Constitution."

I wasn't expecting this so I have to wing it. "You're defying a legitimate court order and refusing to cooperate with this investigation?"

"I'm a reporter and the video is my work product."

"You're refusing to comply?"

"I'm invoking my constitutional protection: freedom of the press."

I imagine Kevin's reprimand: *She double-crossed you. She got what she wanted, an exclusive, and you get bubkes. Told ya that would happen.*

Emma didn't bring the tape to court, so it's not worth arguing about. Besides, I'd lose. The constitution trumps our side agreement. I can't force her to pony up the tape, but I can try to get the information that was on the tape. There's no rule barring me from asking what she observed.

"Did you see Paul Tagala the night Rudy Maddox disappeared?"

"No, not directly."

"You filmed him leaving the ballpark. You were on the roof, weren't you?"

She remains silent for a minute, then smiles so smugly that I want to have her arrested.

"I decline to answer."

"On what basis?"

"I'm asserting my rights under the Fifth Amendment to the United States Constitution."

I'm not sure I heard her correctly. "You're taking the Fifth? That means you think you'd be incriminating yourself by answering my question."

She nods. "I understand."

She understands, but I don't. "You're saying you committed a crime that night, and that by responding to my question, you will implicate yourself in that crime."

We go back and forth for a few minutes, until it's clear she's not going to retreat. The problem is she doesn't have to reveal what she'd be incriminating herself about because that would defeat the purpose of the Fifth Amendment. I can't imagine she has a legitimate issue, but she's adamant.

I think back to the night I was standing on the roof with her. I picture the alley, the fire escape. Then I remember the sign: NO TRESPASSING. Emma's claim is that she broke the law when she took the video—and she's right, she did. Even though trespassing is a misdemeanor, and no one will ever prosecute her for it, under the rules, it's a legitimate reason to take the Fifth.

She got me.

"You are excused," I say, "for now."

I have to push forward. I had planned to ask for a vote today, and there's no turning back. I excuse myself for a minute and grab Kevin, who is pacing around the hallway, talking on his cell.

"I need you to testify to what you saw on the tape," I say.

"You're the one with the fancy-schmancy law degree, but isn't that total hearsay?"

"It's frowned upon, but it's allowed in the grand jury, and it's all we got."

"But that'll never get us to guilty at trial."

"One step at a time. First, let's get an indictment."

Kevin and I have reversed roles. A few days ago, he was eager to roll the dice and get an indictment with barely any evidence; now I'm the one taking chances.

Kevin follows me into the grand jury room. He takes the stand and tells the grand jurors about the tissue with Tags's DNA that was recovered near Wayne's body; Emma's tape of Tags wheeling a laundry bin to the parking lot; Tags's car and license plate; and the Pacer data about Tags's movements the night Rudy went missing. Then he describes the discovery of Rudy's body. It sounds like a lot, but it's not. The evidence is all circumstantial. We don't have an eyewitness who can place Tags at either crime scene, we don't have a confession, and we don't have a motive.

I ask the grand jurors to vote, then leave the room. It takes them almost an hour to decide on two indictments, which is fifty-nine minutes longer than most cases.

The foreman comes out and smiles weakly. "It's a true bill, but it was a close call. How are you going to prove it at trial?"

"Trial is months away. By then, I'll have more evidence," I say.

I hope I'm right.

Chapter Thirty

As soon as I'm done with the grand jury, I give a full confession to Kevin. He's not surprised to learn Emma pulled a fast one on us, but he spares me an *I told you so*. Kevin, not one to waste time, goes out to hit the street again and look for new witnesses. I tuck my tail between my legs and skulk across Pemberton Square, to Bulfinch Place.

I step onto the elevator and swipe my badge on the sensor; a text from Stan's assistant summons me to his office.

"I got the indictment."

"Great. Emma Phelps gave you probable cause?" Stan says.

"Not exactly, but Kevin did." I tell him what happened.

He doesn't take the news well. "Most people with your level of intelligence learn from their mistakes, but not you. First, you arrest him prematurely. Then, you indict him with no evidence. You've backed yourself, and the whole office, into a corner."

"Paul Tagala killed two men. Who knows, he could have been targeting someone else. What if he had gone after a third person, then where would we be? You should be thanking me. I got a dangerous guy off the street."

"The goal is to imprison the murderer for life. As soon as this guy's lawyer takes one look at our case, he'll get the charges dismissed, and Paul Tagala will be back home in time for dinner."

"Nothing is going to be dismissed. I can get a conviction." I sound confident even though I don't feel that way.

Stan's assistant taps on the door. "Paul Tagala's lawyer is on the phone."

"Tell her I'll call her later."

"She is not looking for you, Abby."

Tracey Miller is a fighter, but I didn't expect her to do an end run around me and go directly to the boss. If Stan takes the call, it'll weaken my bargaining power.

Stan, picks up the phone. "Hello?"

As soon as Tracey brags about her chat with Stan, my standing in the legal community will take a nosedive.

"Stan, please don't," I say. "Let me handle Tracey."

Stan puts his hand in the air and waves at me to shut up. As soon as he starts speaking, I appreciate him a little more.

"Tracey, I don't negotiate with defense attorneys. This is Abby's case. You'll have to deal with her." He hangs up and turns to me. "My number one rule of law enforcement: present a united front—even when I want to toss my skipper overboard."

Maybe he's not such a bad guy after all. Surprised, and impressed by his attitude, I try a new tack: I ask him his thoughts and actually listen to his answer.

"Immunize Emma Phelps. That will take away her Fifth Amendment claim on the trespassing."

"That will only solve half the problem. Emma can still hide behind her First Amendment freedom-of-the-press argument."

"Then, maybe it's time to offer Tagala a plea."

"We just got the indictment, I don't want to throw in the towel yet. Besides, Tracey has been around the block—she'll smell the desperation."

He stands, unable to meet my eyes. "I'm thinking about putting another prosecutor on the case."

"It's a minor setback."

"It's not just the case. You've got some personal issues to deal with."

He takes out his phone, types a few words, shows me a photo: me at Anchovies, drunk, kneeling on the floor, looking up. It's not a flattering picture.

"My top prosecutor looks like a train wreck. And that reflects poorly on me, and the whole office."

"I had a rough night."

"From what I hear, you've had a few of those lately."

I start to respond, but Stan picks up his phone, indicating that the meeting is over. More determined than ever, as soon as I'm back in my office, I call Kevin.

"I want to reexamine our evidence, maybe we missed something," I say.

We meet at the crime lab. I glove up and sort through everything: clothing, hair, fingerprint exemplars. I hold my nose and inspect the trash that was collected at the crime scenes. I hold my breath and examine the autopsy photos. Kevin carefully unseals the boxes of items that were seized from Rudy's house, Wayne's storage locker, and his boyfriend Graham's apartment.

"Let's talk motive," Kevin says. "There's a few things staring us in the face."

"Steroids."

"Wayne and Rudy were buying them, but dollars for doughnuts they weren't selling them. Next?"

"Money," I say. "They both lived beyond their means."

"So do a lot of young athletes. They come from nothing, have no idea about financial planning, and get in over their heads."

I look at the bubble-wrapped baseball that we seized from Graham's apartment. "They were both hiding baseballs for some reason, like they were saving them for something. Let's get them tested."

We drop the baseballs off at the crime lab and put a rush on them. Less than an hour later, we get a call.

"The balls have been tampered with," the technician says.

"Can you be more specific?" Kevin says.

"I could discern traces of K-Y jelly."

I'd heard of spitballs, but didn't think they were a real thing—used by superstar athletes.

"What happens when you grease a baseball, besides making it slippery?" I say.

Kevin doesn't wait for the technician's response. "A slick ball moves faster, it has less spin, and it catches the batter off guard, with a late drop."

"Sounds like that only benefits one person," I say. "The pitcher."

"There's our motive. Tags worked for Moe Morrissey. Moe was cheating and his catchers knew it. Maybe they threatened to expose him. So Moe had to get rid of his catchers."

"If that's our working theory, this could have been a murder for hire," I say. "Which means it didn't have anything to do with steroids."

If Moe paid Tags to kill Wayne and Rudy, that would make Moe the instigator. Tags is still responsible for the murder, but Moe is the one we want most. A contract killing never happens without the contractor and whatever incentive he offers to the hit man.

"Maybe we can make Tags a flipper," I say.

"You think he'll turn on Moe?"

"There's only one way to find out."

Chapter Thirty-One

Tracey Miller jumps at the chance to meet me and Kevin at the jail. She has nothing to lose by hearing us out. If she doesn't like the offer, she can tell us to pound sand. Hopefully, that's not the way it will go down.

Tracey, Kevin, and I watch in silence as Tags shuffles into the room. Jail doesn't agree with him. His hair is stringy, his face pale. Kevin stands and pulls out a metal chair, causing it to squeak against the cement floor. Tags flinches at the sound. He looks pathetic as his eyes well with tears. It's a good sign when your defendant cries before you've uttered a syllable.

At my request, the guard unshackles Tags, and as soon as the cuffs come off, he rubs his wrists.

"What's the purpose of the meeting?" Tracey says.

"We've come into possession of new information," I say.

"Is it exculpatory?" Tracey says.

"No, but it could be helpful to your case," I say. "We believe Tags wasn't acting alone."

"We think someone ordered you to carry out the hits," Kevin says.

Tags looks at me, his lip quivering, and starts to mumble something.

Tracey puts up her hand, cuts him off. "Don't say a word. We're not here to answer questions or offer incriminating evidence."

I keep my eyes trained on Tags, but speak to Tracey. "If it's true, and he was acting under someone's direction, we're prepared to offer a deal."

"I'll take it," Tags says, his voice cracking.

"Slow down," Tracey says.

She leans in, whispers to him. He bites his lip, sits on his hands, whispers back.

Tracey shakes her head. "I don't recommend it."

"Ask them," Tags says.

"My client wants to know, what's the offer?"

"He pleads guilty to a second," I say.

"No way," Tracey says.

"Hold on. What does that mean?" Tags says.

"They want you to admit to second-degree murder. And testify against Moe. I don't recommend it."

"Why not?" Tags says. "Will they let me go home?"

"No. They'd put you away for life."

Tags drops his head forward.

"But you wouldn't necessarily serve life. You'd be parole eligible in fifteen years," I say. "That's better than life without the possibility of parole, which is what you're facing."

"Fifteen years is an eternity when you're the one in prison. Plus, he'll serve at least thirty. The parole board will never let him out the first few times," Tracey says. "He'd be admitting to killing two members of the Red Sox."

"Let's not forget, he did pull the trigger," Kevin says. "Twice."

"He's got to serve at least fifteen years," I say.

Tracey cups her hand over her mouth and speaks softly to Tags. I look away, but can hear snippets of what she says. *Let's wait until the trial. . . . They may not be able to prove anything. . . . It's up to you.*

Kevin kicks me lightly, under the table. Time to do some double-teaming.

"Are you a gambler, Tags?" Kevin says. "Because if you take this case to trial, the odds won't be in your favor."

"You're young," I say. "You could get out in fifteen years and still have a full life—finish school, get married, have kids."

Under my own definition of a full life, I'm only one for three.

"Tell us the truth about what happened," Kevin says.

"Don't do the time for someone else," I say. "That's not fair to your grandmother, your sisters, or yourself."

Tags takes a lion's breath, looks at Tracey, ready to talk.

"It's your call," she says, "but for the record, I'm advising against it."

Tags looks at me and nods.

Kevin turns on the recorder. "In your own words, tell us what happened."

"He paid me to do it."

"Who?" Kevin says.

"Moe."

Even though this has been my working theory, it's shocking to hear Tags say it out loud. I cover my mouth to hide my surprise.

Kevin inches his head closer to Tags, gets in his face, and teases out his story. "Moe Morrissey hired you to kill Rudy Maddox and Wayne Ellis?"

"Yes."

"Why?"

"Rudy and Wayne knew he was cheating."

"How was he cheating?"

"He was putting gel on the ball."

"Did they threaten to expose him? Were they extorting him?"

Tags nods. "They wanted money to keep quiet, and Moe paid them. But it was never enough. They kept coming back and asking for more. They were going to take him down, ruin him."

Tags's story has the ring of truth—it explains the money and the baseballs, but not the reason for his own involvement.

"How much did Moe pay you?" I say. "It must've been a lot."

"Two hundred and fifty thousand."

"Total?" Kevin says.

"Each."

"So you got a half-million dollars?" I say.

Tags gnaws on a hangnail, then spits it out. "Not yet, but I will. Moe put it in a bank account."

Kevin and I exchange looks. Tags is still holding back.

"That's not the only reason you did it," Kevin says.

"This wasn't just going to hurt Moe. If they exposed him, they would've taken down the whole team."

I underestimated Tags; he was motivated by greed, but he was also moved by loyalty—a warped sense of allegiance.

"Are we done?" Tracey says.

"One more question," Kevin says. "Where did you get the gun?"

"It was Moe's. He gave it to me."

"What did you do with it?" I say.

"He wanted it back, so I gave it back to him."

Tags is about to say more, but Tracey interrupts. She wants to seal the deal.

"If you want my client to testify, you have to reduce the charges to manslaughter and recommend he serve no more than fifteen years."

I look at Kevin, who nods reluctantly. Neither of us want to lessen Tags's degree of guilt, or his sentence, but it's the only way to get Moe.

"Deal," I say.

Chapter Thirty-Two

The whole city is wondering, worrying, that the steroids scandal is going to have a devastating impact on the team. Meanwhile, the rest of the country is excited about the potential for another Boston sports scandal. Even the grand jurors are obsessed with the subject. When I go back into the grand jury room, they think I'm there to present more evidence about steroids. I wish that's all it were about.

Armed with Tags's confession, including the part that inculpates Moe, I reopen the case. This time I present the grand jurors with two new indictments—first-degree-murder complaints against Moe Morrissey.

Kevin takes the stand and hits the play button on his recorder. We listen to Tags's interview. Everyone is still; there's no fidgeting, no snacking. When it's over, there is a collective sigh of disappointment. No one asks questions. The grand jurors know what they have to do and they're devastated—everyone except the Dodgers fan.

Kevin and I wait outside the grand jury room while they deliberate. We position ourselves close to the door, trying to eavesdrop, but we can't hear any of the discussion. It only takes a couple of minutes. The door swings open, smacks me in the shoulder, almost knocking me over. Kevin grabs my elbow to steady me and keep me from dropping to the floor.

The foreman and I sign the indictments, and I authorize an arrest warrant for Moe Morrissey. I want to get him into custody immediately, before word leaks out. If he finds out we're looking to arrest him for murder, he could harm someone else, or he could flee.

"Where do you think Moe is?" I say.

"The Sox are playing at home tonight and he's in the lineup," Kevin says. "We can pinch him at Fenway."

We can't wait for him to finish the game, that would be giving special favor and caving to special interests.

"It'd be better if we grab him before he gets to the ballpark," I say. "The press is swarming, and we don't need his arrest to be broadcast live."

"Then let's cut him off at the pass."

Kevin issues a BOLO or "be on the lookout" to the local police departments. Moe is likely to be in transit—somewhere between his home in Chestnut Hill and the ballpark in Kenmore Square. We chart out the most likely route and wait in a central location. That way we can be sure it doesn't take us long to get to the arrest scene—wherever that turns out to be. The Fenway Park area seems like a solid option, so we drive to the Fens and wait, cell phones in hand. Less than thirty minutes later, we get a call from Brookline Police. Moe Morrissey's car was stopped in Coolidge Corner, and they have him in custody.

"We captured him without incident," the captain says.

My heart races. "Seal off the area, secure the car," I say. "And be sure no one touches anything. And by anything, I mean *anything*: the suspect, his car, not even the sidewalk around the car."

We jump in Kevin's SUV and race around the ballpark, through Kenmore Square, and up Beacon Street. Pregame traffic is at a standstill; our lights are flashing and siren blaring, but the motorists and pedestrians are unimpressed. A millennial, in a BU Terrier's T-shirt, darts in front the car, daring us to hit him, and yells, "Hey, pedestrians have the right of way."

We finally reach Harvard Street, where a Brookline police officer is directing cars around the arrest scene. Kevin flashes his tin and we're waved inside the perimeter. We pull up behind a blue-and-white—Moe Morrissey is in the backseat of the cruiser, peering out at me. We lock eyes.

"We secured his car, just like you asked," the captain says.

"Great," I say.

"You're not going to believe what we found."

I take a breath. My head is about to explode. "Found? I told you not to touch anything."

Whatever they found, I hope it's not important. I cringe as the captain smiles and holds up a green box marked *Remington .357 Magnum, 125 Grain.*

"You seized that?" My face heats up. "From Moe's car?"

He nods proudly. "It's a box of fifty, but there are only forty-eight bullets inside. That means he used two."

"I can do the math."

"What's your problem?"

"I told you not to touch anything."

"This is Norfolk County, you have don't have jurisdiction over us. But still, it's great, right?"

"No, it is not great," I say under my breath, aware that Moe is watching and hoping he can't read lips.

"Are you jealous that we cracked the case? Is that why you're pouting?" The captain knows what he did is wrong and he's trying to turn it around on me, make me the whiny girl.

I'm not biting. "I specifically told you to wait for me to get here."

"You're nuts, you should be thanking us."

Moe is still staring at me. I swivel around so my back is to him.

"You don't have a warrant to search the car," I say.

"Don't worry about it. My officer told me it was in plain sight."

Moe yells out from the backseat, "That's bull. There was nothing in plain sight, except my sweatshirt and sports bag."

"What's he talking about?" I say. "He's saying you planted evidence?"

"Who cares?" the captain says.

"I do."

Moe calls out, "Those bullets aren't mine. That cop is lying."

"Keep quiet," the captain says.

"He's trying to frame me," Moe says.

"That's what they all say," the captain says.

A voice calls out, "It was on the front seat, plain as day."

It's a familiar voice but not a welcome one. My head starts to throb as I swivel around to face the man. I don't have to look at him because I already know who it is.

"Hey, I know you," the man says. "You're that snotty prosecutor from Boston—the one with the boyfriend."

"Officer Chase," I say.

"*Detective. Detective* Mike Chase."

Chapter Thirty-Three

The Brookline Police department is less than a mile from Coolidge Corner, where Moe was pulled over. Per protocol, he's transported to the station for booking; Kevin and I follow the cruiser, up Harvard Street, toward Brookline Village. Kevin parks in the lot, and we watch as Moe is taken out of the back of the car, his hands cuffed behind his back. As he is led inside the brick building, I think about how Ty and I were stopped and harassed not far from here. Even though Ty was innocent and Moe is guilty, there is a common denominator: Mike Chase. I can't help but wonder if Chase has manipulated the evidence against Moe.

As Moe is being processed, Mike Chase stands next to him.

Chase turns to me, grinning broadly. "I caught the big fish."

"Booking is not a spectator sport," I say. "Go write your arrest report."

He retreats down the hallway.

"What's going on?" Kevin says. "That's how you're supposed to treat the bad guys, not the cops."

"Sometimes the line is blurry."

"Want to tell me what that's supposed to mean?"

"Later."

Moe is photographed and fingerprinted, and his property is

confiscated and inventoried: a custom-made diamond-encrusted iPhone; a Bulgari Diagono chronograph watch; a Ferragamo alligator wallet. He's definitely not your average prisoner. A successful drug kingpin might have one of these luxury items, two at them very most, but I've never known anyone to have all three.

The booking officer hands Moe a pen. "I need you to sign here and here, Mr. Morrissey."

"We only need one signature," I say.

The officer holds up two pieces of paper. "This one is for the property sheet, and the other is for my uncle Joe."

"He's not signing autographs," I say.

Kevin asks the captain for an interview room, where he takes Moe, and closes the door. I watch from a monitor in the captain's office, eager to hear Moe's side of the story. Moe settles into his chair, leans forward, and puts his elbows on the table. He looks as if he were at a postgame press conference.

"I've got a game tonight."

"You're not going to be in the lineup." Kevin starts to recite the Miranda warnings. "You have the right to—"

"Don't waste your breath. I want a lawyer."

Kevin clenches his jaw, looks into the camera. "Having invoked your right to counsel, this interview has concluded."

We give Moe access to a phone, he makes a call, and he is taken to a cell for the night. He has enough money to post bond, but the magistrate won't release him. He's going to have to wait for a judge to set bail at his arraignment tomorrow.

Since there's nothing more we can do tonight, I call Ty to see if I can catch him before he heads off to play at the Regattabar in Cambridge. We're both hungry and agree to meet at Alden & Harlow in Harvard Square. When I was an undergrad at Harvard, the space was occupied by Casablanca, a divey subterranean restaurant, decorated with larger-than-life-size murals of Humphrey Bogart and Ingrid Bergman. Now, it's a foodie's delight, where you can order snail tortellini, roasted bone marrow, and fried rabbit. The menu is a little pretentious, but it's close to Ty's gig, and they have a great wine list.

When I arrive, the place is packed with people waiting for tables. I find Ty in the crowd, seated at the bar. He stands, gives me a kiss, and picks up our drinks—a mug of Ipswich oatmeal stout for himself, and a glass of Cabernet for me—and we relocate to a booth.

"You'll never guess who I ran into today," I say.

"I don't have to guess, it's all over the news."

I look at him, confused.

"Moe Morrissey?" he says.

"Oh, yeah, right."

"Isn't that who you were talking about?"

I take a sip of wine. "I was talking about Mike Chase."

Ty's face tightens, making me wish I'd saved the information until after our first round of drinks.

"Where'd you see him?"

"He made the arrest."

"He's the one who locked up Moe Morrissey?"

Ty takes a long sip of beer. I finish my glass of wine and order another.

"Unfortunately, Chase was the first to find him," I say.

"I hope you have better witnesses than that punk."

Thankfully, the waiter comes and takes our orders: the off-menu "secret" burger for me, and raw pumpkin salad and grilled octopus for Ty.

"I know you're planning to report him for what happened—and I want you to—but can you hold off?" I say.

"Why?"

"Just for a little while?"

"How long is a little while?"

"Until the case is over."

Ty finishes his beer, puts down the glass slowly, doesn't speak.

"Chase searched Moe's car."

"I hope he didn't find anything important."

"He did. He found a key piece of evidence; it could make or break the case."

"Then so be it."

Ty goes up to the bar to order another round. He could have signaled the waiter, who is standing nearby, but he opts to leave the table instead. He takes his time, more time than necessary, chatting with the bartender for a couple of minutes. When he returns to the table, the food has already arrived. It looks good, but all I can stomach is a few nibbles of the Cabot cheese tuile that came with my burger.

We make small talk for most of the meal. Ty tells me about his latest bookings, and we speculate about whether my parents will get back together. After one more glass of wine, I get back to the issue of Mike Chase.

"Moe Morrissey is responsible for a double murder. The entire country is watching. Mike Chase will become a distraction. If you report what happened now, the jurors will focus on him instead of the evidence. It'll give them an excuse to acquit Moe."

"Last week you were itching for me to expose him as the racist that he is."

"I still want you to expose him, just not right now."

"Maybe he planted the evidence. Mike Chase is a danger to society."

"If you had reported him when I asked you to, he would have been put on desk duty while they investigated what he did to us. He would have been taken off the street, he wouldn't have been available to make the arrest, and we wouldn't be having this discussion."

"So this is my fault?"

I reach for my glass of wine but lose hold of the stem and it shatters all over the floor; a shard of glass narrowly misses the waiter. Someone comes to clean up my mess. Ty gives me the worst kind of look: anger and pity.

"Let's put a pin in this and talk about it later," Ty says. "I've got to get to work."

I apologize to everyone within earshot. Ty pays the bill.

"Please don't do anything about Chase before checking in with me," I say.

"Fine. I promise I'll give you a heads-up before I make a move."

He takes my elbow, ushers me out of the restaurant. The cool night air feels good on my face.

"I'm sorry, I didn't mean to make a scene."

He gathers his thoughts, considers his words before responding.

"Abby, I love you. I'm angry, but I'm also worried about you."

I know where this is going, can't meet his eyes.

"Addiction runs in your family. No judgment, just something to think about."

Chapter Thirty-Four

I slip out of bed before dawn, careful not to wake Ty. He promised not to file a complaint against Mike Chase until he's checked with me, so my strategy is to evade Ty for as long as possible. Plus, I'm embarrassed about the wine debacle last night. I know I'm only delaying the inevitable, but avoidance is the best I can come up with right now.

I disappear into the bathroom without making a sound and take the quickest shower on record. I towel-dry my hair—the whoosh of the blow-dryer would make too much noise. I also forgo the electric toothbrush, opting for the disposable one I keep in my purse.

In the living room, I turn on the TV and mute the volume. No surprise, Moe Morrissey's arrest is the lead story on every media outlet—national, regional, and local. Every angle is covered: news, sports, and entertainment. It's not even light outside yet, but Emma is reporting live from in front of the courthouse, eager to catch Moe's arraignment. I make coffee, burn a piece of raisin bread, and wait for the weather report. It's May 3 at 5:00 a.m., and the temperature is already eighty-one degrees. Hottest spring on record. Again.

Luckily, there is two weeks' worth of dry cleaning in the coat closet, which eliminates the need to go back into the bedroom. I rip open the plastic bag and select a black crepe dress. A light-weight, breathable cotton would be more comfortable, but that's not one of the options. Fortunately, I always keep a spare pair of hose in my tote. I take them out of the packaging and slip them on. I apply my makeup in the living room, using the mirror app on my iPhone, and blot my lipstick with a paper towel.

As I'm about to make a clean getaway, Ty starts to stir and the bedroom door creaks open.

"Babe, I didn't hear you get up. . . . Babe? Are you still here?"

Without responding, I grab my tote, tiptoe out of the apartment and into the hallway, and close the door softly. I hope Ty doesn't hear the lock click. Downstairs, on the front porch, I feel something sharp in my shoe. I sit on the bottom step and remove a safety pin from inside the toe of my stiletto. As I stand, my ankle brushes up against the splintery stairs, and the fabric of my hose unzips up the length of my calf, all the way to the panel at the top of my thigh.

As I'm surveying the damage, Kevin pulls up to the curb. I could ask him to wait while I run back in the house and change, but that would involve talking to Ty. Besides, maybe no one will notice a little tear.

I jump in Kevin's car.

"There's a run in your stockings the length of the Northeast Corridor."

"Avert your eyes."

He turns his head and I hoist up my dress, pull down my hose, and roll them up into a ball. Bare legs in court is a no-no, especially before Memorial Day, but I'd rather violate the rules of court than the rules of fashion.

"You seem a little off your game this morning," Kevin says.

He hands me a Dunkin' Donuts bag with a cinnamon roll and unwraps his breakfast, an egg-white veggie flatbread.

I take a bite, lick the sugar from my lips.

"What's eating at you?"

There's no use keeping it from Kevin. He's my partner and we're in this together.

"Mike Chase is a dirty cop."

He finishes chewing his food and considers my comment.

"That's a strong accusation. Where's it coming from?"

"We had a run-in."

Kevin crumples up the tissue paper and places his Styrofoam coffee cup in the center console. "What do you mean, a run-in? Did he do something to you?"

As we drive to the courthouse, I tell him about what happened, leaving nothing out. The bag of Chinese food, the stop and frisk, the accusations about drugs, the racial profiling, the gun. Kevin listens intently, not interrupting or interjecting, an interview tactic that he usually saves for difficult murder confessors.

When I'm done, he seems underwhelmed. "Did anyone get hurt?"

"That's not the point."

"Abby, don't be naïve. I'm not saying it's good; in fact I can't think of anything worse in a cop, but do you know how many cases you've prosecuted with that same set of facts?"

I've read dozens of arrest reports about suspects who were stopped by police because they *fit the description, made furtive gestures,* or were in a *known drug area.* I never questioned it—I never thought I had reason to. Even worse, I stood up in court and argued passionately to defend the legitimacy of the stops. I must have been complicit in racial profiling—at least once, most likely more. I should have been more vigilant. A wave of guilt and shame washes through me. Unfortunately, I can't do anything about the past, but I can do something about the present. Detective Chase is happening in real time, on my watch.

"He crossed the line. It's not even a close call."

"You're the smartest lady I've ever known, so don't go getting any stupid ideas. Proceed with caution."

Kevin knows I won't be able to stay quiet indefinitely.

"What if he's lying about Moe's arrest?" I say. "He's the one who found the bullets, and no one can corroborate his version of what happened. He could have planted the evidence."

"We can report him, but let's think about it first."

Kevin's argument is the same one I used on Ty last night. It doesn't sound any better when someone else says it. Ty was right—as much as it will sink my case, I don't have a choice. Mike Chase can't get away with what he did. And there is a real possibility that he was lying about the bullets.

Chapter Thirty-Five

Government Center is a circus. Every day, the number of news trucks, reporters, and onlookers seems to have grown exponentially. Inside isn't much better; the courtroom is at capacity. Everyone wants to see Moe's arraignment.

As is the custom, the court officer reserved a couple of front-row seats for the victims' families, where Rudy's wife, Rebecca, and Wayne's boyfriend, Graham, are seated, shoulder to shoulder. As I pass Rebecca and Graham, I nod in solidarity. When Cecilia comes through the door, a deputy guides her to a seat on the defendant's side of the courtroom. It looks as if Moe's arrest has driven a wedge between the Bond sisters.

Moe's lawyer, Anthony Cashman, thunders in and files an appearance. Anthony will be a tough opponent. There's nothing subtle about him. He's one of the rare defense attorneys who is actually worth his whopping fee. When I first joined the DA's Office, he tried to lure me away, by offering to quadruple my salary. He made the same proposition again last year. I turned him down both times, without hesitation. I respect his lawyering, but I'll never represent murderers. I'd sooner try patent cases or wait tables.

Moe is escorted into the courtroom, flanked by two burly, but doting, guards. He looks dapper in a pin-striped Zegna suit. After he's seated and unshackled, he turns and blows a kiss to his fian-cée, Cecilia, who smiles nervously. Judge Norman Levine opens the door to his chambers and takes the bench. Judge Levine was recently elevated from the district court to the superior court. He's a former public defender, and we are not members of each other's fan club. When he was a lawyer, we butted heads early and often. He's a true believer, a civil libertarian, who believes his mission in life is to ensure the government is kept in check. He hates prosecutors, especially the ones he can't outsmart. I'm not sure how he got promoted to the superior court, but my guess is he knows someone high up in the government—the same government he finds so abhorrent.

Judge Levine rarely holds people on bail. He says he doesn't like to keep people in "cages." But I'm not worried about this ar-raignment. Since ninety-nine percent of the time, defendants in homicide cases are held without bail. In those rare cases when a cash bail is assigned, it's so high that no one has enough money to get out anyway. The few exceptions are cases involving bat-tered women who claim self-defense, and vehicular man-slaughter cases. Even Judge Levine detains first-degree-murder suspects.

This hearing should be a cakewalk. Nonetheless, I make a force-ful and impassioned argument—for the benefit of the judge, the record, and most important the victims' families. I never want to give the impression that I'm phoning it in.

"The defendant stands accused of two horrific murders. Two men, with brilliant futures and loving families, were gunned down in the prime of their lives. The defendant has millions of dollars at his disposal. He has the means and the incentive to flee the jurisdiction and never return for trial. There is no amount of bail sufficient to assure his return."

When it's Anthony's turn, he stands and gestures for his client to do the same. Moe rises, proudly, chest out, head held high, and listens to his lawyer's argument. Anthony looks and sounds as if he actually believes what he's saying. And that there's a chance he might get his client out of lockup.

"Your Honor, my client has every reason to return to court and clear his name. He has long-standing, deep roots in this community. Even if he intended to flee the jurisdiction, which he doesn't, he wouldn't get very far. He's recognized worldwide. Further, he has no criminal record, not so much as a traffic ticket. And most importantly, he is not accused of carrying out the murders. Even if you were to believe the government's outrageous assertions, Paul 'Tags's Tagala is the triggerman, the real criminal. He's the only one who should be behind bars. We intend to mount a vigorous defense. The deceased were both involved in secret relationships, and they were both engaged in the use of illegal steroids—which could also provide motive for their murders."

My throat tightens as I watch the judge, who is actually nodding in agreement. This can't be happening. I clear my throat and stand to reassert my position.

"Your Honor, the defendant is accused of two counts of first-degree murder, which as the court well knows, carries two mandatory sentences of life with no possibility of parole—"

"I've heard enough. The purpose of bail is to assure the defendant's presence at trial, not to punish him. I find that the defendant does not pose a risk of flight. He's not a danger to the community. I'm allowing him to post bail in the amount of one million dollars cash."

"That amount is nothing to a man like Moe Morrissey," I say, stating the obvious.

I'm shocked. The judge is letting a double murderer back out on the street. "Can you at least set restrictions on his release?"

"Like what?"

"Home confinement."

"My client is having significant health problems, resulting from a recent blow to the head during a game," Anthony says. "He needs to be able to see his physician."

"They have medical care in the jail."

"He also wants to go to church, and—"

"Relax, I'm not ordering home confinement," Judge Levine says. "I take it your client will be able to make the million-dollar bail."

Anthony turns around to look at Cecilia, who stands, reaches into her purse, and pulls out her wallet. "Who should I make the check out to?"

Chapter Thirty-Six

After the arraignment, I walk out of the courtroom past the probing microphones. I stiffen my neck, hold my head high, and take the staircase to the next floor. I don't know how I'm going to explain to Tags that Moe posted bail while he's still locked up. I'll figure that out later because Rebecca and Graham are waiting in the conference room, and I have to at least appear confident, shield them from my despair.

I take a breath, steel myself, and open the door. Rebecca is seated. Graham is standing, pacing.

"What happened in there?" he says.

I don't have a good explanation so I punt. "The purpose of bail is to assure the defendant will return to court; it's not punitive. The judge believes he'll come back."

"He's the reason two people are dead. He shouldn't be allowed to go home and sleep in his own sheets."

"You're preaching to the choir," I say. "The judge made a bad decision."

I take a seat next to Rebecca. She's looking down, peeling the paper label from her water bottle. I touch her forearm but she pulls away.

"This is wrong," she says.

"If you're afraid of him, I can get a protective order or move you to a safe house."

She looks up slowly, meets my eyes. "There's no way Moe killed Rudy. He loved Rudy like family."

A tear slides from her eye, comes to rest on her cheek. I offer her a tissue, but she ignores me and stares straight ahead.

"Are you crazy?" Graham says to Rebecca. "Moe is behind this."

"No way. It doesn't make any sense. Rudy was a little jealous because Moe had all the fame, and the big paycheck, but that's as far as it went."

"Did Moe buy you things?" I say.

"Yes, Moe was generous to our family. He paid for our house, our boat."

Rebecca unwittingly just bolstered my case. She has no idea what was going on. Even though there's already enough heartbreak to last a lifetime, I have to tell her my theory—it's going to come out at trial and it's better that she hear it from me.

"We have evidence Moe was paying for Rudy's silence." I turn to Graham. "And he was paying Wayne too."

"Paying him off?" Graham says. "For what?"

"Moe was cheating." I let this land.

"On Cecilia?" Rebecca says.

"On everyone but Cecilia. He was cheating on his fans, his opponents, his teammates."

"That's a lie," Rebecca says.

"He was greasing the ball. His catchers could tell."

"You think Wayne was extorting money from Moe?" Graham says.

"Yes, and Rudy too."

"No way," Rebecca says. "I don't believe it."

There's a knock on the door. Cecilia peers in the small window and comes inside. "Becca, let's go."

"The DA is saying Rudy was extorting money from Moe," Rebecca says.

"Don't listen to her nonsense. She's looking to make herself famous by taking Moe down. That's what this is about."

Cecilia gets in my face, so close I can smell her coffee breath.

"Mrs. Morrissey, I think you should wait outside," I say.

She doesn't move. "You're not going to destroy my family." She looks angry enough to smack me. "You probably made up evidence, like that dirty cop from Brookline." She gives me a final scowl. "Let's go, Becca."

Without glancing in my direction, Rebecca picks up her purse and follows Cecilia out the door. Graham looks the way I feel— shell-shocked. I fill the silence by giving him the Reader's Digest version of criminal procedure—the grand jury indictment, the case transfer to superior court, the trial.

"Are you really going to be able to prove Moe is guilty?" Graham says.

"I can't promise anything, but, yes, I believe I can."

I text Kevin, who offers to drive Graham home, and then I head to my office. As soon as I step outside, I start to sweat. During the three hours I was in the courthouse, the temperature climbed another ten degrees. The crowd outside has dwindled, but a few hard-core pests remain.

A couple of voices call out.

"Abby, do you want to make a comment?"

"ADA Endicott, does this change your strategy?"

I keep walking, ignore them both.

Emma Phelps keeps pace, sticks her microphone in my face. "That was a blow to the prosecution. Can you recover?" She's taunting me, and I'm not going to take the bait. "Was Moe using steroids too?"

I swat at the microphone and take out my cell. Pretending to listen to a nonexistent caller, cupping my hand over my mouth, as though I'm speaking.

Emma persists. "Moe's lawyer said he has health concerns. Sounds like he still hasn't recovered from that ball he took to the head."

I keep walking, lose Emma halfway up New Chardon Street, and turn the corner onto Cambridge Street. The timer on the pedestrian light says I have two seconds to cross the street. Good enough.

As I step into the crosswalk, a red SUV comes barreling toward me. Boston drivers are notoriously bad, but I have the right of way, so I continue to cross the street. As the car gets closer, the driver doesn't slow down; in fact he seems to pick up speed. He blasts his horn and I start to retreat, but I'm already committed, in the middle of the street.

"Look out, lady," someone says.

I pivot, take two steps back toward the sidewalk. The driver is only a few feet away and is making no effort to jam on the brakes or swerve to avoid me. Left with no option, I jump out of the way, hurling myself to the ground, half in the street and half on the sidewalk. Finally, the driver slams on his brakes, stopping about two feet from me.

He opens his window, exposing only his elbow. I jump to my feet, try to get a look at him. The driver spits out a wad of chewing tobacco. Some of the juice slimes my bare knee before landing—splat—on the pavement. It's Moe Morrissey, all smiles. Cecilia is in the front passenger seat, glaring at me. Rebecca is in the back, looking down.

"What the hell are you doing?" I say.

"You were walking against the light," Moe says. "Be careful, or you'll get yourself killed."

Chapter Thirty-Seven

Stan must have issued an APB for me because when I get back to Bulfinch, his assistant is waiting in the lobby, near the elevators. She gives a half smile and shrugs. Not a good sign.

"I take it Stan saw the arraignment," I say.

"The whole office watched. It was live-streamed."

"Where is he?"

"In his office."

I follow her into the elevator and we get off at the executive suite. I can hear Stan from the reception area. He's berating a junior ADA for giving a three-time shoplifter probation. I can only imagine what he has in store for me.

As soon as I cross the threshold to Stan's office, he dismisses the poor first-year with a "Do it again and you'll spend the rest of your career prosecuting drunk driving cases." Stan starts to launch into me, but stops and gives me the once-over.

"Are you okay?"

I hesitate. "Yes, why?"

"You're sweating, and you're bleeding."

I follow his eyes to the side of my hand, where a trickle of blood has formed.

"What the hell happened?"

"I tripped, I'm fine."

He searches his desk for something I can use to blot the cut, but comes up empty. I take a crumpled-up paper napkin from my purse. I consider telling him the truth about what happened, in an effort to garner sympathy, but decide not to. Given the scowl on his face, he might use it as cannon fodder to yank me from the case. Before I can decide whether to pull the injury card, he loses interest in my well-being and takes something off his printer and waves it in the air.

"What the hell is this?"

I grab his hand to stop the paper from fluttering around. It's a newspaper article: *Brookline Police detective Mike Chase . . . allegations of racism involving stop and frisk . . . raises questions about Moe Morrissey's arrest and key piece of evidence . . . Entire case could be in jeopardy.*

Someone leaked the information. I stand, stunned, in silence, and try to get a read on how much Stan knows about my connection to the story. Ty's name isn't mentioned in the article, but Stan has access to a lot of sources; maybe he's done some digging.

"What do you know about this crap?" he says.

"Which part?"

"All of it."

I have no idea how to respond—fortunately, he doesn't wait.

"Who the hell leaked it?"

I don't tell him what I'm thinking: Ty. "It could've been anyone. The cop has a bad rep."

"The timing is suspect."

"Regardless, it's probably true."

"That's Brookline's problem. Right now, all I care about is this case—someone is trying to sabotage it. Find out who."

When I get to my office, I read the article again, then get online and surf. The story has spread, and not surprisingly, the accusations have multiplied. Three other men, all African-American, felt empowered by Ty's disclosure; they came forward to complain about their own illegal stop and frisks by Chase.

My phone sounds; it's Ty. I hit *decline*, sending him to voice mail. He betrayed me in the worst way—he undermined my work. It'd be more forgivable if he cheated on me. I trusted him, which I rarely do with anyone, and I'm not sure how we'll get past this.

The next call is from Kevin. "Did you see the papers?"

I hold the phone to my ear, unsure of how to respond. "Our whole case is about to fall apart," I say. "We have to stop the bleeding."

"How?"

"By proving the stop was legit."

"We don't know that it was."

"Then we have to find someone to corroborate Chase's story and refute Moe's version of what happened."

"That's for the internal affairs investigation," Kevin says. "We can't unring the racism bell."

"You realize the impact it will have on a jury?"

"Look at the bright side. It's probably for the best that it's out there now, while we're still building our case. It'd be a lot worse if this happened on the eve of trial, or worse, after we've picked the jury."

He has a point.

"As it stands, we can't call Chase as a witness," I say. "It'll turn into a sideshow like OJ."

Kevin knows this means I won't be able to use one of our strongest pieces of evidence—the bullets Chase found in Moe's car.

Chapter Thirty-Eight

For the next few months, I spend every waking moment filing discovery motions, responding to various defense requests, shoring up witnesses, avoiding the press, and worrying—about the case, my family, and my relationship with Ty. On the eve of trial, I prepare for voir dire and put the final touches on my opening statement. I hit the wall at about seven. I'm in need of food and drink, but I don't want to go home yet; Ty is scheduled to play at Wally's, he probably won't leave the apartment until nine, and I don't want to run into him.

I've been avoiding Ty, using work as an excuse, to delay any further discussion about the Mike Chase leak. We've talked about it a little; he hasn't admitted to being the source of the leak, and I haven't probed. In true Endicott fashion, rather than talk about what's bothering me, I've been cold and distant. In true Ty fashion, he's given me space. We both know, however, we can't go on like this indefinitely. I'm hoping to put it off until the trial is over.

I call my sister-in-law and invite her to dinner. Charlie is still at work and she's available. She's also suspicious about the reason for my call.

"Is everything okay?"

"Of course," I say, pretending that a spur-of-the-moment,

midweek social call, in the middle of a high-profile murder case, is an everyday event.

Missy is eight months pregnant and exhausted, so we choose Toscano, on Charles Street, a short walk from her Beacon Hill town house. When I arrive, she's already settled into the coveted window table, sipping Pellegrino. I order a glass of Sangiovese, which comes in a carafe that could easily serve three, and linguine vongole. Missy gets halibut and steamed asparagus.

"What's your secret?" she says.

I take a long haul of wine, wondering which of the many secrets she could be referencing. "Secret? I don't have secrets."

"How do you stay so thin?"

"Nervous energy burns a lot of calories." I rip off a piece of bread and dip it in olive oil. "It's one of the upsides to my job. I'm in a constant state of anxiety."

When our meals arrive, we make small talk about my parents, preschools, and the upcoming trial. Missy knows something's on my mind but she doesn't press. I take a forkful of pasta and twirl it on a spoon, around and around.

"Ty betrayed me, in a big way. I don't know what to do."

"Who is she?"

"No, it's not another woman, but I almost wish it was." I finish my first glass of wine. "He really let me down."

She takes a sip of water and hesitates before speaking. "Abby, disappointment is part of any relationship. You just have to decide how much of it you can tolerate."

"My brother lies to you?"

"I hope so."

"You want him to lie."

"About certain things, yes. I want him to pretend to share my obsession with child safety locks. I want him to act interested in wallpaper choices for the nursery. And I definitely don't want him to tell me when something makes me look fat, especially now."

I signal the waiter and order tiramisu and two forks, even though I know Missy won't partake.

"What about infidelity?" I say. "Would you want to know if he was cheating on you?"

"I don't want him to cheat, and I don't think he will, but if he does, I don't want to know about it." As I consider, she reads me. "This must have something to do with your job."

"Yes."

"I love my career. I worked hard to land a job at Fidelity and I hope to go back after my maternity leave. But no job is more important than a relationship."

I'm not sure I agree, but I let it drop. We finish dessert—or I finish dessert—and she finishes her chamomile tea. I take a final sip of wine and offer to give her a ride up Mount Vernon Street.

"Are you sure you're sober enough to drive?"

"Yes. I only had one glass of wine."

"It was a carafe. More like three glasses."

"I'm sober."

"I could use the air. I'm going to walk up the hill."

When we get outside, I realize I'm a little wobbly after all. I decide to leave my car on Charles Street and Uber to my apartment. I'm disappointed to find Ty is home. He's in the living room, putting on his leather jacket. We exchange tense hellos.

"Hey, babe," he says. "We need to talk."

He meets my eyes, touches my arm with confidence, definitely not the behavior of a guilty man who is about to confess to treason. He leans in for a kiss. Something is on his mind, but I don't want to deal with it right now.

"I think I'm coming down with a cold."

He feels my forehead, looks me in the eye. "You feel fine."

"I'm going to bed." I turn to leave.

"This isn't working. We can't keep dancing around each other."

I stop short. Ty is not one to make false threats. He's as tolerant and patient as any man I've ever known, but he draws the line at prolonged silence. I turn to face him and wait for him to speak.

"I haven't pressed, because I know how you are before your trials, but this is getting out of control. We can't live like this."

I look him in the eye. I want to have a rational, adult conversation but I'm overcome with anger.

"You leaked the Mike Chase story without talking to me. Admit it. You lied to me, you betrayed me, and you screwed up my case."

"I told you it wasn't me."

"I guess I don't believe you. I can forgive you, but I don't believe you." I search his face for a hint of guilt.

He looks at me blankly. "I didn't leak that story. If you can't accept me at my word, then we have serious problems."

He picks up his sax case and walks out the door without looking at me again. As soon as he's gone, I regret being so hard on him. It's possible that I'm wrong. Maybe he's not the source of the story. And even if he did talk to a reporter, it's his story to tell—and I was the one who encouraged him to come forward in the first place. I've been too harsh on him. I call his phone to apologize, but he sends me to voice mail. I hang up, without leaving a message.

I take a lukewarm shower, then check my Twitter feed. Since the trial is starting tomorrow, the Detective Chase controversy has been back in the news. It had quieted for a while; Brookline PD is conducting an internal investigation. But last week, another man came forward to file a complaint. Yesterday, the governor issued a statement, denouncing the detective, and Brookline Police rejected his request to mediate the claims. The headline in today's *Globe* announces "Detective Chase Suspended from the Force amid Increasing Allegations of Racism." Whoever leaked the story has done a great service to the community, but they've done irreparable damage to my murder case, and possibly to my relationship.

Chapter Thirty-Nine

Whenever Kevin and I are on trial together, we have a routine. The day of my opening statement, he volunteers to be my chauffeur, picks me up before sunrise. And he always brings a Grande soy latte with an extra shot of espresso. In his car on the way to court, we review our to-do list, then he gives me a pep talk and helps carry my exhibits to the courtroom.

When I step out my front door, he's waiting in his car. "Your front porch light is still out. You want me to bring a bulb tomorrow?"

"Ty said he'd do it."

He raises his eyebrows, hands me my Starbucks. "Yeah, when was that—like five months ago?"

I take a long sip of coffee. "This is going to make me jittery."

He hands me a paper bag; inside is a cranberry scone. "That oughta soak up the acid in your gut."

I take a bite, set it aside. "I'm nauseous."

He starts the car and smiles. "For a lady who can't pack enough adventure into her day, you're pretty predictable."

When we arrive at the courthouse, we set up shop at the prosecutor's table. My trial box has a file for each witness: the initial police interview, the follow-up detective's report, grand jury minutes, a catalog of corresponding exhibits, and a list of the questions that I plan to ask. Everything is in alphabetical order and color coded. I remove the exhibits from brown paper bags, but keep them in their plastic evidence sleeves. Then, I lay them out on the bench, according to when I plan to use them. I have spent hours meticulously choreographing each move of this trial, well aware that nothing will go as planned.

A few minutes before nine, the court officer unlocks the door, and people start to file in—reporters, a pool cameraman, lawyers, and spectators. Moe's family and friends assume their seats in the front row, on the defendant's side. My side of the gallery is empty, a rare occurrence. In most of my murder trials, the front pew is jam-packed, unless the victim's family has given up caring, can't afford to take a day off work, or both. Today that's not the reason for the empty space. Wayne's partner, Graham, is here, but he's been sequestered because he's on my witness list. Wayne's mother isn't here—she had a heart attack, probably from the stress of losing her son. The Maddox family, including Rebecca, are in the courtroom, but they're seated on the defendant's side.

Moe is seated at the defendant's table, wearing horn-rimmed glasses and holding a Bible. Nice touch.

"All rise," the court officer says.

Judge Levine bounds into the courtroom, with energy and enthusiasm—which makes me uncomfortable. The more alert he is, the tougher he'll be on me. I take a silent breath and steel myself as he gets the ball rolling.

Not surprisingly, Moe's lawyer files a motion to suppress my most compelling evidence—the bullets that were allegedly seized from Moe's car. He assumes I'm going to call Chase as a witness at trial, so he never even bothers to ask. His team wrote an extensive brief deeming Mike Chase unreliable, alleging that the search of Moe's car was illegal, and arguing that the judge shouldn't allow the ammunition to be part of the evidence. It's a valid request, and it's also another way to garner pretrial publicity.

"Does the Commonwealth wish to be heard on the defendant's motion to suppress?" the judge says.

I gather my thoughts and utter a sentence I've never said before.

"The Commonwealth assents to the defendant's motion."

It makes me nauseous but I don't have a choice. Everyone saw the damage Mark Fuhrman did to the OJ case. I'm not going to vouch for Chase's credibility. I know too much; it'd be bad strategically, not to mention morally repugnant.

Jury empanelment goes swiftly and efficiently. This is one of the rare cases where people actually want to serve as jurors. The judge eliminates anyone with strong feelings about sports and the police. Most people have heard about the case, and the judge asks if they can still remain fair and impartial.

The trial is going to be tough, but I've tried cases with less evidence. Hopefully, Tags's testimony will be enough to carry the day. My real concern is the media spotlight. High-profile cases bring out the worst in people—not just lawyers. It impacts the judge, court officers, witnesses; even spectators react in an exaggerated manner. Everyone clamors for attention, hoping to make it on the nightly news. Jurors are never filmed and they're not supposed to read coverage about the case, but they're aware of the cameras and they know their verdict will undergo tremendous scrutiny. Sometimes it seems as if people care more about perception than about getting it right.

It only takes a day to pick twelve jurors and five alternates. We adjourn for the night and start fresh in the morning. Everyone is anxious and excited to get going, but no one else as much as me.

"Ladies and gentlemen of the jury," Judge Levine says, "you are now going to hear opening statements from both attorneys. These statements are like a road map, to let you know what you can expect to hear at the trial."

The road-map analogy is a staple among trial judges. I disagree. To me, an opening statement is a contract, between the jury and me. I tell them how I'm going to prove my case, and if I make good on my promise, I expect them to convict. So, I'm careful not to make promises I can't keep.

When Judge Levine gives me the nod, I stand and center myself in front of the jury box. After establishing eye contact with each juror, I pivot and point at Moe Morrissey.

"It's indisputable that the defendant is many things. He's a husband, a father, a professional athlete. Moe Morrissey is an all-star on the field, a sports legend. But he's also a double murderer. Just like a Mafia boss, he put out a hit on Wayne Ellis and Rudy Maddox."

I pause, survey the panel. My least favorite juror, an accountant from the North End, is staring at Moe. Jurors often look at defendants with contempt. Not this juror. This juror looks as if she's itching to go over and ask for an autograph, or a kiss. The attraction of celebrity. I pause until she turns her attention back to me.

"The defendant has a high strikeout-to-walk ratio and a multimillion-dollar contract, but that doesn't make him any less of a killer. In fact, it corroborates our theory—he had a lot to lose. He was cheating, about to be exposed."

I glove up, take out the baseballs, and hold them up, one at a time, using both hands—as though they were fragile. The jurors lean in, straining to see.

"This is why he wanted Rudy Maddox and Wayne Ellis dead. He was a cheater. He manipulated the balls with a slippery substance and the victims found out and they threatened to expose him. He hired Paul Tagala to do his dirty work, to keep distance between himself and the killings. He didn't pull the trigger, but that doesn't make him any less guilty."

Halfway through my opening, Moe tips his glass and spills his water all over the table, causing a distraction and breaking my momentum. I glance over but keep going; I'm not going to yield control. I walk the jurors through the evidence and talk to them about murder for hire, and how it makes Moe responsible for the murder itself. Then, I talk about some of the witnesses that I expect to testify—the medical examiner, the detectives, the crime lab technicians.

"The most important witness you will hear from is Paul Tagala. He knows what happened because he was there. He will take the witness stand and tell you about Moe Morrissey's directive to kill, and the compensation he was promised. He will describe the horror of what happened."

Before I conclude, I move to Moe's table. He sits up straight and we lock eyes.

"At the end of this trial, you will know that this man is a murderer." I turn back to the jury. "And I will ask you to return a verdict of guilty."

Anthony stands and starts talking before I get a chance to put my butt in my chair.

"Ms. Endicott's case is all smoke and mirrors. There isn't any evidence of a conspiracy or an agreement to kill, nothing to tie my client to a murder. Moe Morrissey loved Rudy Maddox, like a brother. He grieved his death like everyone else in this city. And he is an innocent man."

Anthony picks up one of the baseballs, tosses it in the air. "Pardon the pun, but I'm asking you to keep your eye on the ball. Don't be fooled or misled by an overzealous prosecutor."

Anthony is entertaining, and worse, he's convincing. He tells the jurors about the steroids scandal, to make the victims look bad and to raise another motive for someone else to have done the murders. He wraps up by insulting Tags, calling him an opportunistic liar with an immunity deal.

When Anthony is done, the judge calls a recess so we can take the jury on a view. Moe joins his family in the hallway. It's unsettling to see him, walking around, without as much as an ankle bracelet.

In the hallway, a couple of spectators approach Moe, shake his hand, and ask for his autograph. The stenographer asks him to sign a baseball that she pulls from her tote. A detective who is on trial across the hall smiles and takes a selfie. When I see an ADA from my office move toward Moe, palming her cell phone, I throw her the stink eye. Reluctantly, she backs off. Then, the accountant juror comes into the hallway and stands in place, waiting to catch Moe's attention. If I were allowed to talk to jurors, I'd tell her to keep moving.

Fortunately, a court officer steps in. "Ma'am, why don't you follow me."

"I wasn't trying to talk to Moe or anything. I can be fair and impartial."

She is unconvincing—and unable to take her eyes off Moe.

Chapter Forty

Pictures may speak a thousand words, but they're no replacement for a jury view. A field trip to the crime scene is always creepy, scary, and invaluable. Jurors can stand where the victim took his last breath. They can imagine the horror he experienced, especially if I'm lucky enough to have a location where bullet holes are still in the ceiling or specks of blood spatter on the walls.

We all get on the bus at the courthouse, and the driver takes us to our first stop, Fenway Park. Taking the jury into the ballpark would be fun, and taking them on the roof where Emma filmed Tags would be an adventure, but neither sets the tone I'm going for.

I stand and turn to face the rear of the bus.

"Members of the jury, I'd like you to take note of the location of the ballpark. And pay particular attention to Gate D because I'll be talking about that exit during the trial."

They all look out the windows as I speak. Some seem eager to get off the bus. I have to deliver the bad news, in case they don't hate me enough already.

"We're not going into the park. I'd like you to notice the distance between this location and our next stop."

We travel the route Tags took, to the transfer station. When the bus arrives, we see that Kevin, along with a dozen uniforms, is positioned near the front gate. Yellow crime-scene tape is up to keep the crowd away. Workers, reporters, and lookie-loos—all with cameras—lurk nearby, hoping for a money shot of Moe. He nods but keeps his game face on.

The stench of rotting trash is heavy in the air. I'm not sure where it's coming from, but I'm glad it's here. I prefer a trial that assaults all the senses.

Kevin leans in and whispers, "You'd better make this quick—a couple of jurors look a little green around the gills."

I filed the motion in court, and the judge allowed me to have the view, but my role is limited. I'm not allowed to do much more than point things out. I direct the jurors' attention to the entrance of the dump and the spot where Rudy was discovered. Later, I'll connect the dots, through witnesses and photos.

As I speak, Anthony and Moe hover, as though they're spectators; a subtle way of distancing themselves from the crime. On our way back to the bus, one of the jurors, the accountant, stumbles on a loose piece of scrap metal; Moe rushes to her side, catches her elbow, and steadies her. She smiles and blushes. He hasn't said a word, but he's scoring a lot of points.

Our next stop is the Fens. Traffic is heavy and the driver seems to hit every pothole on Massachusetts Avenue. Halfway there, it starts to rain lightly. Then there's a quick downpour, complete with a burst of thunder.

Anthony, who is seated in the row behind me, leans on my headrest and whispers, "Having fun yet?"

I smile but he knows I'm aware that the jurors are mumbling and grumbling in the back of the bus.

When we arrive at the Fens, I lead the pack down the path, which is now an obstacle course of puddles and soggy grass. At our destination, I see Kevin talking to an ice cream vendor.

"Do you mind moving for a few minutes?" Kevin says.

The man has planted himself on a bench and refuses to budge. "It's a free country."

Kevin, not wanting to make a scene, stands in front of the man, blocking him from view. I direct the jurors' attention to the streetlights and ask them to take note of the distance between the entry points of the park. Tags will testify to how he dumped the body in the swamp under the cover of darkness.

The ice cream vendor steps out from behind Kevin and interrupts, "Hey, does anyone want a Hoodsie?" The man holds up a red-and-white paper cup, and a wooden spoon. "I'm running a special, two for three dollars."

A couple of jurors reach for their pockets. Moe beats them to it. He takes out his wallet, gives the man a $100 bill, in exchange for the entire stash.

It was a brilliant move. He looks like a good guy, and I can't object—unless I want to deny my jurors their treat. I look to Judge Levine, hoping he'll intervene. He steps up, and instead of admonishing Moe, he reaches into the box of Hoodsies and helps himself.

The man puts the money in his billfold and then looks back at Moe. "Hey, you're Moe Morrissey."

Moe puffs out his chest. "That's right."

"Didn't you kill someone?"

Moe moves back a few steps, slumps against a light post.

The man keeps talking. "Wait, you killed *two* people, right?"

Judge Levine tries to run interference. "Does the Commonwealth have anything else to present?" Judge Levine's words are muffled because his mouth is full of ice cream.

"No, Your Honor."

"Then this view is over."

Two of the jurors toss their unopened Hoodsies in the trash. I suppress a smile as I lead the jurors out of the park and we all climb back into the bus.

Chapter Forty-One

I'm exhausted from the view but still have to put in a couple of hours at Bulfinch. I want to organize my exhibits and prepare questions for tomorrow. If all goes according to plan, I should get through my opening statement and at least three witnesses. Nothing, however, ever goes according to plan during a trial, so I have to be ready to shoot from the hip.

At about eight, my phone rings. It's Missy. "Your mother and I are having dinner at the Gardner Club. Can you join us?"

"I'm in the middle of trial."

"You still have to eat." A hint of desperation is in her voice.

"What's going on?"

"I think she wants to tell us something."

I agree to meet them at the club, one of my least favorite places in Boston. It's the default location for Endicotts to observe various rites of passage. It's where my parents celebrated their twenty-fifth wedding anniversary, where Charlie and Missy were married, and where Uncle Minty had his last meal before going to prison for tax evasion.

When I arrive, my mother is in rare form, flitting around the dining room. She looks as if she were hosting a private dinner party, moving from table to table, Missy in tow. Missy is carefully monitoring the conversations, to be sure my mother doesn't say or do anything to shame herself or the family.

I tell my mother I have to get up early and coax her to the table, where a bottle of champagne is waiting on ice.

"We don't need a whole bottle," Missy says, patting her expanding baby bump. "I'm not drinking."

"That's ridiculous—my generation drank when we were expecting, and our children turned out fine," my mother says. "Abigail will join me in."

I'd love some alcohol—it'd help numb the pain, both familial and professional—but seeing my mother drink drives home Missy's and Ty's point—my gene pool is loaded with addiction. I have to be mindful of my own behavior.

"I'm not drinking tonight."

My mother rolls her eyes and turns to the waiter, who is ready to take our dinner orders. Beef Wellington for me, lemon sole for Missy, and shrimp cocktail for my mother, who prefers to drink her calories.

"Are we celebrating something?" I say.

My mother smiles at the pop of the champagne cork. She waits for the sommelier to fill her glass, then raises it as though making a toast. "I have an announcement." She takes a sip, holding the suspense.

Missy catches my eye.

"What's the news?" I fidget with my silverware.

"Will and I are moving in together."

A piece of my dinner roll goes down the wrong pipe. I try to clear my throat, but can't stop coughing. Missy hands me a water glass and I take a few small sips. A waiter stands nearby, ready to perform the Heimlich.

My mother, who is not at all concerned, waves him off. "Don't be so dramatic. You of all people should understand the desire to cohabitate."

After a minute, I'm able to clear my throat and regain my breathing.

"When are you moving?" Missy says.

"I'm not actually relocating."

My mother signals the sommelier, who tightens the napkin around the champagne bottle and refills her glass.

"He's moving into our house?" I say.

"It's my house now, at least it will be when the divorce is final."

"Does Dad know?" I say.

My mother shrugs. "That's not relevant."

"What's the rush?" Missy says.

"Will has been staying at the Harvard Club since his divorce. He has to live somewhere."

"Whose idea was this?" I say.

"That's it, end of subject," my mother says.

When the waiter arrives with our food, none of us are hungry. My mother nibbles on a shrimp and polishes off the bottle of champagne. Missy takes a forkful of fish and moves the snow peas around on her plate. I ask for a doggie bag because I'll be hungry later—and because it'll annoy my mother. She thinks it's crass to take uneaten food home.

Since Kevin drove me to work this morning, and I don't want to spend money on a taxi, I ask Missy to drive me home. My mother lives three blocks away, but she's barely walking a straight line. We drop her off first.

When we arrive at the house on Louisburg Square, our house-keeper opens the door. Will is standing in the foyer, behind her. The housekeeper takes my mother's coat; Will takes her arm.

"Let's have a nightcap," Will says.

As he ushers her upstairs, Missy clocks my look of concern.

"You don't trust him?"

"I know he's got money of his own, but, no, I don't trust him."

Chapter Forty-Two

Normally, I call witnesses in chronological order, starting with the first responder—an EMT or patrolman, who talks about finding the body. That's not going to work today. I have to go off script and begin with a witness who is recognizable, someone with gravitas, someone who can tarnish Moe.

"The Commonwealth calls Donnie Rourke to the stand," I say.

Donnie, the team manager, is a celebrity in his own right, and he's the only person who can drive a wedge between Moe and Boston's beloved ball club. He races in the courtroom as though he were trying to catch a bus, stopping short in front of the clerk, who administers the oath. Cameras click and people sit up a little taller. Everyone in Boston has seen Donnie on TV, and they feel as if they already know him, which allows me to tick off the introductory questions quickly: name, occupation, background, and training.

Then, I get to the point, ask the million-dollar question. "What is Moe's current status with the ball club?"

"Inactive." Donny remains his usual loquacious self.

"He's been suspended from the team?"

"Yes."

I display photos of Moe with Wayne at an away game, and

Moe with Rudy at a family function, and Donnie identifies both victims.

"Did Paul Tagala know both men?" I say.

"Yes."

"As far as you could tell, was there any animus between them?"

"Nope."

When I'm done with my direct examination, Anthony dives in and does his best to rehabilitate his client. "Moe has been suspended, pending the outcome of this case."

"Correct," Donnie says.

"If he's acquitted, as he should be, he could be back on the team. And they could start winning games again."

I jump out of my seat. "Objection. Calls for speculation."

"Would he be allowed to play again?" Judge Levine wants to know the answer as much as the rest of the sports fans in the courtroom.

"Possibly," Donnie says. "Can't say for sure."

Two jurors, seated in the front row, glare at me, as though I were the only thing standing between the Red Sox and another World Series championship.

"Nothing further," Anthony says.

Anthony smiles and sits.

Before I have time to figure out my recovery, Judge Levine prompts me to move on. "Call your next witness."

I need to humanize my victims. I turn to look at Rudy's family. His mother, June, offers a faint smile, which could be tacit assent. Or at least that's how I choose to interpret it. She wouldn't allow me to prep her, and I know she's probably going to be a hostile witness, but I need her testimony.

I turn to the judge. "The Commonwealth calls June Maddox to the stand."

Mr. Maddox leans in to whisper something to his wife, but she shakes her head. She doesn't want to hear it. She's doesn't look me in the eye, and it's obvious to anyone who's paying attention, she's no longer on my team. She stands, smooths her suit skirt, and tugs on the cuffs of her shirt. Anthony must have prepared her for the possibility that I'd call her. The court officer opens the swinging door that separates the audience from the partici- pants, and June tromps through to the front of the courtroom.

Once she's settled in, I tread lightly. Maybe the jury didn't no- tice the seating situation; it's possible they don't know that the mother of my victim is sitting with the family of the accused.

"Could you please state your name for the record," I say.

She crosses her arms and looks at the ceiling.

"Mrs. Maddox?" I say.

No response.

"Did you hear the question?" Judge Levine says.

She nods. "I heard, but I don't want to talk to her."

"Why not?" the judge says.

"My daughter-in-law, Rebecca, told me she's a sneaky lawyer and she's out to get us."

I clock the jurors. The lunch lady twists her body away from me. The accountant holds her purse in her lap as though she's ready to get up and go home as soon as the judge gives her the go-ahead. This is a disaster, but I've backed myself into a corner.

"Your Honor, perhaps it's time for the afternoon recess," I say.

The judge consults his watch. "No, we still have thirteen min- utes."

He's enjoying my pain. I clear my throat, shuffle my papers, and glance into the gallery. Kevin throws me a *Go get 'em, tiger* look. I take a photograph from the top of my pile of exhibits: Rudy, wearing a Red Sox uniform, flashing a toothy smile. I proj- ect the image onto a screen.

"Do you recognize this man?" I say.

She tears up, as I'd hoped. I hate to bring her pain, but I have to get her to stop snarling long enough to answer my questions.

"That's my son, the day he signed with the team."

I have the picture marked with an evidence sticker and pass it around to the jury. Then, I show them Rudy's contract with the Sox. Hopefully that will take their minds off me, and back onto what this case is about. The jurors study the contract; maybe I've neutralized a couple of them. Regardless, I've killed enough time to make a second request for a recess, which the judge allows.

The courtroom empties, and I look for Kevin in the hallway. He's waiting with a gooey, sugary cinnamon roll.

"I've dealt with hostile witnesses before, but the victim's mother has never refused to cooperate." I take too big a bite of the roll and chew until it's safe to swallow.

"No time for self-pity. What's your plan?"

"I need to put Tags on the stand. Can you arrange to have him brought over from the jail?"

"You sure you want to call him so soon?"

"My options are diminishing. If I have any hope of a conviction, I need the jurors to stop hating me and start hating Moe. ASAP."

"I'll see what I can do."

Chapter Forty-Three

It will take at least an hour to transport Tags from the jail to the courthouse. I fill in the time by putting the transfer-station worker on the stand. I go slowly, methodically, dragging it out as long as I can.

He helps me get in some gory details about the condition of Rudy's body and the horror of finding him. When I hold up a photograph of Rudy partially buried in the scrap heap, I hear a sound from the jury box. Someone is hissing at me. Hissing—the courtroom equivalent of rotten tomatoes. I want to turn to him and tell him this isn't my fault—I wasn't the one who killed Rudy.

Anthony is so confident about the case he doesn't even bother to cross-examine the witness: "No questions."

I turn and look at Kevin, who gives me a thumbs-up, signaling that Tags is here.

"The Commonwealth calls Paul Tagala to the stand," I say.

The court officers escort Tags into the courtroom. He's wearing his orange prison-issued jumpsuit; his lawyer, Tracey Miller, keeps pace by his side. This should turn things around. Tags will set things straight. As the clerk swears him in, Anthony and Tracey exchange the hint of conspiratorial nods. Wait. This can't be happening.

"Your Honor," Tracey says, "may we approach sidebar?"

I try to stall. "Objection."

"On what grounds?" the judge says.

"Um, it's unduly prejudicial."

"To have a sidebar?" Anthony says.

Judge Levine rolls his eyes and waves us all forward.

"My client wishes to invoke his rights under the Fifth Amendment to the United States Constitution," Tracey says.

"No way," I say. "We had a deal."

Tracey smiles and shrugs. "He changed his mind."

"When?"

"Does the time really matter?" Anthony says.

I ignore Anthony, stay focused on Tracey. "If he doesn't cooperate, we'll withdraw the plea offer."

"Yes, he understands that."

"He'll do life, no chance of parole."

"Only if he's convicted at trial," Tracey says.

"At the rate you're going, that's not going to happen—to either Tags or Moe," Anthony says.

"Your Honor," I say, "I demand that the court enforce our agreement with Mr. Tagala."

"No can do," Judge Levine says. "Your request is denied."

I'm being triple-teamed.

"It's a few minutes before five." Anthony points to the clock. "Perhaps we could break early. My client has plans to go to Las Vegas for the long weekend."

Judge Levine addresses the entire courtroom. "We're in recess. It'll give us all some time to rest and recharge. See you on Tuesday."

I wish he were that amenable when I needed to buy time. He gets off the bench and disappears into his chambers.

After the jury is dismissed, Tags get off the stand and walks past Moe's table. Tags signals solidarity with a quick chin raise. Moe looks over at me and smiles. I hold his gaze—a game of who will blink first—until Kevin calls me over.

He's got a piece of paper in his hand. "It's the visitors' log at the jail. Guess who visited Tags last night."

"It couldn't be Moe. Tell me the guards didn't let Tags's coconspirator visit him in the jail."

"It wasn't Moe."

"Did he send his lawyer? Did Anthony visit him? That'd be cause for reprimand."

"Nope. It wasn't Anthony."

I grab the paper from Kevin and scan the list.

"It was Cecilia," he says. "Moe sent his fiancée to do his bidding."

Chapter Forty-Four

M oe gets permission to travel to Las Vegas for the weekend. While he and Cecilia are playing blackjack, shopping at Cartier, and dining at CUT, Kevin and I do some digging. Bank records don't show a transfer of funds from any of Moe's accounts to Tags, but $500,000 was recently withdrawn from Cecilia's investment account. We can't figure out where the money went, but it's reasonable to infer that it went to Tags. Or at least that's what I plan to argue in court. It's not proof beyond a reasonable doubt that Moe bribed Tags, but maybe we can use it as leverage.

On Saturday afternoon, Kevin and I make the drive to Cohasset. It's not even October, but an unexpected storm has left Jerusalem Road slick with a thin layer of ice. The sky is dark and the road is slick with fallen leaves. We park behind the Maddoxes' home, knock on the door. Rebecca answers but doesn't invite us in.

"We won't stay long," I say. "Please hear us out."

Rebecca steps aside and we enter the kitchen, wipe our feet on the mat. Chloe is crawling behind her mother. Rebecca picks her up, holds her in her lap as we all take seats around the table.

Rebecca speaks first. "Moe is innocent. I don't understand why you're doing this to my family."

"We're doing it *for* your family—for you and for Chloe," I say.

"Even Tags says Moe wasn't involved. You pressured him into lying."

"Tags didn't exonerate Moe," I say. "He took the Fifth—it's different."

Chloe whines and starts to fuss. Rebecca bounces her on her knees and sings the words that every Boston-born baby loves to hear: "Trot, trot to Boston. Trot to Lynn. Look out little Chloe or you might fall in." With that, Rebecca opens her knees, but keeps hold of Chloe's underarms, while pretending that the child might slip through. Chloe knows the routine. She squeals in delight.

"Your sister paid Tags money, to stop him from testifying," Kevin says. "Moe doesn't want the truth about what happened to come out."

Rebecca shakes her head. "I don't believe you."

Kevin shows her the printout of the visitors' log from the jail and directs her to her sister's signature. I show her the bank records. Rebecca chews her bottom lip as she studies the documents.

"Cecilia protected Moe, knowing he killed your baby's father," I say. "That's what the evidence shows."

Kevin shows Rebecca the security tape from the jail, time-stamped from Thursday night. It shows Cecilia checking in at the front desk, putting her coat and bag in a locker. Rebecca looks at her daughter, who is humming to herself. Rebecca struggles with what she wants to say.

"I saw Cecilia."

Kevin and I exchange looks, but mask our excitement.

"Your sister? When?" Kevin's voice is calm.

"The day after Rudy went missing."

Rebecca pauses, puts Chloe in her play seat.

"Where did you see her?" Kevin says.

"At their house, in Chestnut Hill. Cecilia and I were in the living room, drinking coffee, waiting to hear from Rudy. Moe called."

"Did she talk to him?" I say.

"For a minute."

"How did she seem?" Kevin says.

"Nervous, she was pacing around, whispering. Then, she left the room."

"Could you see where she went?" Kevin says.

"To the garage—Moe was there. I thought it was weird that he called when he was right outside."

"Was anyone else there?" Kevin says.

"Tags."

"What happened?"

Rebecca hesitates, looks at her child. "Moe handed Cecilia a laundry bag."

"How big was it?" Kevin says.

Rebecca shrugs. "It was all bunched up. It looked like it could have come from the locker room at Fenway. Cecilia took the bag and got in her car and drove away."

"What do you think was in the bag?" I say.

She starts to speak, stops herself.

We wait.

"Moe kept a gun in the garage."

"How do you know?" I say.

"I've seen it."

"It must've been the murder weapon," Kevin says, looking at me.

"You think your sister stashed it somewhere?" I say.

Rebecca eyes the baby, who is gnawing on her stuffed Paddington bear's paw, and nods.

"When your sister came back to the house, did you ask where she went?" I say.

"Yes, but she didn't really answer, so I let it drop."

I take out my iPad. "I'll draw up a subpoena, call her as a witness."

"She'll never testify against Moe," Rebecca says.

"If she doesn't, she'll go to jail," Kevin says.

Rebecca drops her head and starts to cry. "She won't care. She'll do anything for him."

I get a tissue from the counter, hand it to her. Then, pour her a glass of water from the dispenser near the fridge.

"If she's locked up, she'll be separated from her kids," I say.

Chloe sees her mother in distress, starts to cry.

Rebecca scoops her up. "She won't turn on him."

"What makes you so sure?" I say. "Is she scared of him?"

Rebecca stands, keeping her daughter in her arms. "It's nap time. You can see yourselves out."

Chapter Forty-Five

Kevin and I drive out to Logan Airport on Sunday night. We're optimistic that forcing Cecilia to testify is the break we need. We scan the arrival board until we find Moe's flight information, then position ourselves near the luggage belt. Dozens of suntanned passengers are already at baggage claim. I look around, scout out a man in a dark suit, holding a sign: MORRISSEY.

Moe rounds the corner first, holding a Vuitton duffel bag. Cecilia is close behind, wrapped in a plush cashmere sweater.

If Moe is surprised to see us, he doesn't show it. He puffs out his chest slightly, as though he's emboldened by our presence. "Did you come to tell me you dropped the charges?"

We're not allowed to speak to a defendant who is represented by counsel, not even the arrogant ones who need to be knocked down a peg.

"Cecilia, we have a gift for you," Kevin says.

She looks at Kevin, then at Moe.

"Whatever it is, we don't want it," Moe says.

A small crowd is starting to form around us. *Hey, that's Moe Morrissey. Did you do it, Moe? Why'd you kill them? Can I have your autograph?* A couple of cell phone cameras snap. We've got to serve the subpoena and split, otherwise we'll be on the eleven o'clock news.

Kevin holds out the papers. "It's a court order."

"Go ahead, take it," Moe says. "There's nothing more they can do to us."

Cecilia extends her hand and accepts the subpoena.

"Tomorrow morning, nine o'clock—be there," Kevin says, "or instead of that diamond tennis bracelet, you'll be wearing hand-cuffs."

Kevin drives me home. When we arrive, the porch is dark. I'm annoyed to see Ty still hasn't changed the bulb. I'd do it, but we don't have a stepladder, and I'm not tall enough to reach the light fixture. When I get upstairs, I decide not to nag him. We've got bigger issues right now.

I stay up all night, preparing for Cecilia's testimony. It's going to be stressful in the moment and I don't want to forget any-thing. I draw up dozens of questions, starting with the basics. *Name, address, relationship to Moe.* Then I move on to ques-tions that will elicit information about Moe's relationship with Rudy. *How long did they know each other? How often did they interact socially?* I'll save the best for last. *Where were you the night Rudy disappeared? Was there a gun in the laundry bag? Did Moe tell you to dispose of it? Where'd you put it?*

The pages fill up quickly. When my head starts to throb, I take a break to shower and dress. It's cold and dark when I set out for the courthouse. Out of habit, I grab a coffee at Starbucks, but what I really need is a beta-blocker, to slow my heart rate and dull the physical symptoms of anxiety. I'm amped up and jittery, but excited to face off against the Morrisseys. This is going to be my day. Things are going to turn around. The jury will come over to my side.

In my office, I stare at the clock, waiting for the courthouse to open. No need to review my questions again; I committed them to memory. At eight o'clock, I pack my trial box and walk toward Pemberton Square. The temperature has risen in the last couple of hours, and by the time I climb the steep stairs at Center Plaza, my forehead has developed a film of sweat.

In the lobby, near the elevator bank, Emma Phelps breaks away from her cameraman and catches up with me.

"You look flushed," she says. "Is everything okay?"

"Never better."

She jumps on an empty elevator car, holds the door. "Coming?"

"I'll wait for the next one."

I don't trust myself alone with her. I'm so excited, I might blurt out something I regret. *Moe Morrissey is going down.*

Anthony calls the clerk to say he's going to be late for court. He says he's tied up at home. His kid is sick. I don't think he has children, but I let it slide. He's probably at his office, furiously trying to prepare his cross-examination of Cecilia. He can prepare all he wants, the truth doesn't change.

An hour later, Anthony strolls in. Kevin tells me Cecilia is in the hallway. The court officer calls order, and Judge Levine takes the bench.

"Ms. Endicott, who is your next witness?" he says.

I stand and look at the jury. "The Commonwealth calls Cecilia Bond."

The jurors look back at me; one even shows the hint of a smile. They take out their notebooks, uncap their pens. Cecilia sashays into the courtroom as though she were on a runway, dressed to the nines in a turquoise pantsuit. She passes Rebecca, who has switched seats. Today, she's on the prosecution side of the aisle, next to Graham.

The clerk swears her in and Cecilia takes her place on the hot seat. As I move to the lectern, I catch a glimpse of Moe. He looks as confident as ever, game face on. Nothing seems to ruffle him.

I want to start slow, build the tension, and find my rhythm. "Please introduce yourself to the members of the jury."

She takes a sip of water, smiles. "My name is Cecilia Morrissey."

"Where do you—" I stop short. Wait. Cecilia *Morrissey*? "You mean Bond, Cecilia Bond."

"No, I mean Morrissey. Moe and I got married yesterday, in Las Vegas."

She holds up her ring finger—for the jury, the cameras, and me. The lower half of her finger is covered by a sparkly emerald-cut diamond. This is not how I expected it to go.

Anthony shoots out of his chair. "Your Honor, may we approach sidebar?"

"Approach. You too, Mrs. Morrissey."

We huddle; the jury strains to listen. The clerk turns on the white-noise machine.

Anthony speaks first. "The witness has informed me she intends to assert her marital privilege. Pursuant to the General Laws, Chapter 233, Section 20, she must be excused."

The judge looks at Cecilia. "Is that true? Do you intend to assert your spousal privilege?"

"I don't want to testify against my husband, if that's what you're asking."

The judge looks at me.

I try to keep my cool, but only because the jury is watching. "Your Honor, the marriage is a sham. The Morrisseys are trying to take advantage of a loophole in the system."

"We've been engaged for two years. We have kids together," Cecilia says. "We were in Vegas and we decided it was as good a time as any."

"While the timing is suspect, I'm bound by the rules, Ms. Endicott," Judge Levine says. "Mrs. Morrissey, you don't have to testify. You are excused."

Cecilia flashes her million-dollar CoverGirl smile, winks at her husband, and takes her place in the front row of the gallery. When this trial started, I didn't have a lot of evidence, but I had hope. Now, I don't have either.

Chapter Forty-Six

For me, Moe's nuptials have not been cause for celebration. Cecilia was going to be my Hail Mary, and her refusal to testify is a major setback. Since I had planned to spend most of the day with her on the stand, I only have one witness on deck: the junkie who found Wayne's body in the Fens.

He's pacing around the hallway, twitching and sniffling, ingesting as much sugar as he can get his hands on. I gave him my lunch—a Mounds bar and a pack of Oreos. I can't call him to testify in this condition—the jury doesn't trust me as it is. It'd be the final nail in my coffin.

"Who is your next witness?" Judge Levine says.

I'd like to summons someone from the Brookline Police to testify, to show the jury the ammunition that was found in Moe's car, but I can't. I look around the gallery, at all the people who could help, but won't: Emma Phelps, Cecilia Morrissey, even Paul Tagala's grandmother is here. My eyes land on Rebecca.

"The Commonwealth calls Rebecca Maddox."

I turn to look at Rebecca, who is shaking her head back and forth. I walk over to her, cover my face with a legal pad, and lean across the rail. Kevin joins the huddle.

"I need you," I say.

"I can't testify against Moe. I can't."

"You don't have to testify *against* anyone," Kevin says. "Testify for Rudy."

"All you have to do is tell the truth," I say.

The judge calls out. "Let's go, Ms. Endicott."

Rebecca hesitates, then stands and follows me up the aisle. As we cross the bar, Moe turns his entire body around to glare at her. She stumbles. I hold on to her elbow and help her regain her balance.

"Raise your right hand," the clerk says.

She's shaking so much that she has to use her left hand to steady her right one. Her breathing is loud and purposeful as she takes the oath. As soon as she sits in the witness box, I launch in. We make it through the foundation questions.

"Please introduce yourself to the members of the jury."

"My name is Rebecca Maddox."

"How old are you?"

"Twenty-three."

"What is your marital status?"

She takes a breath. "I'm a widow."

I project a photo of Rudy onto the screen. He's smiling, his arm around Rebecca, holding their baby.

"That's my husband."

As Rebecca dabs at the corner of her eyes with a tissue, my least favorite juror, the accountant, unfolds her arms and looks at me. She might be warming up to me. Maybe she sees I'm not the enemy.

"Do you know the defendant, Mr. Morrissey?" I say.

"He's my brother-in-law."

Anthony jumps out of his chair. "May we be heard at sidebar?"

"Approach," Judge Levine says.

Anthony leads the charge to the judge's bench. In an effort to overpower the white noise, he raises his voice. "Ms. Endicott didn't give notice of this witness. It's a violation of the discovery rules."

"I didn't know your client was going to marry a key witness," I say.

"What's your point, Counsel?" the judge says.

"Mrs. Maddox should be excluded and her testimony stricken."

"She's a necessary witness," I say.

The judge looks over our heads, at the reporters in the gallery. "I'm going to split the baby. I'll allow her to testify, but I'll give you time to prepare. We'll adjourn until tomorrow."

"I don't know if I'll be able to get her back here tomorrow," I say.

"That's your problem," the judge says. "We're in recess."

The courtroom starts to empty. Rebecca looks as if she's about to bolt.

"If you're worried about safety," I say, "we can put you in a hotel for the night."

"And then what?"

I wish I had a good response, but I don't. I wish Kevin could make a preemptive arrest for failure to appear, but that's not one of his superpowers. Rebecca promises to come back tomorrow, but she's not very convincing. I remind her that the judge will issue a bench warrant if she doesn't show. Hopefully, her fear of arrest is at least equal to her fear of Moe.

Chapter Forty-Seven

Back at the office, I line up witnesses for the next day, including some backups in case we have to issue an APB for Rebecca. As I'm packing up for the night, my phone rings. It's my sister-in-law.

"I'm downstairs, and I was wondering if you could grab dinner."

Missy has never stopped by my office before, and she's due to give birth any day now. Something is up.

"Is everything okay?"

"Charlie is working and I'm kind of lonely." Her speech is clipped and tentative.

"I'll be right down."

Since I don't have a lot of time for dinner and Missy is craving sauerkraut, we go to Zaftigs in Brookline, not far from my apartment. I order a Reuben sandwich; it's heavy, greasy, and exactly what I wanted. I'd love a glass of wine.

"I'll have a seltzer," I say.

As soon as the waiter is gone, Missy pleads her case: "I think your mother's beau, Will Dorset, is a fraud."

I dip a french fry into mayonnaise, fully aware that I'll regret this whole meal before the waiter brings the check.

"I'm staying out of it. My mother isn't interested in my opinion."

"Charlie said your mother is burning through money. That trip they took to Palm Beach—she paid for it. She even bought him a new car."

I'm taken aback by this. Still, none of my business. "She's enjoying her life. That's not a crime."

Missy takes a fry from my plate, a sign she's not thinking clearly. "Can't you run his record, or something?"

"No, I can't. It'd be a violation of CORI laws."

"Charlie saw Will at the Harvard Club, said he was wearing a Patek Philippe. I think it's the one your grandfather used to wear."

I'm getting more uncomfortable with each morsel of information, but I'm not getting involved. "The watch is hers to give."

"He's the reason she's drinking again. Charlie thinks he wants to impair her judgment so he can rob her blind."

That's where I draw the line. Taking advantage of my mother, preying on her weakness and vulnerability, is cause for interference. "I'll look into it."

Missy drives me home and when we pull up to my apartment, she asks to use the bathroom. Missy hasn't been inside my apartment yet, and I'm embarrassed to invite her upstairs, but I can't deny a pregnant women use of the facilities.

The front porch is dark. Either the stairs are more warped than when I left for work this morning, or I'm hyperaware of the shabbiness of my new home.

"Your bulb is out. Someone could trip and fall."

"Ty keeps promising to fix it."

I take Missy's elbow to be sure we don't have a mishap. We reach the top of the landing and I dig around the bottomless pit that is my tote, looking for my key. Suddenly, Missy screams.

I drop my tote and turn around. "What? What happened?"

Missy is speechless, staring at the bottom of the steps. Someone is there, in the darkness. It looks like a man—he's wearing a hoodie, pulled tightly around his face, exposing only his eyes. His hands are gloved and he's brandishing a knife—sharp and shiny, with about a four-inch blade. We both freeze. He lunges toward us.

The man grabs Missy and holds the metal to her throat. "Don't do anything stupid."

I stand, throw my hands in the air. "Don't hurt her. She's pregnant."

Missy starts to hyperventilate. "Please, take my money." She drops her bag on the steps of the porch.

"Leave Moe alone." He waves the knife in the air.

I could take out my pepper spray, but that might make things worse. Ditto if I scream. And I can't run for help—that'd mean leaving Missy alone.

"I'm having contractions," she says.

The man isn't dissuaded. I lean against the wall, trying to press the doorbell with my elbow. The living room light is on, Ty must be upstairs. I've never heard our buzzer before, and I don't know if it's supposed to make a sound on this floor, or if it's broken.

Suddenly, liquid splashes onto the porch, trickles down the steps.

"My water broke."

The man lets go of Missy, pushes me up against the door.

"I have to get her to the hospital," I say.

As he grabs my throat, the door swings open, knocking into us. The man and I lose our balance. As we go down, I feel his knife plunge into me; first the cold metal, then the warmth of my own blood. I grab on to my left side, under my rib cage.

Ty comes out of the foyer. "What the hell is going on?"

Ty charges onto the porch, makes a grab for the knife, but the man takes off. I look over at Missy. She's holding on to the railing, trying to control her breathing. I look at my hand, red and sticky with blood.

"The baby is coming," she says.

"Get in the car," Ty says. "I'm taking you both to the hospital."

Chapter Forty-Eight

I sit in the back of Ty's Corolla. Missy is next to me, lying with her head in my lap. As soon as Ty starts the engine, we get into an argument about which hospital we should go to. He wants to go to the closest emergency room, St. Elizabeth's. I have nothing against the hospital. I've been to the emergency room a few times to visit victims, but Missy had planned to have her baby in the Mass General. That's where her doctor is. The least I can do is get her there safely. Missy is screaming and sweating, and for the first time since I've known her, she's almost swearing.

"Call Charlie and tell him to meet us at the freakin' Mass General," she says.

Ty gives in and veers on Storrow Drive. I call my brother, sparing him all but the most essential details.

"I'm on my way," he says.

When I hang up, I yell at Ty, "It's your fault."

"My fault?"

"I told you to change that lightbulb."

Ty is having none of it. "This has nothing to do with the porch light. This is your fault. It's your job."

"Both of you—shut up!" Missy says. "The baby is coming."

Ty accelerates; he's driving so fast a police car pulls behind him and activates the light and siren.

"Don't slow down," I say.

"I have to or we'll have a police chase on our hands."

"Listen to me for once and drive."

I call 911 and tell the operator what's going on. She radios the cruiser, tells us to let him pass, and he leads us to the emergency room. As soon as we arrive, Missy is rushed to the delivery room.

A nurse points to my side. "What happened?"

"Nothing."

"Your blouse is wet with blood."

I look down at the stain. "Oh, I was stabbed."

"That's definitely not nothing."

She has a point. She gets me on a gurney, pulls up my shirt, and takes a look. "It's not too deep. You're lucky."

I don't feel lucky. Ty holds my hand as she cleans the wound and summons a doctor, who stitches me up.

"I'm sorry," I say to Ty as soon as they're done. "I never should have said that. It wasn't your fault."

He kisses me on the forehead. "Your parents are right, you should quit your job."

"That's not what I need to hear right now."

"It's exactly what you need to hear."

We sit in silence for a while, waiting for Charlie to arrive. I close my eyes and pretend to doze off, until Ty nudges me.

"You have a visitor. I'm going to see how Missy is doing."

I don't have to ask who it is—I can tell by Ty's tone it's Kevin.

"I haven't even reported it yet," I say. "How did you know I was here?"

"I don't sell shoes for a living."

Ty and Kevin exchange a quick handshake, then Ty disappears.

"You should rethink your career path," Kevin says.

"Not you too."

He looks at his watch.

"You're due in court in a few hours. I'll go tell the judge what happened and ask for a continuance."

"I don't need a continuance."

I sit up, slowly. The pain is sharper than I had anticipated. I flinch.

Kevin clocks it. "Ouch."

"I'm fine," I lie. "I want to go upstairs and meet my niece."

"You have to file a report. You were attacked and stabbed. And the assault was probably funded by Moe."

"Later. There's no rush. I can't ID the guy—none of us can. It was dark and his face was obscured."

Kevin knows this isn't an argument he can win. "I'll get you a wheelchair."

I ignore him, hobble to the elevator on my own. My side feels like it's burning. Kevin follows me down the hallway, pushing an empty wheelchair. I ignore his plea to sit down. When I get on the elevator car, he abandons the chair and joins me.

Chapter Forty-Nine

Kevin and I stand in the doorway of Missy's room, unnoticed. Missy is in bed, hugging the most adorable baby I've ever seen. Charlie is sitting on the side of the bed, admiring his new family. My parents are there, sans Will, and Ty is explaining what happened.

"Why won't you go in there? Are you afraid of your family?" Kevin says.

"I'll take a gangster over my angry family any day of the week."

He touches my arm, looks me in the eye. "See you in court."

"You're not supposed to leave your partner on the battlefield."

I enter the room quietly; the area around my wound stings when I drop into a chair. I release a quiet moan. No one looks over. I sit and listen to the sounds of dysfunction.

Missy: "We're naming her Joy."

My mother: "Did you say Joy? Did she just say Joy?"

Ty: "Yes, she did. I think it's beautiful."

My father: "It certainly is unusual."

My brother: "Her middle name is Elizabeth, after grandmother. Joy Elizabeth Endicott."

My father: "What about Elizabeth Joy?"

My mother: "What about Eleanor, after my side of the family?"

229

There's a tap on the door.

"Knock, knock," Will says.

Will enters, carrying a bouquet of wilted carnations. He probably got them from the guy who sells them out of a plastic bucket in front of CVS. Missy and Charlie exchange looks.

My mother races over and accepts the flowers. "How lovely." Her chirpy delight over a bunch of cheap flowers is proof positive she's not in her right mind.

She looks over and acknowledges me for the first time. "Abigail, please get a vase. They might have one at the nurses' station."

I ignore the command. "I wanted to meet my goddaughter, but I can't stay. Congratulations, she's beautiful."

Missy and Charlie don't look at me or acknowledge my presence. I guess I deserve it.

"I'll walk out with you," Ty says.

As Ty says his goodbyes, no one even looks in my direction. The elevator is crowded, relieving us of the burden of having to speak to each other. Downstairs in the lobby, Ty starts to walk to the parking garage.

"It'll be quicker if I walk to the courthouse," I say.

"You're not going to work. There's blood on your shirt."

"I have to. Rebecca will be there."

He leaves without pressing further. When I arrive at the courthouse, Moe is seated on the bench outside the courtroom. I ignore him, find Anthony, and then ask the clerk to see the judge. Anthony and I wait outside his chambers.

"Didn't you wear that suit yesterday?" Anthony says.

"I was attacked last night. By someone who wants me to drop the charges against your client."

Anthony eyes the bloody evidence of my assault. "Sorry to hear it. Did they get the guy?"

"Tell Moe I'm not backing down. I'm going to nail his ass."

"Look, Abby, I hope you're okay, but we can't be held responsible for the acts of crazy fans."

"Moe is behind this and we're going to prove it."

"Sounds like another baseless accusation."

The door to the judge's lobby opens and Judge Levine motions us inside. "I know it's not proper to comment on a woman's appearance, but you don't look well."

"I don't feel well. I need a one-day continuance."

Surprisingly, Anthony doesn't object, which makes me wonder what he's up to.

"If you bring in your witness, Ms. Maddox, I'll recognize her and order her to be here tomorrow," Judge Levine says.

Outside in the hallway, a couple of jurors straggle in, but there's no sign of Rebecca. Kevin gets off the elevator. I expect to see Rebecca with him, but he's alone.

"Where is she?" I say.

"I went to pick her up this morning, but she wasn't there. Rebecca Maddox is among the missing."

Chapter Fifty

Rebecca is nowhere to be found. Her home in Cohasset is dark and a FedEx delivery from yesterday is sitting on the back porch. We ask the local police to do a safety sweep of the house, and when they're done, they report there's no sign of a struggle. That's little comfort. Rebecca could have been abducted in the driveway or someplace else.

She's not answering her phone so we track down her *namaste* nanny at a Mindfulness-Based Harmonica retreat at the Kripalu Center in Stockbridge. The yogi tells us she's tied up in a purposeful-breathing session, but he'll relay the message. As soon as she's done, Holly returns our call.

"Do you know where Rebecca and the baby are?" I say.

"I don't work there anymore."

"She fired you?"

"Not exactly. She can't afford to pay me."

The connection is staticky, I'm not sure I heard correctly. "She doesn't have enough money to pay your salary?"

"She told me she's going to lose the house."

There's nothing wrong with the connection. Turns out, Rudy left Rebecca in bigger debt than we realized. He was making millions but he was spending a lot more. I apologize for interrupting

Holly's retreat and she promises to contact me if she hears from Rebecca.

"Where do you think she is?" I say.

"I'm not sold on the idea of a kidnapping," Kevin says. "Someone could have disappeared her, but it's more than likely she disappeared herself."

"Do you know if they have a summer house? Or a winter place?"

"Negative."

"Then we should check out Rudy's apartment in Weymouth. She probably knows about it. That's where I'd hide."

"You wouldn't last ten minutes at that dump," Kevin says.

An hour later, Kevin and I are at the door. The walls are thin enough to hear a baby's cries coming from inside the apartment.

"Bingo," Kevin says.

We knock, and after a little back-and-forth, Rebecca opens the door and invites us in.

"I'm sorry I subpoenaed you to testify, and I know you feel sandbagged, but I had to make a judgment call," I say.

"She's my sister. She's blood."

"Remember, she's protecting the man who killed your husband."

The baby starts to wail. Rebecca picks her up, but she's inconsolable. Rebecca starts to lose it too. She stands, passes me the baby. "Please, hold her."

I take the baby, who is kicking and drooling on my jacket. I hold her on my shoulder, walk around, rubbing her on the back. She burps, then barfs all over my suit and my hair.

"Sorry about that," Rebecca says.

"Anything for the cause."

She takes the baby and hands me a wet cloth, which only increases the size of the stain.

"Did Moe offer you money to hide from us?" I say.

Rebecca doesn't respond.

"How much did he offer?" Kevin says.

"When the case is over, he's going to set up a trust fund."

"You can't rely on that."

"I don't have a choice. I'm broke."

"He's made a lot of empty promises to a lot of people. When he's convicted, we can get court-ordered restitution," I say. "They can freeze his bank accounts."

"I can't wait that long." Rebecca looks at her baby. "Please, leave us alone."

"Did he threaten you?" Kevin says.

She walks to the kitchen, pours herself a glass of water. I'll take that as a yes.

"Is Cecilia afraid of him too?" I say.

"I think so."

"We'll find you a safe place to live," Kevin says.

"I'm not going into witness protection."

I try to convince her to cooperate but decide not to force her. I know what it feels like to be afraid, and I know Moe is capable of making good on his threat. Plus, I know it won't do any good. She'll disappear again, or worse, she'll take the stand and damage my case even further. I'll have to figure out another plan.

When I return to the office, I spend the rest of the day preparing to cross-examine Moe. It's no guarantee he'll take the stand—he doesn't have to testify, and he doesn't have to tell me what he's going to do—but I have to be ready.

The next day, I file a motion to revoke Moe's bail.

"He threatened my key witness," I say. "And I have reason to believe he attempted to threaten me."

I explain what happened on my front porch. Anthony lets out a groan and jumps to his feet. "There's no evidence my client had anything to do with it. It's an inflammatory, baseless allegation."

"Do you have any reasonable reason to believe you are in jeopardy?" Judge Levine says.

I start to tear up, check myself. "Two years ago, a member of my office was gunned down by a man he was prosecuting."

I don't have to explain further. Even Judge Levine won't dispute the horror of what happened to Tim Mooney. No jurist wants that type of incident on his or her watch.

"Deputies, take Mr. Morrissey into custody," Judge Levine says.

"Hold on," Moe says.

The deputies look at each other, as though they're unsure about whom they answer to—the judge or the all-star.

"There's no basis for bail revocation," Anthony says.

"The trial is almost over," the judge says. "If he's acquitted, he'll be released."

The deputies apologize to Moe but they do as they're told. Moe is cuffed and removed from the courtroom. Suddenly, it feels as if being attacked outside my home, seeing my sister-in-law almost lose her baby, was kind of worth it.

Chapter Fifty-One

Kevin and I go back to the lab to double-check the security tapes of Moe's home, focusing on the backyard and the driveway. We come up empty. If Moe passed a gun to Cecilia, he must have done it outside the range of the cameras.

"If you can tap-dance for a few more days, I'll figure something out," Kevin says.

"I've got nothing left. The judge is going to issue a directed verdict and dismiss the case."

Kevin starts to shut down the monitor.

"Not so fast," I say. "I'm going to queue up the video to the day before Rudy went missing."

Kevin and I sit in front of the screen, squinting, until we want to rip our eyes out. I get a splitting headache, but we finally find what we're looking for. Kevin takes a screenshot—the image is fuzzy and the gun is blurry, but there's no mistaking what's going on. It's Moe and he's holding a gun.

"Now all I have to do is figure out how to get it into evidence," I say.

"He's standing outside his house. With what could be the murder weapon. It's relevant—even to this lefty liberal judge."

"It's relevant to us, but that doesn't mean it's admissible. I need someone who can authenticate it. Someone who can say that it's

237

a fair and accurate representation. And I have to be able to tie it to the murder."

"Work your magic."

When court reconvenes, I'm excited to show the picture of Moe with the gun. I set up the projector and smile as Moe is escorted into the courtroom. The court officers remove his shackles, the judge takes the bench, and the jury is brought in.

"I'd like to offer a photograph, taken from one of the surveillance tapes in Moe Morrissey's home."

Anthony stands to object. "We already established there's nothing of value on the tapes."

"The tapes are blank on the days Rudy and Wayne were murdered, and I'd submit that's evidence of the defendant's consciousness of guilt."

"Do you have proof that the defendant erased them?" Judge Levine says.

"No, but I have something better. There is important evidence from earlier in the week."

I struck a nerve with that one. For the first time since he took this case, Anthony looks unsure. "I haven't . . . I don't . . . she didn't."

"Come on up here." Judge Levine motions us up to sidebar.

Anthony keeps an eye on Moe, who walks slowly. Moe seems unfocused and has to stop at my table to gain his balance. When they step in front of the bench, I show them the still photograph, pulled from the security video. I can tell they've been dreading this moment and I couldn't be more delighted. Anthony takes a long look at the picture. He clasps his hands, purses his lips.

"It looks like a gun," Judge Levine says.

"It's relevant and admissible," I say.

"Not unless you can prove it's the murder weapon," Anthony says. "Otherwise it's irrelevant and inflammatory."

"Can you prove it's the murder weapon?" the judge says.

"I don't have to." I realize that sounds a little bossy, even for me, so I rein myself in. "Respectfully, case law, directly on point, states that if the weapon could have been used to commit the crime, we don't have to prove that it was the actual weapon."

I give the judge the citations, and he pulls the cases from the books behind him. When he's done reading and rereading, he looks disappointed by what he's found. "She does have a point."

"This is an unfair surprise," Anthony says.

I speak quickly, before the judge rules against me. "One more thing."

I signal Kevin, who walks up to the front of the courtroom, holding a shiny, new .357 Magnum. Being this close to a firearm, even though I know it's not loaded, brings back memories of the night I was almost shot. I can almost hear the deafening sound of a bullet being ejected.

"What the hell is this?" Anthony says.

"I'd like to show this firearm to the jury," I say. "It's for demonstrative purposes. So they can see what the murder weapon looked like."

A camera snaps as I take the weapon from Kevin's steady hands.

"I'm not going to let you play the speculation game," Judge Levine says. "If you can't find the actual murder weapon, then I don't want to hear about it again."

Moe blurts out, "They're never going to find it."

Anthony grabs his arm to quiet him and tries to deflect: "That's because only the killer, Paul Tagala, knows where it is."

My motion is denied, but I made my point. Hopefully, the jury got a peek at the .357. When we adjourn for the day, I find Kevin in the hallway.

"Moe was a mess in there," I say.

"He's afraid we're going to find the weapon."

"Which means it's hidden somewhere accessible."

"We checked his property with a fine-tooth comb."

"We searched the buildings, and the gardens, but we didn't check the woods."

That evening Kevin assembles another search team and we get a warrant. It doesn't allow us to go back in the house, but it authorizes us to check the grounds. Officers fan out with metal detectors. Canine cops bring in dogs. City engineers set up a pump to drain the lake.

As they scour every inch of those woods, I go home, prepare for the next day, keeping one eye on the phone. It doesn't ring. I fall asleep somewhere between 2:00 and 3:00 a.m. and wake up at 5:00 to the sound of my cell. I wipe the drool off my chin and check the screen. My heart sinks when I see Stan's name.

"If you lose this case, it's on you," he says.

"I know."

"The entire city will want your head on a platter. I told you, if you charge Moe Morrissey with a crime, you'd better be able to prove it."

I don't remember the warning but point taken.

"You know, if you lose, I'll have to fire you."

"Thanks for the pep talk. I appreciate the support."

I drag myself out of bed and into the shower. To give myself a treat, I find the free gel sample I got at the Saks cosmetics counter last month.

As I'm soaping up, Ty opens the bathroom door. "You have a visitor."

Ty's abrupt manner tells me it's not family, which means it can only be one person. I wrap myself in a towel, secure it by folding it under my armpit, and walk to the door. Clearly Ty didn't invite our visitor in for coffee; Kevin is waiting at the threshold to the apartment, holding his hands behind his back.

"I got something for you."

Kevin reveals a brown paper sack; he unfurls it and pulls out a plastic evidence bag. Inside is the most beautiful thing I've ever seen: a black semiautomatic .357 Magnum, caked in mud, smelling like swamp water. My fear of firearms is cured.

I'm so excited that I grab the bag and plant a kiss on Kevin's cheek. My hands are a little wet and the plastic almost slips through my fingers. I fumble with the bag, almost drop the weapon. I manage to save the gun, but my towel comes loose. I try to grab it but it falls to the floor, exposing me in the most embarrassing way. And at that exact moment, Ty walks in the room.

Chapter Fifty-Two

I walk into the courtroom slowly, carrying the brown paper bag as though it were a diamond tiara atop a purple velvet pillow. The press corps smiles, speculating, drawing their own conclusions about what I'm holding. Anthony pretends not to notice. Moe hasn't been brought up from the lockup yet and the jury box is empty.

At my request, the court officer ushers me and Anthony into the judge's chambers. We take seats in front of his desk.

I hold the evidence bag in my lap. "I'll cut to the chase. We found the proverbial smoking gun."

"You've got to be kidding," Anthony says.

I unfurl the top of the bag and let Anthony peek inside.

"Big deal, it's another gun."

"Ballistics test results were conducted this morning. We can prove this is the murder weapon."

Anthony clears his throat.

The judge asks the million-dollar question: "How are you going to tie it to the defendant?"

I fight the urge to smirk. "We found it on his property."

"Objection," Anthony says.

"Grounds?" Judge Levine says.

"It's prejudicial."

"Everything we present is prejudicial, that's the whole point," I say.

Anthony's voice is strained. "Someone could have planted it."

"You can argue that to the jury," I say.

Anthony keeps pressing. "It's a violation of the discovery rules. It should be suppressed."

"We didn't have it. And the reason we didn't have it is because your client hid it from us."

Judge Levine puts up his hand. He's heard enough. "I'm going to allow it. Go downstairs and talk with your client. See how much time you need to prepare for cross-examination."

Anthony goes downstairs to deliver the bad news to Moe. I find Kevin in the hallway. We walk in awkward silence to a conference room; neither of us wants to relive towelgate.

Kevin closes the door, raises his hand. "High five."

"Not yet. You know I'm superstitious."

We prep for Kevin's testimony about finding the gun, until the court officer calls us back into the courtroom.

"I don't want to keep the jury waiting any longer," the judge says. "Let's bring up the defendant and then break for the day so I can release the jurors."

The court officer goes down to get Moe and Anthony. He returns a few minutes later—alone. "We have a problem. Moe is down in the lockup, and he's refusing to come to the courtroom."

"Tell him it's not an invitation, it's an order," Judge Levine says.

"I think you oughta come down and see him for yourself."

Judge Levine gets off the bench and we all trudge down three flights of stairs to the holding cells. I've been here a couple of times to talk to witnesses, but usually I have the prisoners brought to me. In a communal cell are a half dozen men, all of whom look and smell like they could use a shower.

Moe is in his own cell, seated on the floor, head in hands. He looks disoriented. Anthony is standing over him.

"He just collapsed. He was sitting on the bench, eating a bologna sandwich, and then he dropped to the floor," Anthony says. "Moe, it's me, Anthony. Can you tell the judge what's going on?"

"Why is everything blurry?" Moe says.

"You've got to be kidding," I say.

"Do you hear that?" Moe says. "There's a buzzing noise. Like a bee."

"I think we should call 911," Anthony says.

"The room is spinning," Moe says.

"He's not injured," I say.

"He might need medical assistance," Judge Levine says.

The judge tells the court officer to unlock the cell and to help Moe to his feet. Moe stays on the ground, lets out a whimper.

"He's in distress," Anthony says.

Moe doesn't budge, mutters something about having a headache, feeling weak.

"I was afraid of this," Anthony says.

"Afraid of what? He was fine a couple of hours ago," I say.

"He's been putting up a good front, but he's been suffering. The symptoms have been intensifying."

I think I know where this is going, but ask the question. "Symptoms of what?"

Anthony crosses his arms, takes a beat. "Repetitive head trauma."

Even Judge Levine is skeptical. "That's for football players and boxers."

"New research is emerging," Anthony says. "Baseball players can get it too. Especially pitchers. He's been hit on the head by speeding balls more than a few times. You can check the video of his games."

"What do you suggest we do?" the judge says.

"I have no choice, I'm filing an insanity defense."

"Convenient," I say. "The defendant creates an illness at the exact moment his case falls apart."

"Not true," Anthony says. "He says he's been experiencing

blurred vision, poor balance, and, most importantly, impaired judgment for months, if not years. The symptoms have been getting worse since that blow to the head on opening day."

"The symptoms didn't starting showing up until he hired you as a lawyer," I say. "And they got worse after we found the murder weapon in his backyard."

"I'm not going to deprive a defendant his right to offer a defense," Judge Levine says. "This works out well for both of you. I'll give you a couple of days to prepare for both the gun evidence and the insanity defense."

The gun evidence will be moot if Moe prevails on his insanity claim. The focus won't be on guilt or innocence, the issue will be whether Moe is insane. And if the jury gives him a verdict of not guilty by reason of insanity, he won't be the only one with mental health issues.

Chapter Fifty-Three

There's no debating that chronic traumatic encephalopathy is serious. Athletes, particularly professional football players, are at risk for it. It can be debilitating and there is no known cure. Moe Morrissey does not suffer from it.

I should have seen this charade coming. As my case has grown stronger, Moe has been building his counterattack. His so-called blurred vision, problems with balance, alleged confusion. The dropped water glass was a nice touch. Anthony probably coached him, helped him lay the pipe, gave him the tools to carry it out. They chose the perfect mental defect. CTE often doesn't show up on scans, so the diagnosis is based on a report of symptoms. The condition can't be verified until after the patient dies, at the autopsy.

Any juror who has been in Moe's corner, searching for a reason to acquit, now has something to hold on to. And even if they don't buy it as an insanity defense, Anthony will give them an alternative—diminished capacity, which will lessen both the degree of murder and the length of the sentence.

I spend hours in my office, studying up on the medical aspects of the defense, becoming a quasi expert on the brain, but what I really need is something to prove Moe is malingering. His wife's not going to out him as a liar, and neither is Rebecca, so I have to figure out how to communicate that to the jury.

As I start to pack up for the night, I get a call from my brother Charlie. He hasn't spoken to me since the night Joy was born. No doubt he's still angry with me for putting everyone in danger—and I can't blame him. Once again, my job put my loved ones in jeopardy.

"Is everything okay?" I say.

"Missy and I are worried about Mom. She's not making rational decisions. We have to do something."

"She never listens to me."

"She will if you tell her Will has a police record."

"I checked, he's never been arrested."

"Probably because his victims are too embarrassed to press charges."

"You don't know there are victims."

"There's no way she's the first woman he's taken advantage of. Just lie to her, tell her Will has been charged with fraud before. She'll do anything to avoid a scandal."

"After my trial is over."

"Please don't let work take priority. You owe me one. And don't forget—the baptism is Sunday."

"You still want me to be the godmother?"

"Yes, of course, but promise you won't take her on a police ride-along until her sixteenth birthday."

"Promise."

"Call Mom." Charlie hangs up.

Charlie is right. I do owe him. I owe everyone. Besides, I'm worried about my mother too. I stop by the house on my way home from work. Our housekeeper lets me in.

"Is my mother home?"

"She's upstairs."

"Is Will Dorset with her?"

The housekeeper shakes her head and whispers, "He just left."

"Who is it? Who's there?" My mother's voice floats down two flights of stairs. "Will, is that you?"

"It's just me, Mother."

I find her upstairs in the library. She tilts her head but doesn't look up when I give her an obligatory kiss on the cheek.

"If you're here about Will, don't bother."

I select a wine from the silver tray. I know I shouldn't, but I need fortification. Before I pour myself a glass, I reconsider and put the bottle down.

My mother is quiet, thumbing through the latest issue of *Town & Country*, sipping a clear cocktail, probably straight gin, and definitely not her first for the evening.

"Fix me another, please."

"You haven't finished the one in your hand."

"Before you take my inventory, you might want to clean up your own side of the street."

She's drunk, quoting AA. This is testing my patience, but I'm here to help not judge.

"We're all worried about you," I say.

"I can stop drinking anytime I want."

"That's not what I'm talking about. You've taken up with a deadbeat."

"The same could be said of you. At least my deadbeat has a Harvard degree and a membership to the Union Club."

She's hoping that her insult will shut me up, but I know her games, and I'm not going to let her throw me. I came here on a mission, and I'm going to finish.

"He's run through all his money, and soon he'll run through all of yours."

"Darling, I know all about Will's financial situation."

That's a surprise. "Then why are you with him?"

She smiles, takes a sip of her cocktail.

"You're doing this to get to Daddy. Aren't you?"

"It'll get his attention. You'll see."

I knew she had a plan. She's clever, even when intoxicated. If this is a ploy to get my father back, then I'm all for it.

"Please don't take Will to the baptism. Let it be Charlie and Missy's day," I say on my way out the door.

When I arrive home, Ty is in the living room, watching TV. There's been so much tension between us lately—first because of the Mike Chase leak, and then because of the lightbulb and Missy. Tonight, however, I'm glad to see him.

"They've got all kinds of medical experts on CNN, talking about repetitive brain injury," he says.

I take a seat next to him and click off the television.

"I'm thinking about talking to my father about Will Dorset. It's getting out of hand. I'm afraid my mother is going to get hurt."

"He probably already knows. He hired a private eye to investigate me, and he did the same to Missy. My guess is he's fully investigated Dorset."

"She's only doing it to make him jealous."

Ty rubs my back, gives me a kiss. "Every couple's got their games."

I bury my head in his chest and well up with tears. I've put Ty through the wringer. He's not a cynic, at least he wasn't a cynic until he met me.

Chapter Fifty-Four

When court resumes, Moe agrees to come upstairs and join his lawyer at the defense table. He was probably getting tired of being alone in the dank cell. Plus, this way he can put on more of a show. He sits, slumped in his chair, and looks around the courtroom as though in a daze.

I try to ignore him, but everyone else seems more interested in Moe than my witnesses. When I call Kevin to the stand, I'm able to win back the attention of about half of the jurors—mostly the women. Kevin's wearing the tie I gave him last Christmas, and it brings out the blue in his eyes.

He testifies about the search of Moe's property, draining the lake, and finding the gun. The evidence goes in smoothly, but Anthony manages to do some damage on cross-examination.

"Anyone could have tossed the gun in that lake," Anthony says. "Especially if they wanted to frame Moe. Right?"

"I suppose."

"It could have been planted there last month, or last week."

"It could have."

"You didn't find any fingerprints on it."

"It was caked in mud."

"No DNA was recovered."

"We didn't expect to find anything of forensic value. The gun was dragged from the bottom of a lake."

"You can't prove my client even had knowledge that the weapon was there."

"It was on his property."

"It wasn't registered in his name."

"It wasn't registered in anyone's name. In my experience, people don't commit murder with a gun that can be traced back to them."

After the medical examiner testifies, I rest my case. Anthony kicks off the defense with a highlight reel of Moe on the mound. The video serves two purposes: it reminds the jury that Moe is a superstar, and it shows Moe getting hit on the side of the head with a baseball—twice. The first time was about a year before the murder; a fastball knocked him over when it whizzed into the side of his head. The second time was on the day Rudy went missing; I witnessed that one in person.

I can't cross-examine a videotape, so I remain seated. Anthony moves on to his first witness: Dr. Jane Davidson. I had to tell him about Jane as part of the discovery process. I knew he'd use her to muddy up my victim, make Rudy out to be a cheater and a drug user, but I didn't have a choice. Jane testifies that she's suffered as a result of her involvement with Rudy. She lost her medical license and was humiliated in the press, and her husband filed for divorce. I don't ask any questions on cross, and she seems grateful when the judge excuses her. I'm glad Rebecca wasn't here to hear her testimony.

The next defense witness is Jeffrey Messinger, Harvard-educated psychiatrist. The defense goes on the offense.

"People with brain injuries of this nature often don't recognize, or admit to the symptoms, until they've developed into advanced stages. Then, it's usually too late," Dr. Messinger says.

"And it can only be diagnosed postmortem?" Anthony says.

Messinger nods. "Currently, degenerative brain disease, chronic traumatic encephalopathy, can only be definitively diagnosed as part of an autopsy."

"Is there a link between chronic traumatic encephalopathy and sports?"

"Yes."

"Violent, uncontrollable behavior and lack of impulsivity control can be among the symptoms," Anthony says. "Right?"

"Yes."

"Sometimes the behavior mirrors that of schizophrenia."

"It can."

"And if my client suffers from the condition, it would be impossible for him to comport his behavior in accordance with the law."

"Objection!" I say. "Calls for speculation."

"Overruled," Judge Levine says.

"I believe he would have difficulty understanding the wrongfulness of his actions and being able to comport himself in accordance with the law," Dr. Messinger says.

"In your medical opinion, does Mr. Morrissey suffer from CTE?" Anthony says.

"I can't say for sure until he has been autopsied, which hopefully won't be for many decades, but he does exhibit many of the symptoms."

Anthony sits. I stand. Stan helped me prepare my cross. Finally, he brings something to the table. Before being named DA, Stan was a forensic psychologist, a profiler for the FBI.

"Moe Morrissey's so-called symptoms are all self-reported," I say.

"That doesn't make them any less real," Dr. Messinger says.

"No objective tests back up his claims."

"Not yet."

"These so-called injuries didn't show up on any scans."

"That's not unusual."

"It's convenient, don't you think, that the defendant didn't develop the symptoms until we found the murder weapon, in his own backyard?"

"Objection," Anthony says.

"Sustained," Judge Levine says. "The jury will disregard that comment."

"He could be malingering," I say.

"As I understand it, that's your burden to prove, not mine."

I'd like to cut my losses and sit down, but a couple of jurors are chuckling at my expense.

I have to fight back. "How much are you being paid for your testimony?"

"I'm paid for my time, not my testimony."

"How much are you charging Moe Morrissey?"

"Eleven hundred dollars an hour."

That could cut both ways. Some jurors will think he's expensive and, therefore, worth it. Hopefully, others will see him for what he is—a hired gun.

"Is this the first time you've ever seen a baseball player with this type of diagnosis?"

"Yes."

"Nothing further."

Anthony stands. "This diagnosis is more common among boxers, isn't it?"

"Yes."

"Moe Morrissey was a boxer in high school, wasn't he?"

"Yes, he was."

"He was hit in the head countless times."

"That's what I've been told."

"And the baseball hits could have made it all worse."

"Most definitely."

As if that isn't enough, Anthony cues the projector and shows a series of photographs of Moe in a boxing ring, getting punched in the head. It's contrived, but judging by jurors' expressions, effective.

Next, Anthony calls Moe's high school coach, then a sports doctor, and then an engineer. He pulls out all the stops. He even brings in the CEO of the company that manufactures the baseballs and a physicist to talk about dimensions and weight. He wants to show that baseballs are like missiles, able to inflict serious bodily harm.

When court breaks for the night, Kevin helps me carry my trial boxes out to the Plaza, where his car is parked. It's a short walk, but I can't face the media. Reporters are doing live shots and I don't want to be put on the spot.

Kevin stashes my boxes in the backseat while I climb in the car, keeping my head down. Emma Phelps sees us and runs over to my window.

"What makes you so sure he's not telling the truth?" The camera is pointed at me, so the viewers can't see the smirk on her face.

"If this were a legitimate diagnosis, he'd have offered it before the trial," I say, "not after he started losing."

Kevin pulls away before I say anything more. "Don't let her get to you. The jurors will see through the nonsense."

"Someone really screwed up my case."

"How so?"

"If he hadn't leaked the information about Mike Chase, I'd be able to use the ammunition found in Moe's car. And the jury would know that the bullets matched the murder weapon. That'd help us prove premeditation, and lack of insanity."

Kevin parks the car. I unclip my seat belt but he remains still.

"I think Ty did it," I say. "He denied it, but we're the only ones who were there. I don't know who else would have reported it."

Kevin takes a breath. "Ty didn't leak that information."

"What makes you so sure?"

"Because I know who did."

"Who?"

"Me."

I laugh, until I realize he's serious. "You torpedoed our case?"

"That wasn't my intention but someone had to out the guy."

"I was planning to do it. Afterwards."

"I guess I beat you to the punch."

Chapter Fifty-Five

Kevin was the leak. I never saw it coming. I have to apologize to Ty for accusing him, and even worse, I have to tell him it was Kevin. He's working tonight at the Regattabar, so I call him to see if he can have dinner before he heads to his gig. I offer to meet him in Cambridge, near the club.

Henrietta's Table in the Charles Hotel is the logical choice. It's one flight down from where he'll be playing, and it has the most comforting comfort food—Yankee pot roast. They don't serve dinner, they serve supper, as if that makes the artisanal cheeses and homemade sorbets any less precious.

When I arrive, Ty is waiting at the table, sipping ice water.

"Anything to drink?" the waiter says.

"Just water," I say.

Nonalcoholic beverages seem like the best way to go. The waiter takes our food orders. As soon as he's gone, I change my mind, flag him down, and order a glass of wine. It's been a rough week. I'll think about my alcohol consumption another time.

I tear off a piece of cranberry nut bread, smear butter on it, and take a bite.

"I shouldn't have accused you of lying to me."

Ty meets my eyes. "I know."

"Turns out, Kevin released the information."

"How did Kevin know?"

It's a rhetorical question, but I feel compelled to fess up to what I did. "I told him."

"After you made me promise I wouldn't tell anyone."

The waiter puts a wineglass in front of me. I put my fingers on the stem, but don't pick it up. I know what Ty is thinking.

"Nothing has ever happened between me and Kevin."

"Yet."

Another sign of cynicism from Ty. I feel like I've corrupted him. He was so perfect when we first met—trusting, patient, calming. We lock eyes.

"You have no reason to be jealous."

"I can see where it's going and I don't like it. You wouldn't like it if I spent that much time with another woman."

He has a point. I've been pretty dismissive of his concerns. Maybe I need to make more of an effort to put Ty's mind at ease.

I reach across the table and take his hand. "Kevin and I had a talk a few months ago. You don't have anything to worry about."

That definitely didn't have the intended effect. Ty pulls his hand away, takes a gulp of water.

"Don't you think that's kind of weird—that you two had to discuss it?"

I take a breath. I don't know how to diffuse this. "Are you saying you don't want me to work with him anymore?"

"That's not what I said."

"Then what?"

"It's just something to think about."

"Duly noted."

When the food arrives, I push it around on my plate. The pot roast is rich and tender. The mashed potatoes look creamy. I take a forkful of both, then lose interest. Ty bites into his roasted chicken and changes the subject, and I'm relieved that we can move on.

Ty moves the conversation to a tried-and-true subject. "How's your trial?"

"I could use some witnesses."

A couple at the next table pose for a selfie, which normally annoys me, but tonight it gives me an idea. As soon as we're done eating, and Ty gets ready to go upstairs for his gig, I give him the car key and tell him where it's parked.

"I'll Uber home."

After he's gone, I look at the Uber app on my phone and see that there's a car two minutes away. Instead I call Kevin.

"Can you pick me up in Cambridge?"

I can hear his wife in the background. "Who are you talking to? Is that Abby? Again?"

I guess she's not happy with our relationship either.

"We were just getting ready to turn in," he says. "What do you got?"

"Jail cells in the courthouse have security cameras."

"I know."

"Anthony talked to Moe in his cell, ergo—"

"I don't speak French."

"*Ergo* is Latin. It means 'therefore,' as in therefore, when Anthony went down to talk to Moe, they were recorded. We need to find the tape."

Kevin puts his hand over the receiver but I can still hear him. "Hon, I'm going to have to go out and deliver a subpoena."

Not exactly true, but close enough. I can't hear exactly what Kevin's wife says in response, but I can tell by the hushed tone she's not happy with the news.

Chapter Fifty-Six

Kevin and I scour the video of the courthouse cells, paying particular attention to the time between Kevin's testimony about the gun and Moe's pseudobreakdown. We watch the play-by-play, hitting the pause button frequently. We see a court officer let Anthony into the cell. He sits on the bench and talks to Moe. They huddle for a few minutes. Then, Anthony stands and walks with an exaggerated limp; it's a demonstration. Moe imitates him for a few steps. Anthony talks as Moe plops down on the bench, drops his head in his hands. Anthony puts his arm around Moe's shoulder, encouraging him. All they need is a wad of chewing tobacco—then it would look exactly like a coach talking to a player in the dugout.

"We struck gold," I say. "Anthony is teaching Moe how to fake the symptoms."

"That's sleazy, even for a defense attorney."

"It's more than sleazy. It's suborning perjury."

"We can have two defendants for the price of one."

As much as I'd like to stick it to Anthony, I'm not going to take out a perjury complaint against him. It could be grounds for a mistrial in this case and I don't want to have to try it again. Retrials never benefit the prosecution. Memories fade, evidence gets lost, and witnesses start to contradict themselves.

When court resumes the next morning, Anthony rests his defense. Moe eyes the jurors; some look back with sympathetic smiles and understanding nods.

"Anything else from the Commonwealth?" Judge Levine says.

"Yes, we have a rebuttal witness."

"I haven't been given notice," Anthony says.

"We became aware of new information as a direct result of the defendant's newfound medical condition."

The judge calls us up to sidebar.

"I'd like to play a video," I say.

"What's on it?" the judge says.

I deliver a summary of Moe's coaching session. Anthony's face starts to redden—from both anger and shame. Still he remains sharp. He knows what's coming and tries to stop it.

"Objection. These conversations are protected by attorney-client privilege."

"There are no conversations, there is no audio," I say.

"It's still a consultation. And it's protected."

"He does have a point," the judge says.

"There is no expectation of privacy. It's an open space. Anyone could walk by."

"It's a private jail cell. We're out of hearing distance. There's no one in the vicinity."

"Let me see the tape," Judge Levine says.

The judge calls a recess and retreats to his chambers. He's in there for over an hour, probably calling his pals and trying to figure out a way to suppress the tape. In spite of all the evidence, he's still rooting for Moe.

Kevin and I wait in the conference room.

"If we get a not guilty, I'm going to indict Anthony for conspiracy to commit perjury," I say.

"We're going to get a conviction."

I wish I had Kevin's confidence. "The jurors love Moe, even now."

I start to think about all the flaws in the case, working myself into a full-blown panic attack, until the court officer summons us back. I take a few shallow breaths until I can get a full inhale and exhale, then walk to the prosecutor's table.

"I've made my decision." The judge clears his throat, as though what he's going to say pains him and he wants to delay it, which I take as a positive sign. "I am going to allow the tape into evidence."

I want to do the Snoopy dance but restrain myself.

"Before you start your rebuttal," the judge says, "does the defense have any more witnesses to present?"

"Mr. Morrissey would like to take the stand on his own behalf," Anthony says.

We've backed Moe into a corner. My guess is he wasn't planning to testify; Anthony would have advised him to remain silent. Opening himself to cross-examination when he doesn't have to would be a bad move. But now that we have the tape, he has some explaining to do.

"We'd pray Your Honor's indulgence. Can we have the night to prepare?" Anthony says.

"Any objection?" the judge says.

There are a couple of hours left in the day, and normally I'd object and force the issue. I don't want to give Anthony time to sharpen his assault, but I could use the extra time.

"No objection," I say.

"Fine, we'll adjourn," Judge Levine says. "Tomorrow we'll hear testimony, we'll play the video, and then we'll go right into closing arguments."

The judge excuses the jury and we recess for the day. The pressure is on. For Anthony. For Moe. And for me.

Chapter Fifty-Seven

Bulfinch is a secure building. Nonemployees can get on the elevator in the lobby, but access is limited to the second-floor reception area; beyond that, the elevators and stairwells are locked. Receptionists sit behind bulletproof glass; visitors check in and have to supply a photo ID, and someone escorts them to the meeting place. Usually, my assistant, Amber, greets my visitors and brings them up to my office.

Amber knocks on my office door and pops in. "Moe Morrissey's lawyer is in reception. His fiancée . . . I mean wife . . . Cecilia is here too."

"What do they want?"

Amber shrugs, applies a fresh coat of lip gloss—as though being one degree of separation from Moe requires beautification.

"Want me to go down and get them?"

"I need to handle this one. Call Kevin and ask him to come by."

The reception area is jammed. I have to elbow my way off the elevator and through the crowd. Cecilia is seated; Anthony stands by her side. They're surrounded by a motley crew of visitors and employees. Everyone in the city has been following the trial on TV; Cecilia was already recognizable from her modeling days, and Anthony has become a minor celebrity in his own right. I've never been in a mosh pit, but this is how I imagine it starts.

I push my way past a couple of organized-crime detectives who are giving Anthony their take on this year's rookies.

"Let's go up to my office," I say.

On our way to the elevator, a drug dealer takes out his cell phone and asks for a selfie with Cecilia. With little choice, she leans in and forces a smile. An assault victim with a bandage covering her forehead and three missing teeth Instagrams a photo. A prosecutor from the gang unit holds out a slimy, chewed-up pen and asks for an autograph. I grab the pen and throw him a nasty look.

I escort Anthony and Cecilia to the conference room and tell them I'm going to wait for Kevin. Without him, it's two against one—I need a witness to the conversation in case there's any dispute about what is said. I close the blinds to keep away the lookie-loos and leave them alone.

Kevin and I devise a game plan on the phone. We assume Moe wants to plea. We agree that the best plan is to listen but not to make any promises. When Kevin arrives a few minutes later, we begin the meeting.

"I'm going to cut to the chase," Anthony says. "Moe needs help."

"You didn't have to come all this way to tell me that," I say. "He can get all the help he needs in state prison."

Kevin throws me a look. So much for my listening without comment.

"He needs medical help," Cecilia says.

"You're gonna have to be more specific," I say. "What are you asking for?"

"He'll plea to manslaughter," Anthony says. "Give him six years."

He can't be serious. "That comes out to three years for each murder," I say.

Kevin breaks his silence. "With good time, he'll practically be out on parole next Tuesday."

"He's sick and he needs medical care," Cecilia says. "Where's your humanity?"

"He'll agree to check in to a locked rehab facility," Anthony says.

"Not going to happen," I say. "Not on my watch."

"I wouldn't be so quick to turn it down." Anthony's smiling, signaling he's got something up his Thom Browne shirtsleeve.

"Why's that?" I say.

"We came here to reason with you, but you're forcing me to play hardball. You withheld exculpatory evidence. Detective Chase—you knew all about his prior incident and you didn't report it. You could be sanctioned if anyone finds out."

My heart starts to race. I put my hand over my mouth to cover my reaction.

Kevin steps in. "I know you're not trying to blackmail a prosecutor because you're too smart for that."

"I'm just stating a fact."

"I knew about Chase," Kevin says. "If anyone is going to get in hot water, it should be me."

This isn't the first time Kevin has stepped in front of a bullet that was intended for me.

I can't let him take the hit. "I knew and I was planning to disclose. In the meantime, I didn't put Mike Chase on the witness list, so there was nothing to disclose. We didn't offer the bullets into evidence. It wasn't an issue."

"That's for the judge to decide," Anthony says.

No defense attorney is going to strong-arm me into a plea. I'd rather be disbarred than give Moe Morrissey one less day in prison. Kevin shows them the door and walks with me to my office.

"I have no one to blame but myself," I say.

"Don't beat yourself up over this. You did what you thought was right for the case."

"I have a higher duty."

"God?"

"Justice."

Chapter Fifty-Eight

For the first time since I've known him, Anthony beats me to court. When I arrive, he's all smiles. Nothing gets a defense attorney more excited than an allegation of prosecutorial misconduct—except maybe a not guilty on a double murder rap.

Judge Levine is running late. I make good use of the time, eating chocolate and developing a migraine. By the time he calls us into his chambers, I've taken two aspirins and bitten my lip so hard, I need a tissue to blot the blood.

Anthony uses the strategy he prefers when negotiating a plea—asking for twice what he expects to get. "The defense moves for a mistrial with prejudice."

"Denied." Fortunately, Judge Levine doesn't want to start the trial all over again either.

"Disclosure would not have impacted the outcome of the trial," I say as if some random ADA were involved. "The defense knew about the allegations and we did not call the detective as a witness."

"It's a violation of the rules of discovery," Anthony says. "You knew before it hit the papers."

"We revealed the substance of the information." I'm not going down without a fight.

"The trial is going to continue," the judge says.

I unclench my jaw, take a breath, until—

"But I am going to instruct the jury of the violation."

This is almost worse than a mistrial. The jury won't understand that this was a technical violation of the rules. They'll think I'm a liar. Credibility is a prosecutor's currency. Without it, I'm just another lawyer.

As soon as the jury is seated, Judge Levine delivers the bad news. "Ms. Endicott withheld a critical piece of evidence from the defense. I am instructing you that you can hold it against her during your deliberations."

There's a lilt in his voice, as though he's soothed by the promise of antiprosecution sentiment. A few jurors shift in their seats. Others won't meet my eyes. I'm screwed.

On the heels of my admonishment, Moe takes the stand—literally—as if he owns it. His posture, his self-confidence—he might as well be on the mound, hurling a fastball, in the middle of a no-hitter. He denies any conspiracy with Tags. He says he learned about the murder like everyone else. If Tags did it, he should be punished.

Then Anthony tosses him some softballs.

"Did you kill Rudy or Wayne?"

"They were my teammates, my friends, my family." As Moe speaks, he pauses to look each juror in the eye.

"Nothing further," Anthony says.

I'm on my feet before Anthony has gathered his papers from the podium.

"Then why was the gun on your property?" I say.

"You'll have to ask Paul Tagala. He must have tried to hide it there. He had access to my land, was over at the house all the time."

He's using my theory of the case against me. Anthony did a good job prepping him.

"Mr. Tagala had no motive to kill, other than the fact that you paid him."

Anthony jumps up to prevent Moe from answering. "Objection. Ms. Endicott is stating facts not in evidence."

Technically that's not the proper objection. He could have complained that the question called for speculation or a conclusion, or that it was badgering—but he's trying to further disparage me. And by the scowls on the jurors' faces, it's working.

"Sustained," Judge Levine says.

"It was your gun, wasn't it?" I say.

"No."

"Paul Tagala returned the gun to you."

"Is that a question?" Anthony says.

I don't need to hear the judge's ruling. Some witnesses are impossible to trip up, and Moe is one of them.

"Withdrawn," I say. "Nothing further."

As I move toward my table, I hear a screech and a loud thud from the witness box. Moe has fallen off his chair. Court officers rush to his side. The jurors stand to get a better look. He appears to lose consciousness for a minute. It's an act, but he's a performer, especially in the clutch.

"Mr. Morrissey," Judge Levine says, "are you okay?"

Moe opens his eyes, rolls over onto his knees, and the court officers hoist him to his feet.

"I'm sorry, Your Honor," Moe says. "I don't know what happened."

Perfect timing. His lawyer doesn't need to redirect him because Moe just testified. He said, *Remember I have a medical condition. Remember to feel sorry for me.*

When Anthony stands to rest his case, I make sure the jury knows I'm not ready to throw in the towel.

"The Commonwealth has a rebuttal witness."

The accountant in the jury box looks at me, almost disappointed, as if she was ready to vote not guilty and I've foiled her plan.

I recall Kevin to the stand so he can describe the circumstances surrounding the video of Moe and Anthony in the lockup. Then I hit *play*. Everyone watches as Anthony coaches Moe, and Moe hobbles around the cell.

"Nothing further," I say.

Kevin stands, to get off the stand, but Anthony stops him. "I have a few questions."

Anthony doesn't move to the podium, opting to stay at the defense table. He leans in and whispers to Moe. Anthony's up to something.

"Detective Farnsworth, you have no idea what I just said to my client, do you?"

"No, I don't."

"I could have said, 'How are you feeling?' "

"Sure."

"I could have said, 'Everyone knows you're not guilty.' "

I'm on my feet. "Objection."

Anthony doesn't wait for a ruling. "I could have said, 'The jurors are too smart to fall for the prosecutor's cheap antics.' "

"Your Honor!" I say.

"Sustained," Judge Levine says.

Too little, too late.

"Likewise," Anthony says, "you couldn't tell what my client said to me, could you?"

"Correct," Kevin says.

"He could have been discussing his symptoms."

"I don't know what he was saying."

"Exactly. You're showing the jury a video and you want them to believe it's incriminating, but you can't prove it." Anthony turns to the jury. "Nothing further."

This did not go as well as I had expected. In fact, it was a disaster.

"I think this would be a good time to break for the day," Judge Levine says.

Chapter Fifty-Nine

I stand in front of the mirror to rehearse my closing argument, but get distracted by the dark circles under my eyes. I should try to live a healthier life—eat better, exercise more. Since that's not going to happen anytime soon, I make a note to buy better concealer.

The judge has ruled I can't argue Tags killed Rudy and Wayne for money because I can't prove he actually accepted any money. I can show that Cecilia withdrew the cash, but that's where the money trail ends.

I pick up the phone and call Kevin.

"What do you need?" he says.

I can hear a ball rolling, a crash, and a series of fast clinks. "Bowling night?"

"Yup."

"Who is that?" his wife says.

"Work," he says to her.

"Can you try to run Tags's family's financials one more time?" I say. "Maybe his grandmother deposited the money in the last few days."

"I flagged the accounts. They'd call if there's any activity. His grandmother has been spending like a billionaire though. She took the kids on a trip to Bermuda, bought some high-end electronics, even got a new car. Can't you use that?"

"It's all on credit. They haven't paid any of the bills yet."

"The funds could be anywhere—in a locker at the train station, buried in the sand at Crane Beach, or in an offshore account. You used to have money, you know there are a million legit places to hide it, never mind the illegit places."

I did used to have money—a lot of money—but not anymore. My parents would give it all back to me if I quit my job.

"Maybe they're living on credit because Tags expects to get money, but we can't prove it," I say. "Wait, what if he never gets the money?"

"Moe isn't exactly a stand-up guy."

"If we're lucky, maybe he stiffed Tags."

"If Moe stiffed Tags, then what did Cecilia do with the five hundred K?"

"Maybe we're following the wrong trail. Maybe Cecilia spent the money on herself."

I spend the night with Kevin—at headquarters—sorting through Cecilia's financials: bank records, credit card records, insurance records, utility bills. After a couple of hours, Kevin finds something: a payment to Southern California Edison.

"Why would Cecilia need her lights turned on in Los Angeles?" Kevin says.

"It's a Beverly Hills address. Do you have any contacts at the LAPD?"

Kevin makes a few calls, and a short time later, a police officer sends us a text. It's a photo of a mailbox, with Cecilia's name on it. A real estate trace of the property shows Cecilia bought the house through a straw.

"My guess is she's planning to leave Moe after the trial, and she wants a place to land," I say.

"Bad news for Tags—"

"Good news for us."

Tracey agrees to meet with us. Armed with piles of financial reports and real estate documents, we head over to Nashua Street to meet with her and Tags.

"Moe didn't put anything in a trust for you," I say.

"I don't believe you," Tags says.

We show him the papers. He reads them carefully, puts them down, unimpressed.

"Moe is never going to pay you," I say. "If he gives you money, we'll have the link we need to prove his guilt. He'd be incriminating himself."

"You and your family won't get bubkes," Kevin says.

Tags sits back, crosses his arms, remains silent.

"I know Moe can be both charismatic and scary," I say. "But your grandmother is in debt up to her ears, and you won't be able to help her because you'll be doing life without parole."

"I want to go back to my cell," Tags says.

"Don't get too comfortable," Kevin says. "They'll be moving you to maximum security as soon as your trial is over."

"You'll have to convict me first."

Tags is not going to budge. I'm wasting time that I don't have. On our way out of the jail, as we pass through a series of locked doors, Kevin and I do a postgame analysis.

"Do you think it's money or loyalty that's motivating him?" I say.

"None of the above. Not anymore."

"He thinks he's going to beat the case?"

Kevin nods. "He thinks both he and Moe are going to walk."

"He could be right."

"What's worse is Tags thinks it's in his best interest for Moe to walk."

"Do you think Cecilia believes her life would be better if Moe did life without parole?"

Kevin shrugs. "I don't know. But I wouldn't mind being the one to give her a glimpse of her future."

Chapter Sixty

We take the drive to Cecilia's house in Chestnut Hill. On the way, we pass Fenway Park, another Boston landmark that will forever remind me of my victims and my murderers. No place is sacred for me anymore, not the stately brownstones on Commonwealth Avenue, or the golden dome of the statehouse, not even the Green Monster.

There's no traffic at this hour and the ride takes less than twenty minutes. Cecilia will probably be hostile, but she isn't a defendant so we don't have to notify a lawyer that we're going to see her. We decide not to call ahead and let her know we're coming because she'd probably hang up on us or tell us not to bother or, worse, call Anthony.

We don't expect a warm welcome. When she answers the door, she exceeds our expectations.

"You've got nerve coming here."

Kevin lodges his foot in the door before she has a chance to slam it. "Hear us out."

"Please leave me alone."

"You might like to hear what we're offering," I say.

"Is it a plea? The only thing I want to hear is you're offering Moe a deal."

At least we have her attention.

"We're not here to talk about Moe, this is about you," I say.

"It's a lifeline," Kevin says.

She starts to turn away.

"We know about your place in Beverly Hills," I say.

She stops, spins around, and, for the first time, shows a hint of vulnerability. "Does Moe know?"

"Can we come in?" Kevin says.

She steps aside and we follow her into the kitchen. A pot of coffee is on the counter, and a plate of freshly made brownies is on the table, with a stack of unopened bills. My stomach grumbles, but she doesn't offer us snacks. She doesn't even offer us seats.

We stand around the kitchen table.

"We know you're afraid of him," I say. "You went to great efforts to hide ownership of the home. Nothing is in your name. Well, almost nothing."

She stiffens; her tough exterior is back. "What do you want?"

"We can protect you," I say.

"I don't want anything from you."

"You don't want Moe back in the house, do you?" I say.

"Your sister told us she's afraid of him too," Kevin says.

Cecilia spins the plate of brownies around on the table. Kevin looks at me and I give him a quick nod. We didn't want to resort to threats, but it seems like the best thing for everyone.

"We'll have to tell his lawyer about Beverly Hills. It'd be a violation of discovery rules to keep it to ourselves."

She pulls out a chair, sits at the kitchen table, and puts her head in her hands. Encouraged, we sit too.

"Don't you want him to stay in prison?" I say.

She takes a breath, exhales loudly. "What if I help you but he still gets out? Then what am I supposed to do?"

"If you help us, tell us about the gun, he won't get out," Kevin says.

"His lawyer said I'm an accomplice."

"I'll give you immunity. You won't be prosecuted," I say.

"If Moe is convicted, how will I live? How will I support my-self and the kids?"

"You're married. If he goes to prison for life, you and your kids will have a claim to his money," I say.

"But now that we're married, I can't testify against him. That's what his lawyer said."

Anthony must've been worried Cecilia would flip. He's cov-ered all the angles.

"That's not entirely true," I say. "I can't force you to testify against him, but you can if you want to. In Massachusetts, spou-sal privilege belongs to the witness, not the defendant. So it's up to you."

She starts to tear up, finds a tissue, and blots her eyes. "I don't know if I can do it."

"Your sister's husband is dead because of him," Kevin says. "Is this the kind of home you want your kids to grow up in? You want everyone to live in fear?"

We've given her a lot to think about. If she makes a decision on the spot, she could change her mind. Whatever she decides, we need it to be definitive.

I give her my card. Kevin gives her a subpoena. All I can do is hope that she shows. A lot is riding on it. If Cecilia doesn't tes-tify against Moe, it could be the end of the case.

Chapter Sixty-One

Word spreads that we have a surprise witness, and the rumor mill goes into full gear. The press corps somehow got ahold of the jail visitors' log; reporters know we went to Nashua Street and they think Tags has flipped. Other theories float around as well. People speculate that the rebuttal witness could be Rebecca, or the team owner, with new information. By the looks on their faces, no one was expecting me to call Cecilia Morrissey to the stand, not even Moe.

She arrives at the courthouse late and refuses to talk to me or Kevin. She's not giving me a hint of what to expect, but she's here and she's willing to testify. She could take the Fifth or claim spousal privilege, but no lawyer has filed an appearance on her behalf, which gives me hope.

I gather my thoughts as the clerk swears her in. Somewhere between *Do you solemnly swear* and *So help you God,* Anthony objects. He comes up with an arsenal of reasons why she shouldn't be allowed to testify, starting with marital privilege and ending with his not being notified.

"Overruled," Judge Levine says. "Let's hear what she has to say."

Cecilia moves to the witness box, sits up straight, and fixes her gaze on me, avoiding eye contact with Moe and the jury. On my way to the podium, I catch Kevin's smile out of the corner of my eye.

"Could you introduce yourself to the members of the jury," I say.

"Cecilia Bond."

Moe stands and leans over the table and speaks directly to her. "Cecilia Morrissey. You took my name when we got married."

His tone is sharp, his demeanor is menacing. I couldn't have scripted this any better. A couple of jurors are startled by the outburst. Three jurors lean away in disgust. The court officers take a step closer to Moe and I take a step away. A defendant hurled a table at me once, and it wasn't a pleasant experience.

"Sit down, sir," the judge says.

Anthony whispers to Moe, who reluctantly complies with the judge's order. People are scared, which means this is the perfect time to ask the clerk for the gun that has been entered into evidence.

"Have you seen this weapon before?" I say.

Cecilia seems empowered by her audience. I barely have to ask any questions. The words flow as though she's been holding back for years.

"I told him a million times, I never wanted a gun in the house. I didn't know why we needed one. He insisted. That's the gun he gave me after the murders. That's the murder weapon."

"Objection," Anthony says. "There's no question in front of the witness."

"Ask another question," the judge says.

"Did you see him with the gun after the murder of Wayne Ellis?" I say.

"I can do better than that. I saw him give it to Tags before both men were killed and I saw him take it back after they were dead."

"Do you know what he did with it?"

She nods. "Yes."

"Objection," Anthony says. "Hearsay. Calls for speculation. No foundation."

"How do you know what he did with the gun?" Judge Levine says.

"Because he gave it to me."

"Why did he give it to you?" I say.

"He told me to get rid of it. He said he paid Tags to kill them."

"Objection," Anthony says.

"Sit down," the judge says.

"What did you do with the gun?" I say.

"I tossed it in the lake."

I take a breath, look at Kevin to be sure I didn't miss anything. He gives me the nod.

"Nothing further," I say.

Anthony leans in and whispers to Moe for a full minute. Then, he flips through his legal pad and stares at a blank page. Finally, he stands.

"You didn't see your husband kill anyone."

"Nope."

"And you don't know who did."

"I wasn't there."

"Your husband's behavior has been erratic, hasn't it?"

"Sure."

"That's all."

I stand. "How long have you known Moe Morrissey?"

"Since high school."

"Has his behavior changed? Or was he always like this?"

"This is him. He's always been angry and violent."

Moe yells out, "You didn't seem to mind when I was paying the bills."

I could object and ask the judge to admonish Moe for his outburst, but I want the jury to experience his rage.

"I loved you before you had money," Cecilia says. "And I love you now. But I don't love what you did. And I think you need to be punished."

On my way back to the table, I glance at the jurors. Two men, the firefighter and the retired history professor, are shaking their heads in disgust—I hope it's meant for Moe and not Cecilia. The accountant is clucking her tongue. I'm not sure what to make of that.

Chapter Sixty-Two

As soon as Cecilia gets off the stand, both sides rest. All that's left is closing arguments and jury instructions. Since I wasn't sure what Cecilia was going to say, I wasn't able to fully prepare my closing. I'll have to think on my feet. Fortunately, the defense goes first, which gives me a little extra time.

Anthony is effective. He uses all the standard defense arguments: the case is based on circumstantial evidence, there are recanting witnesses, police corruption. He hits his stride when he points at me and goes on a rant about prosecutorial misconduct. After about an hour of insults and accusations, he pauses, looks at his client. Then he turns to the jury and sums up:

"Moe Morrissey did not commit one murder, never mind two murders. He wasn't anywhere near the scene of the crime. He never pulled the trigger, and he doesn't know who did. He is an innocent man, suffering from a debilitating condition—a good man who has done great things for this city. There's only one just verdict in this case. Find my client not guilty."

I have the burden of proof, so I go last. I argue that Moe didn't have to pull the trigger. He was the mastermind. I remind the jurors of the testimony and the exhibits. And I talk about motive.

"The defense wants you to believe that Moe didn't do it, but that if he did, he's crazy. You can't have it both ways." I take a

285

breath, look the jurors in the eye, as though it pains me to say what comes next. "Moe Morrissey may have been the pride of Boston, but not anymore. No one wants to believe he did what he's accused of, but you have to put your emotions aside and look at the evidence. Moe Morrissey is responsible for the murders of two innocent men. He should not be celebrated, he should be punished. Find him guilty."

When I'm done, I take my seat. The case is over. There are no more witnesses, no more evidence, no more arguments. All that's left is the judge's jury instructions, and the verdict.

As soon as the jury goes out to deliberate, I go out the back door of the courthouse and take a walk. I always need to clear my head after closing arguments, and I usually take a stroll with Kevin, but last time we got a little too close. We talked about keeping our relationship platonic, which upset Ty. Out of respect for Ty, I'm going to try to avoid those situations.

As I pass by the back of the statehouse, I see a familiar face and do a double take. It's Mike Chase, wearing a suit and tie using his remote to unlock his car.

We lock eyes.

I can't help myself. "Are you here to beg your state rep to help get your job back?"

"You and your boyfriend made sure that'll never happen."

"Good." I wish I could take credit for his demise, but he doesn't need to know it wasn't me.

"Thanks to him, and to you, I got kicked off the force."

"Don't thank us. You can thank yourself for that."

They took away his gun, but still, he looks like he could smack me. Before this gets any more heated, I head down the hill and back to Bulfinch. Chase has lost his job, but that's not a fair punishment. Something more needs to happen.

I go directly to Stan's office, and his assistant buzzes him. He's in a meeting but he comes out to the reception area, anxious for information about the case.

"They couldn't be back this fast. Could they?" Stan says. A quick verdict in a complicated double homicide would not be good for the prosecution.

"No, I'm not here about the verdict. I'm here to ask for a favor."

He tilts his head, gives me the side eye.

"You're supposed to wait until after the jury finds him guilty before you ask for time off, or a raise, or whatever it is you're looking for."

"This isn't for me. It's for justice."

Stan laughs.

"Can you call a former colleague at the FBI? I want to take out a criminal complaint against Mike Chase. He should be charged with civil rights violations."

"Go to the Brookline District Court. The clerk can issue a complaint."

"I want to make a federal case out of it."

As he considers, I push the button I know any elected official will respond to. "You can take the credit. I don't care—as long as he has to answer to civil rights charges in the United States District Court."

When Stan agrees to make the call, I text Ty and ask him to meet me at the FBI office across from the courthouse. Special agent in charge of the public corruption unit, Ken Kramer, interviews me. He's a just-the-facts kind of guy, which in this case is perfect.

He asks a series of questions to test the strength of the case, as well as my memory and my resolve.

"What hand did Detective Chase use to hold the gun?"

"The right."

"Did your boyfriend obey his commands?"

"Yes."

"Did Chase identify himself as a police officer?"

"Not until after the assault."

"Are you willing to testify in a federal grand jury?"

"Tell me when and I'll be there."

When he's done with me, he leaves to talk to Ty. While he's gone, I pace around, checking and rechecking my texts. I don't expect a verdict, but the jury could have a question and I have to be available. About an hour later, Agent Kramer and Ty return.

"I'll run it up the flagpole," Kramer says, "but I'm pretty sure they're going to want me to open an investigation."

When we get in the elevator, Ty faces me, puts his hands on my shoulders. I can barely meet his eyes.

"I know you did this for me," he says. "Coming forward, you're risking exposure. You could lose your job."

"It's just a job."

Ty kisses my forehead. "Putting killers in jail wouldn't be my first choice for you. It's stressful and dangerous. But I know how important it is to you. It's a big part of who you are, and your passion and commitment are part of the reason I love you."

"And your patience and kindness are part of the reason I love you." This time, I'm the one who moves in for a kiss. "Plus, you're really handsome."

Chapter Sixty-Three

Ty and I walk hand in hand into the courthouse and we settle in a conference room, where we wait for any word from the jury. A couple of hours later, Kevin knocks on the door.

"Come on in." Ty stands and shakes Kevin's hand. "I want you to know I appreciate what you do."

Kevin looks at me, as though he's wondering, *Am I being punked?*

"I'm serious. I didn't want Abby to tell you about my run-in with Chase, but I'm actually glad she did. Out of all of us, you were the one who handled it appropriately. So thanks for that."

"You're welcome."

"But that doesn't mean I want you spending so much time with my girlfriend." Ty smiles, even though he's not kidding.

Kevin checks his phone. My phone starts to vibrate too.

"The jury's back," I say.

Ty, Kevin, and I walk up three flights of stairs, but halfway up, I have to stop and catch my breath. I'm winded, not from the exercise—from the anxiety. A feeling of dread takes hold. I'm frozen in place and I can't seem to get my feet to move.

"Babe, you're sweating," Ty says.

"I know you're in lousy shape, but we take this walk practically every day," Kevin says.

"Give me a minute." I hold on to the railing while I gather my thoughts.

"You put on a good case, especially considering what you were up against," Kevin says.

I wish he would stop. I don't want a pep talk right now, I want an Ativan.

"Come on, baby," Ty says, "I got you."

Ty takes my arm and we continue up to the courtroom. We're the last to arrive; even the judge is on the bench.

"Bring in the jurors," Judge Levine says as soon as he sees us walk in.

I take my place at the table. My mouth is dry and I want to pour myself a glass of water from the pitcher, but my hands are shaking and I don't want to draw attention to myself.

The jurors file in. As they pass Moe, they all look him straight in the eye. This is a bad sign. Usually jurors avoid eye contact right before issuing a guilty verdict. My heart sinks into my stomach.

"Has the jury reached its verdict?" Judge Levine says.

"We have," the foreman says.

"What say you, is the defendant Moe Morrissey guilty or not guilty?"

"Guilty."

There is a blur of reactions behind me; the most audible is from Moe: "I want a recount."

This isn't a foul ball, where the ump can call for an instant replay, but the judge can poll the jury, and that's what he does. Moe glares at each juror as they announce their findings. *Guilty. Guilty. Guilty.* After juror number twelve speaks, it's official. As Moe is cuffed and shackled and taken away, I realize that I've been holding my breath.

Chapter Sixty-Four

Guilty verdicts in a first-degree-murder case provide both a sense of relief and validation, but it's not cause for celebration. Nothing good has happened. Someone has died. Someone is going to prison for life. Both the victims' and the defendants' families are devastated. It's a waste all around. Still, when I wake up the next morning, I can't help but smile a little.

I spend most of Saturday in bed, only getting up a couple of times—to make thank-you calls to Cecilia and Rebecca, to touch base with Rudy's and Wayne's families, and to eat the homemade cranberry scones that Ty has prepared.

On Sunday, I have no choice. I have to get out of bed; it's the baby's christening, and I'm surprisingly excited about it. I haven't had a chance to spend any time with Joy Elizabeth, or Elizabeth Joy, as my mother insists on calling her, and I'm looking forward to seeing her. My parents and their drama, however, not so much.

The ceremony is at the Advent Church on the bottom of Beacon Hill. It's where Charlie, George, and I were all baptized. My father was baptized there too, as was my grandfather and great-grandmother. I attended services there as a child, but I've only been here once in the past decade—after Tim was murdered. I was looking for a sign from the universe that things would be okay. All I got was a migraine, so I never returned.

When Ty and I walk in, we see Charlie and Missy are across the room. I catch Missy's eye, and she smiles. They both seem to have forgiven me. Fortunately, it's difficult to stay angry when Joy is around. She's adorable, with big blue eyes, a full head of brown hair, and the sweetest smile.

"She's wearing my brother George's baptism outfit," I say to Ty.

I hold back tears and look around the church; the dark wood and heavy adornments seem to contradict the reason for our visit. Ty and I join my parents in the front pew. I'm relieved to see that they're seated next to each other, my mother seems sober, and neither has brought a date.

When it's time for the ceremony, I join Charlie, Missy, and Charlie's roommate from Harvard at the front of the church. The white-robed bishop begins a series of questions, and Missy and Charlie provide the responses.

"What do you ask of God's church for Joy Elizabeth?"

"Faith."

"Do you renounce the evil powers of this world which corrupt and destroy the creatures of God?"

"Yes."

When it's my turn, Missy puts the baby in my arms and I instantly fall in love. I listen and respond to what is asked, but my focus is on Joy—her curiosity, her innocence, and her trust.

"Will you by your prayers and witness help this child to grow to the full stature of Christ?"

Even though I'm not religious, I will do anything for this child. Someday, I might even want one for myself.

"I will."

I glance over at Ty, who smiles and nods. He looks down and my eyes follow his. My mother and father are holding hands.

When the service is over, I join Ty, give him a kiss.

"You look like a natural up there holding the baby," he says.

"I can't lie; it felt pretty good."

For the first time in as long as I can remember, I can see it: hope and possibility. Maybe, someday, Ty and I will create a family of our own.